"Are you free for dinner this weekend?" Monica asked, her voice quivering ever so slightly.

Preston grinned. "How's Saturday night?" he asked quickly.

Monica smiled back, nodding her head slowly. She turned toward the foyer, heading to the front door, then spun back around to face him. "I have to ask . . ." she started, her gaze dancing across his face. "What about your girlfriend? Where are you with that relationship?"

Still seated, Preston could feel the smile across his face disappear, thoughts of Donata, and Monica's misinterpretations, tainting his senses. He shook his head. "She's not my girlfriend. I have never been involved with that woman. She was one of my students only, and she has some serious emotional issues that she's trying to work through." He came to his feet, moving to stand beside Monica. "I would not be trying to start a relationship before I ended one. I'm not that kind of man."

The heat around them was steadily rising. Monica took a step back, wishing for cooler air to come between them.

Preston closed the space, stepping in toward her for the second time. He pulled her hand into his, his gaze still locked with hers. "Thank you for stopping by," he said softly, his voice barely a loud whisper. "Maybe we can do it again tomorrow?"

BOOK YOUR PLACE ON OUR WEBSITE AND MAKE THE ARABESQUE ROMANCE CONNECTION!

We've created a customized website just for our very special Arabesque readers, where you can get the inside scoop on everything that's going on with Arabesque romance novels.

When you come online, you'll have the exciting opportunity to:

- View covers of upcoming books

- Learn about our future publishing schedule (listed by publication month and author)

- Find out when your favorite authors will be visiting a city near you

- Search for and order backlist books

- Check out author bios and background information

- Send e-mail to your favorite authors

- Join us in weekly chats with authors, readers and other guests

- Get writing guidelines

- AND MUCH MORE!

Visit our website at
http://www.arabesquebooks.com

Deborah Fletcher Mello

FOREVER AND A DAY

ARABESQUE
★BET
BOOKS

BET Publications, LLC
http://www.bet.com
http://www.arabesquebooks.com

ARABESQUE BOOKS are published by

BET Publications, LLC
c/o BET Books
One BET Plaza
1900 W Place NE
Washington, DC 20018-1211

All Kensington Titles, Imprints, and Distributed Lines are available at special quantity discounts for bulk purchases for sales promotions, premiums, fund-raising, and educational or institutional use. Special book excerpts or customized printings can also be customized printings can also be created to fit specific needs. For details, write or phone the office of the Kensington special sales manager: Kensington Publishing Corp., 850 Third Avenue, New York, NY 10022, attn: Special Sales Department, Phone: 1-800-221-2647.

First Printing: July 2005
10 9 8 7 6 5 4 3 2 1

Printed in the United States of America

*To my grandmother, Susie M. Cole.
Thank you for your love;
you will always have mine.*

Acknowledgments

As always, to God be the glory. It is because of Him that all of this has been possible, and I am grateful to be so blessed.

To Aunt Nellie's baby girl, thank you for letting me borrow your name, cousin!

To my princess brigade: Mariah Bennett, Ebony Blake, Abrianna Broomes, and Blaire and Chakylah Mello, sing girls! Sing, dream, dance, and play! Sing and be little girls for as long as you can. Before you know it, you will each be a young woman, and Aunt Debb will have to remind all of your mommies just how old they really are!

To my cousin Bryan Willis and the staff of Alpha Omega Technology. I love my Web site, and it couldn't have happened without you!

To Tealecia Fletcher, thank you, little sister! Once again, your insight and advice have been right on target. Now stop peeking out that window!

And last, but not least, to my editor, Demetria Lucas, and all the other incredible people that make up the Arabesque family, and who do what they do to bring my stories to life. I cannot begin to tell you how much I appreciate everyone's insight, the kind support, and all the invaluable assistance. My sincerest gratitude to you all.

Prologue

The young woman made one last check of her makeup, staring at her reflection in the rear view mirror of her car. After touching up her cherry red lipstick, she tilted her head to one side, and then to the other, pleased with what she saw. Stepping out of the vehicle, she looked around anxiously, grateful for the blanket of darkness that had taken over the sky. The sliver of a faint moon gave off more than enough light for her needs.

Although it was exceptionally warm outside, eighty-plus degrees and humid, she wore a dark trench coat, newly purchased for just this occasion. She'd come fully prepared to make this an evening the man would surely remember for some time. She was his special delivery, the pretty package he'd pretend to be surprised about receiving, knowing in his heart that she was the one present he'd yearned for more than any other. She was so sure of herself, and of him, that she could barely contain her excitement. Her smile stretched across her chocolate face like that of the Cheshire cat with a big secret.

Easing her way toward the center courtyard, her eyes flitted from one door to the other, scanning the numerous windows for any indication that someone might see her there. Eight town houses sat in the enclave of upscale, luxury homes just inside the northern line of the Wake County community. Side by side,

the U-shaped subdivision of traditional, brick-fronted
housing units bordered a meticulously landscaped
courtyard of lush, green Bermuda grass, exotic flora,
and a splattering of tall, crepe myrtle trees that dot-
ted the landscape with bold sweeps of fuchsia.

Each two-story townhome boasted some three
thousand square feet of living space. The designer
interiors included stainless-steel appliances, plush
carpets, hardwood floors, marbled bathrooms; and
the public amenities included two Olympic-sized
swimming pools, tennis courts, and a community
clubhouse.

What it lacked, the young woman thought as she
maneuvered herself into position behind a large ab-
stract sculpture, was better security. For what these
homes cost, she would have thought someone would
have at least insisted on a twenty-four-hour rent-a-
cop, even if he only carried a pretend badge and
fake gun, and wore a nifty blue uniform.

From where she stood in the center courtyard, she
could see directly into the man's home, the large bay
window of the corner unit devoid of any substantial
window treatments. The micro-thin window blinds
were wide open, and she could see him clearly. He sat
comfortably in his living room, his partially clothed
body extended across the length of a black leather
sofa. A pillow propped easily behind his head inclined
his torso ever so slightly, and she smiled with much appreciation at the broad, buttercream chest that shifted
up and down with each exchange of breath.

She could feel her excitement rising at the sight
of him. This was promising to be a night she and Dr.
Preston Walker wouldn't soon forget. Taking a deep
breath, she tugged at the belt around her waist, adjusted the coat covering her body, and headed for
the man's front door.

One

The provocative flow of her voice was like silk against a listener's ear. When Monica James spoke, her lilt caressed the microphone, whispered seductively over the airwaves, and made love to an audience like they'd never been made love to before. Since her return to Raleigh-Durham, and her arrival at the WLUV-FM radio station, the critics had nicknamed her Black Velvet, quoting the 1989 lyrics by Canadian songstress Alannah Myles. Monica had only smiled when the first reviews paid homage to her slow southern style.

So good was she at what she did and how she did it, no one was surprised when Monica James reached number two in her timeslot. After a six-month run, she was only a step behind King-John Vega, the man crowned emperor of talk radio, and she was working diligently to dethrone him. Every evening, between the hours of eight and midnight, the liquid balm of her voice was pushing and pulling on the legs of the man's royal seat, willing him to fall flat on his very round behind.

With his daily tirades against her, women like her, and the whole female sex in general, Monica knew he was feeling the pressure. When he'd had the audacity to claim southern black women didn't talk like Monica James, she'd called him on it, enlisting an entourage of articulate, chocolate-toned females to put him squarely in his place. The man had made their personal rivalry public, and Monica had ensured he regretted every moment of it. King-John had snapped like a cornered dog, but it was Monica who'd gotten the bigger bite out of his hindquarters, and his ratings.

When Monica spoke, men wanted her, women wanted to be like her, everyone respected her, and all listened intently as she dished out no-nonsense advice, laced with quick, sometimes caustic wit. The voice may have been molasses in the sky, but the female behind it was a tidal wave of intelligence, common sense, and a sharp sense of humor.

"We've got time for one more caller. Who's on the line?"

"Hi, Monica. This is Gail. I just love your show, girl!"

Monica tossed a smile toward her sound engineer, Bryan Bailey, who rolled his eyes in her direction. The short, brown man, whom she depended on to ensure the technical details of her show ran smoothly, pretended to gag as the young woman on the other end continued to gush compliments.

"Thank you, Gail. So, tell me something good, girlfriend. What do you want to talk about tonight?"

"Well, I've been seeing this guy for a while now, and things have been real good, girl. We moved into his mama's house together and he even gave me a ring last month for my birthday. Now he wants us to have a baby. But I don't know if I want to do that. What do you think, girl? What should I do?"

Monica closed her eyes and took a deep breath before responding. "Exactly how long has 'a while' been, Gail?"

"Just about six months now."

"And you've been living together for how long?"

"Only a few weeks. It makes it easier when he needs to borrow his mama's car."

Monica rolled her eyes, and Bryan stifled a laugh. "How old are you, sweetheart? You said you had a birthday last week, right?"

"Yeah, girl. I'm twenty now. Getting old!" The young woman giggled.

"There's not a thing old about twenty, Gail. Be thankful for each day. Far too many young people will never see twenty. Be glad you have."

"Oh, I hear that," Gail responded.

"Do you and your man have jobs, Gail?"

"I'm working on my GED. My man's between jobs at the moment. That's why I'm not so sure about having a baby."

"You're a smart girl, Gail, and I want you to stay smart. Personally, I don't think a baby right now is a smart thing for you to even be thinking about."

"But I'd do anything for my man!" the young woman exclaimed.

"And there's nothing wrong with that, Gail. But this is what I think you should do to help both of you. First thing, you need to finish that GED. When you're done, you should think about taking some classes down at the community college. The fact that you're even working on your GED tells me you're smart enough to know that you need an education.

"After that, you need to lay out a game plan for your man so his behind knows what you expect from him. Babies need security, girlfriend, and that doesn't come cheap. If he loves you as much as you love him, then he'll want to make sure you both have that security before you bring another life into this world. You hear what I'm saying?"

Monica continued, not bothering to wait for a response. "Let your man know you want a home of your own, not his mama's home. That's her house.

You and a baby deserve your own place, and a ride he doesn't have to borrow, and he can't do that without being gainfully employed. Once that baby is here, it's going to be on both of you to do what needs to be done, not just you. If he's not up for the task, then he needs to step off so you can do your thing without all that drama that comes with having a baby on your hip. You can do badly by yourself, Gail. You don't need any man to do bad with you, and you sure don't need a baby if you don't have all your stuff together. You hear me?"

"I hear what you're saying, Monica. Thank you, girl!"

Bryan disconnected the call, spinning his hand in the air to signal her time was up.

Monica spoke into the microphone. "Do your thing, Gail. I have faith in you. Well, that's all the time we have here this evening, people. Stay tuned for Dr. Blue Mood and his midnight magic. I'll be back on Monday, same time, same place, so make sure you call to tell me something good. This is Monica James. Peace and love. I'm out of here."

Chaka Khan and the group Rufus crooned in the background as Monica's call sign faded into the distance. Bryan flicked switches, moving them to an automated sound track that would play until the next crew was ready to take over. "You're getting soft," Bryan said sarcastically as they made their way out of the sound booth. "You were easy on folks tonight." He flashed her a big, toothy grin.

Monica smiled back. "I was in a good mood. I'm sure someone will irritate me tomorrow, and I'll be back in form."

The man shook his head, his large Afro waving atop his head. "I know that's right. Well, let me get home. My wife cooked, and if I'm lucky, she might even be waiting up for me."

"Any plans for the weekend?" Monica asked as they strolled down the length of hallway and into the building's elevator. She stared intently at her partner as he pushed the button for the parking garage.

"I have a dozen kid things to catch up on. Junior has a Little League game, we're working on some school project with Tanya, and my wife promised to make love to me at least twice before I have to report back here Monday night. Three times if I act right."

Monica laughed. "Danielle is going to spoil you. I need to talk to her."

"You stay away from my woman. I got things just like I want 'em. You start putting your two cents in the mix and you'll be messing up my flow," he said with a deep laugh. "What about you? What's on your agenda this weekend?"

The woman shrugged. "I am finally going to unpack and put my house in order. I've made four payments on my mortgage, and my pots are still sitting in a box in my living room. You know that's a crime."

They laughed warmly as they stopped beside Monica's 2004 Nissan Quest, the metallic blue color shimmering under the fluorescent lights. As Bryan opened the door for her, she leaned to give him a quick hug, then waved good-bye, took a seat behind the wheel, and headed home for the night.

Treading a slow path between a collection of corrugated boxes, Monica made her way from the front door of her condominium, through the living room, and into the kitchen. The automatic timer on her new Black & Decker coffeepot had worked as promised, and a pot of freshly brewed coffee sat waiting for her. The rich aroma greeted her in the entranceway. A large ceramic mug with the WLUV-FM logo was sitting on the countertop, waiting to be filled to the brim with the hot fluid.

From where she stood in the kitchen, she could see a light filtering across the courtyard, shimmering from the town house directly opposite hers into her living room window. *Her neighbor must still be up,* she thought as she eased her way over to peer outside. Since the day she'd moved into her home, she'd been watching the good-looking man from her windows, stealing glimpses like a thief on a mission. He'd caught her once, the only time she'd forgotten to cut off the lights in her bedroom before peeking through the window blinds. She'd been rattled by the deep gaze that had passed between them, and then she'd stood foolishly, swatting at the window treatments, hoping he'd not been able to tell what she'd really been doing.

When he'd caught glimpse of her standing in a baby-doll nightgown, a shimmer of a blush had crossed his pale peach complexion. The silk garment had been very short and very sheer, and the matching lace G-string had barely covered the wealth of her assets. The man had tossed up his fingers in what was meant to be a casual wave, then had retreated behind his closed blinds, cutting off her view. Monica smiled at the memory.

Beneath the veil of darkness, she peered out her window into his, her presence obscured by the thin blinds and sheer, white curtains that hung against the glass. He had company, and from where she stood watching, she could see that the conversation between him and the woman he was with was not going well.

In what was supposed to be an alluring striptease, his companion, a very young girl with a Hershey-kiss complexion and platinum blond microbraids, had opened the gray trench coat she was wearing to expose a black, lace-trimmed push-up bra and matching thong. Baby fat spilled out in every direction, and Monica would have wagered the woman's body had never before seen the inside of a gym. She sported ten pounds of excess weight, typical of young college students who tend to eat too much junk and get too little exercise. Sheer, black thigh-high stockings, lace garters, and four-inch, red love-me pumps finished the ensemble as the woman struck what was supposed to be a seductive pose.

When she'd snatched the outer garment closed, an incredulous expression crossing her face, Monica knew the moment had not gone well. She felt for the sister—the girl's embarrassment filled the space around herself and the man as he stood with his hands raised shoulder high, a look of astonishment blanketing his face. As the woman stormed out the door, slamming it profoundly behind her, Monica laughed out loud, returning to her cup of coffee.

Shock filtered across Dr. Preston Walker's spirit, holding him hostage where he stood. As the last vibration of the slammed door stilled, he felt himself exhale. Donata Thompson showing up at his door unannounced had definitely been a surprise. But it was her lurid discourse on what she wanted to do to him, combined with the very graphic exposure of all her private parts, that had shaken his composure. Sweat beaded across his brow, and he reached with the palm of his hand to brush the moisture away. Wiping his hands against the leg of his cotton sleeping pants, he hurried to his front door to lock it, turning the deadbolt before leaning back against his living-room sofa. He heaved a deep sigh.

He'd been teaching literature and language arts

at State University for over twelve years, and in all that time no student had been as brazen as Ms. Thompson had just been. During his tenure he'd waved off many a flirtation and had continually ignored the efforts of any undergraduate who dared to threaten the boundaries of their teacher-student relationship, but this stunt had thrown him right off guard. The young woman had obviously fallen down and bumped her skull, he thought, shaking his head. Had he been a man who drank, he would definitely have had use for a straight shot of scotch.

A quick movement across the way caught his eye, and he looked out his large bay window right into the home of his new neighbor. The stunning woman stood at the granite counter in her kitchen, slowly stirring a teaspoon into a cup. She was giggling at something funny, clearly amused. Preston scanned the room, his gaze intruding into the woman's space, but he saw no one else with her as she stood alone.

For two complete strangers, he and the woman had shared many an intimate moment, he thought, remembering the last time, when he'd looked over to see her standing nearly naked at her second-floor window, tugging at the window blinds. The slip of black lingerie she wore had felt like the only barrier between them—that is, if he ignored the two panes of window glass and the twenty yards of lawn between their two units. His gaze had raced along the fine lines of her lush curves until the flicker of energy through his groin had incited a raging stiffness that pulled him back to his senses. A sliver of a smile crossed his face, and the memory caused a recurrent wave of electricity to flood his body.

Almost simultaneously, the two crossed over to their respective windows, reaching for the pull cords to close the blinds and block out the other's peering eyes. As Monica's gaze met his, she smiled, then gave him a quick wave of her hand. Preston smiled back as he nodded his head slowly, and then both drew back their blinds, allowing darkness to fill the space between them.

Two

When Monica's doorbell rang, she had already consumed three cups of Jamaican coffee and had unpacked half the boxes sitting in her living room. Outside, the sun had risen nicely, settling its golden orb against a bright blue sky. Not one cloud sat in the oceanic expanse of space, promising a bright, hot summer's day. Still dressed in the nightclothes she'd slept in—an oversized, white T-shirt and pair of gray sweatpants—Monica pulled the wooden door open, flooding the room with sunshine and warmth as she did.

Diondre James stood front and center, plastic grocery bags in hand. He smiled widely as his baby sister stood shaking her head in greeting.

"I thought you said you were going to be here by seven o'clock," Monica said with a smile, peering at him through the screen door.

Diondre lifted the bags and gestured in her direction. "I knew your refrigerator was empty. Thought I'd be a sport and give you a hand. Besides, I was hungry."

She shook her head. As she pushed open the door to let him inside, she saw her neighbor standing in the parking lot with two uniformed police officers. The man was visibly agitated, and one of the officers, a tall white man with bright red hair, was motioning for him to calm down. Placing a hand on

Diondre's shoulder, she pushed him into the foyer, moving him out of the way so that she could get a better view.

"What's that all about?" she asked, glancing at Diondre quickly before staring back out into the yard.

He shrugged, pushing his broad shoulders up. "Don't know. They were there when I pulled up. Something about the man's car. What kind of neighborhood have you moved into?"

Monica rolled her eyes at her older brother as he headed toward the kitchen to drop the bags of groceries on the countertop. Stepping out into the courtyard, she sauntered toward the man, who stood staring out at the police car as it pulled out of the lot and onto the main thoroughfare.

"Good morning," she said, smiling sweetly. "Is everything okay?"

Glancing in her direction, Preston appraised her as she came to stand at his side. Her attire was comfortable, but not overly flattering to her voluptuous figure. Since he had been privy to the round curves of her body, he knew the T-shirt and sweats served only to hide them from view. Standing just over five and a half feet, she was as nearly as tall as he was, her dark, ebony eyes meeting his evenly. Her jet-black hair was cut in a short, precise style that curled in wisps at the crown and tapered at the delicate nape of her neck. She wore no makeup, and he couldn't help but think that she was one of only a handful of women he'd known who didn't need it. He found her natural beauty intoxicating. Her skin tone was a cool brown, chocolate with only a mild touch of milk. Preston felt himself staring at her mouth; full lips pulled back into a deep smile, and perfect snow-white teeth glimmered like expensive pearls. She licked her lips lightly, her small, pink tongue lightly grazing the surface, and the movement sent a shiver straight into the pit of his stomach.

Monica extended her hand in his direction. "Hi. I'm your new neighbor," she said, gesturing toward her town house. "My name's Monica James. I thought I should finally introduce myself." Her voice was a rich, deep timbre that lifted her words out and up, as if she were offering him a special present meant only for his ears.

Preston smiled back, his agitation dissipating into the warm morning air and nervous excitement filling the empty space. "Hello, Monica. It's nice to meet you. I'm Preston, Preston Walker."

"So, what was all that commotion about?"

The man shook his head. "Just some minor vandalism to my car," he responded, pointing toward a royal blue Isuzu Rodeo that sat two spaces down from Monica's own vehicle. Monica inhaled sharply as she spied the four flat tires and the splattering of bright yellow paint that now covered the hood and sides of the automobile.

She shook her head, her eyebrows raised ever so slightly. "Some women don't take rejection very well."

Preston cut his eye toward her, then laughed, the sound rising from deep in his midsection. "So, you saw that last night, did you?"

She shrugged, a wry smile gracing her face.

He waved his head from side to side. "It really wasn't what you're thinking. She's one of my students, and it was totally inappropriate. I had to tell her so, but I didn't handle it very well."

Monica laughed. "Obviously."

Preston heaved a deep sigh, pushing his hands deep into the pockets of his khaki slacks. A rush of red flooded his pale cheeks, and Monica could sense his embarrassment at being in the middle of so much drama. She studied him as he started off toward his vehicle, shock still registering. Preston Walker was a man some would definitely call pretty. With his neatly cropped haircut that faded to almost nothing along the sides of his head, his features were classic and perfectly proportioned, from the spacing of his light brown eyes to the slight slope of his thin nose. He had beautiful cheekbones that accentuated the line of his chin with its faint cleft. He sported a thin mustache that spilled down into the fine line of a beard, the medium brown hair flattering his peach-toned complexion. A brief second of silence tripped between them as they stood staring at one another.

"So what do you teach?" Monica asked, her eyes lifting with the tilt of her smile.

"English and literature, at the university," he responded, focusing his attention back on the delicate lines of her face.

The conversation was interrupted when her brother called her name from the doorway. "Monica . . . telephone," he shouted loudly, gesturing for her attention.

Monica smiled again as they both turned toward Diondre, who stood staring in their direction, with the telephone receiver in one hand and a cup of coffee in the other.

Preston eyed the man curiously, then turned back to Monica. "Well, it was nice to meet you. I hope we'll see each other again some time."

Monica winked as she turned toward home. "I'm sure we will. Good luck with your car, Mr. Walker."

Preston watched her until she reached the tall, mocha-hued man in her doorway, a man who made a point of waving in his direction after passing the woman the telephone. It was the first time he'd seen her with someone, and out of the blue, he found himself wishing that whoever this man was, that he didn't have plans on hanging around long.

The last of Monica's personal possessions were finally in place. Diondre had spent the better part of the afternoon helping her empty boxes and shift furniture. She owed her brother a steak dinner and had promised to pay up the following week. There were other things on her mind tonight, though, Preston Walker being at the head of her list.

The real estate broker who'd sold her the town house had spoken highly of the man who lived directly across from the empty unit. As the two women had wandered through, inspecting the closets, the bathroom tile, and the living space, the woman had given Monica more than an earful. Rattling off as much information as she could remember, she had noted that he was a professor at the local university, lived alone, had an impeccable reputation, and was as sexy as sin. In their search for her new home, Monica had also heard the sob story about the realtor's very brief experience with one of her neighbor's male friends, a man who apparently was trying to break the world record on the number of conquests he could manage in a lifetime.

As Monica sat at the dressing table in her bedroom, brushing the short length of her hair, she could feel Preston staring. She sensed his eyes upon her, and had their circumstances been different, had he been someone else, it would have unnerved her. But knowing that it was Preston Walker sitting across the way watching was oddly exciting, and she could feel her heart beating rapidly at the possibilities.

The hot shower she'd taken an hour earlier had warmed her flesh nicely, and the silk robe wrapped around her naked body felt delicious against her skin. Lifting herself from the seat, she put her left leg on the edge of the bed, exposing the length of the limb as she pressed her foot against her down comforter. Pouring a fair amount of cocoa-scented lotion on her palm, Monica proceeded to draw the moisturizer down the line of her firm thighs to her thin calves, and back again. Pressing the length of her manicured nails up and down her legs, she stroked them slowly, methodically, the sweeping motion hypnotizing. When satisfied with her performance, she moved to the other leg, the palms of her hands massaging her brown flesh easily. The light emanating from the hallway into the bedroom and the glow of candles positioned around the room illuminated her figure nicely, her body shadowed seductively in the distance.

The radio played in the background, and the Saturday night disc jockey was spinning love tunes back to back. As Marvin Gaye was pleading to get it on, Monica eased her body into the rhythm, her hips swaying slowly from side to side, her pelvis grinding into the evening air as she put three years of belly dance lessons to good use.

I should not be watching, Preston thought as he sat back in an oversized wing chair just out of view of the window. The darkness around him served only to make her appear larger than life, seemingly closer, the physical distance between them closing ever so slightly.

He sensed she knew what she was doing, and the thought made him smile. As he watched her touch herself, her hands caressing first one leg and then the other, he could feel his excitement building. Perspiration rose to the surface of his palms, and he imagined that it was his fingers and not hers that pressed against her legs. He inhaled deeply, filling his lungs with oxygen.

Across the way, Monica had finished lotioning her legs and was now dancing solo, her erotic movements lighting a low flame between his thighs. The gyrations of her body were temptation personified and caused his manhood to surge to attention. Hopeful for more, Preston pulled himself up to the edge of his seat, fixated on what was happening across the way. His hands fell to his crotch, gently stroking the length of maleness that pressed against the fabric of his pants.

As she glanced over her shoulder, he could see her smile ever so slyly, and he smiled back, watching as she moved to loosen the belt tied around her waist. He waited with bated breath as she paused, her head tilting ever so slightly, and then she crossed over to the window and slowly pulled the curtains closed, staring straight into his room as she did.

Three

As he paced the halls outside room 249, Preston Walker wrung his hands anxiously. His skin was smooth, the flesh along the length of his fingers drenched in aloe moisturizer. Tilting his wrist upward, he checked the time. The gold timepiece adorning his wrist read nine-fifteen. He sighed, leaning back against the stark white wall behind him as he crossed his arms over his chest.

Inhaling deeply, he was suddenly aware of the faint scent of formaldehyde, the obnoxious odor tainting the lining of his nostrils. He frowned, reminded why he'd chosen the arts and not the sciences. He detested the science lab and the smell of dead things that seemed to linger amid the walls and furniture.

Pushing his shoulders back against the wall, he pressed the palms of his hands against his eyes. His head hurt. The morning had barely begun, and his nerves were already frazzled. Students lumbered past him, heading to their classes. Grating noises rang incessantly around him, dancing with the migraine that pressed at the front of his brain, destroying his equilibrium. One or two bodies called out his name as they strolled by, acknowledging his presence as he stood waiting for his best friend and associate, Dr. Godfrey Davis.

The two men were polar opposites, but had shared a brotherly connection since their days at college and their induction into the Alpha Phi Alpha fraternity. As different as night and day, they brought a unique balance to their friendship. It worked, and neither could imagine what he'd do without the other supporting him.

As the large black man finally lumbered down the hallway, a female admirer clutching his arm unabashedly, Preston could only shake his head. His friend never ceased to astound him with his blatant disregard for the university's rules on ethical protocol. The man stood imposingly, a tailored gray suit, pale pink dress shirt, and printed tie fitting the massive muscle of his large, football player's frame. He stepped heavily in gray leather shoes that looked as if they could have been dyed to match the suit. Godfrey smiled warmly as he and the woman stopped in front of the classroom door where Preston stood patiently.

"Good morning, Dr. Walker. How are you this fine morning?"

Preston chuckled. "Very well, Dr. Davis. I just needed a minute of your time this morning. I know you have a class in a few minutes." Preston smiled faintly at the woman, who stood staring from one to the other.

Remembering his manners, Godfrey gestured in her direction. "Do you know Ms. Chatelain?"

"Yes, I do. How are you, Jennifer?"

"I'm fine, thank you, sir. I was just telling the professor that I'm thinking about changing my major to biology."

Preston nodded his head. "Well, I'm sure Dr. Davis will be a great source of information for you. I hope you won't mind my interrupting, but I need to speak with him for a moment. Duty calls."

The girl grinned. "No. Not at all." She turned her

attention back toward the other man. "Will I see you later, Dr. Davis?" she asked coyly.

The man smiled, winking slyly. "Of course. Why don't you stop by later this afternoon so we can finish our conversation?"

Nodding her head, the girl shook the length of her blond hair and spun back down the hallway, her lean hips leading the way.

"Do you ever stop?" Preston asked. "One of these days, one of these young girls is going to lose you your job."

Godfrey grinned. "Please! All I'm doing is offering them some advice."

"You advise the boys like you do the girls?"

The man laughed, placing a large hand atop the doorknob of his classroom. "So, what brings you here so early?" he asked, changing the subject as they entered the room and closed the door behind them.

"Do you know a student named Donata Thompson? She's a junior. Transferred here from Meredith College."

Dropping his briefcase against the desk, Godfrey paused, deep thought etched against the lines of his dark face. "Pretty girl, built like a brick house. I think she's a blonde this month. Girl has thighs like two slabs of southern ham. All I would need me is a plate of biscuits and some old-fashioned molasses." The man laughed loudly, tossing his head back.

Preston rolled his eyes, dropping his body into one of the thirty or so chairs arranged neatly in even rows. He shook his head, not at all amused by the man's humor. "Miss Thompson showed up at my front door Friday night wearing nothing but her bra and panties. I had to throw her out."

Godfrey laughed. "And you hadn't invited her?"

"She's one of my students," Preston responded, his expression incredulous.

The other man shook his head, wiping at a tear in his eye. "I should have it that easy. Send her to me. I've got a thing or two I can teach her."

"I don't find this funny. Saturday, someone trashed my car. I think it was Donata."

Godfrey shook his head, amusement crossing his face. "You need to lighten up. I wouldn't worry about it. Girl had a crush, and you blew her off. She'll get over it. She'll find someone else to give it up to before the quarter is over. One of the boys on the football team, or if I can get lucky, a science professor. Don't sweat it."

As Godfrey's students began to enter the room, Preston came to his feet, still shaking his head. His friend hadn't said one word to ease his anxiety. "I don't know why I waste my time coming to you for advice," he said, making his way back toward the door.

Godfrey laughed as he followed his friend, both pausing in the doorway. "Is that what you were looking for? You should have said so. I'd have told you to give Monica James a call. I hear she's got a wealth of good advice for men like you."

Preston looked at him curiously. "How do you know Monica James?"

The man laughed. "Boy, do we need to get you out more! Call the WLUV talk line, my friend. I hear it said that Monica James is the answer to a dying man's prayers, and all she does is give out advice to weak brothers such as yourself."

Donata Thompson touched up the last of her makeup, as her roommate, Tijuana Fields, sat on the edge of the bed waiting for her. The two shared a sparsely decorated dorm room that had more wall than floor space, the tight quarters meant only for studying and sleeping.

"So, what happened?" Tijuana asked, pulling for the information her friend was struggling to keep secret.

The other girl smiled weakly, still staring at her reflection in the mirror. "What do you want to know for?" she asked, dabbing at an abundance of blue eye shadow across her eyelids.

"I want to know what the professor's working with, 'cause he is sure 'nuff fine!" Tijuana giggled.

"Well, let's just say this sister is not only satisfied, but the professor will still be thinking about it long after I graduate from this place. And I will be passing that literature class with an A-plus this semester."

"You go, girl."

"The man was begging me to stay, but you know I couldn't roll like that. Had to leave him wanting more, you know?"

Tijuana nodded, her head bobbing like a loose ball bearing against her pencil-thin neck. "You are so lucky," she exclaimed, blowing out a low whistle under her breath. "I wish I could find me a man like the professor. These little boys around here get right on my nerves."

"Well, Professor Walker is definitely no little boy, if you get my drift." Donata grinned, gesturing crudely with her hands.

Tijuana laughed. "So, when are you going to see him again?"

Donata forced the muscles in her face to pull her lips upward, her grin stretching across her face to fuel the lie that spilled past her lips. "He wants to take me to dinner tonight. Someplace romantic. I told him I'd let him know if I could fit him into my schedule." She laughed, the sound of it jarring to her ears.

Her friend giggled again, rising from her seat to head for the door. "You are so lucky," she repeated, drawing her book bag into her arms. "We better get going or we're going to be late for class."

Nodding her head, Donata rose to follow, then turned to stare, one last time, at the stranger staring back at her.

Donata glanced up at the clock on the classroom wall. Her sociology class only had twelve more minutes before it would be over and she could focus her attention on getting ready for her afternoon English class. Professor Walker would be anxious to see her. She'd made sure of that with her Saturday-morning visit to the condominium complex where he lived.

She did not intend to let him disregard her like he'd done. She hadn't shown up on his doorstep dressed in a month's worth of dinner money to have him act as if he weren't interested in what she had to offer.

She wasn't crazy. That man had been making eyes at her for weeks now. His offer to help her study for that last exam hadn't been just a professional gesture. Donata knew when a man wanted her, and clearly, Dr. Preston Walker wanted her. After she'd thrown open her coat to offer him a taste of her juicy fruit, she could see it in his eyes that he had wanted to sample what she offered. A man didn't sweat and stammer like that for nothing. But he wanted to play hard to get, throwing her out like she was trash to be discarded. The memory caused her to bristle with anger. It was okay, though. She'd ensured he didn't make that mistake with her again. Donata Thompson didn't play that, and the professor now knew he was going to have to step to her correct, or else.

Four

Monica was locking up her home before heading to work just as Preston was making his way up the graveled pathway toward his own front door. He stopped and waited as she approached him, heading toward the parking lot.

"So, you're the Monica James on the radio. I hear your show is the one to listen to these days."

Monica smiled. "Good evening to you, too, Preston, and you heard correctly. I am, and it is."

Preston grinned, words suddenly escaping him. "Well," he said, then paused, searching for something else to say. The woman's gaze was piercing, nipping at his usual confidence.

"I . . . was . . . um . . . wondering . . . um . . . if—" he stammered.

"Yes," Monica said, studying him intently as she interrupted. "I'd like that."

Preston shook his head. "You don't know what I was going to ask."

"But I know what I said yes to."

"And what might that be?"

"You giving me a call some time so that we can get to know one another better," Monica said softly, stepping in closer. She brushed her fingertips gently against the front of his dress shirt. The gesture caused Preston to choke on his own air, and he gasped loudly.

"I was hoping for dinner, too," he finally said.

As Monica exhaled, blowing air gently past her lips, Preston could feel the flow of her breath against his cheek. The scent was wintermint, intense and cooling.

"Call me. We'll talk about it," she said, her tone inviting. Monica eased past him, heading toward her car.

"Aren't you going to give me your number?" Preston asked behind her.

Her laugh was low and enticing. It caused a shiver to run up Preston's spine.

"Just call me at the station," she responded. "Between eight o'clock and midnight is the best time to reach me."

As Monica slid into the driver's seat, her eyes never left Preston's, the gaze between them spinning energy like an electrical current gone awry. When she pulled out of the parking lot and onto the main road, heading east toward the radio station, Preston was still staring after her.

Pushing his keys into the lock, Preston opened his front door and stepped into the foyer of his home, closing the door behind him. He flipped quickly through the stack of mail he'd retrieved from the mailbox, then dropped it all against the large oak table that sat in the hallway.

He replayed the encounter with Monica over in his mind. His workday had not ended on a high note, but seeing Monica had more than made up for it. As he thought about his day, he could feel his stress levels rising, tension spreading across his back and shoulders.

Godfrey had joined him for lunch, and after some intense discussion, had persuaded him there was no need to report what had happened with Donata to his department's chair. Godfrey had convinced him that

Donata was probably as embarrassed as he was and that it would be in both of their interests to let the matter drop without bringing any further attention to it. "No point in blowing heat in her beehive for nothing," Godfrey had said with a laugh. "A scorned woman's sting can be lethal."

That afternoon he had tried to ignore Donata's presence in his last class. Her entry had been as rambunctious and as congenial as usual, and he'd treated the girl no differently from how he'd treated her before the weekend's fiasco. When she'd approached his desk, leaning across it to say hello, he'd responded politely, directing her to take a seat so that he could begin the lesson. When she'd lingered after the last bell, pressing for his attention, he'd grabbed his briefcase and personal items and had excused himself. Directing his comments at two other students who were also loitering, he'd advised them that he needed to take his automobile to his car dealership to see what could be done about the remnants of yellow paint that marred the surface. He'd made sure his comments were loud and clearly heard, and he'd only given her a brief glance before exiting the room and rushing to the parking lot.

A large, oak replica of an antique radio sat on his kitchen counter. He turned it on, spinning the knob until he got clear reception on the FM station 109.5. They were playing a new cut from Heather Headley's newest CD and he found the lilt of the songstress's voice soothing. Peering into his Jenn-Air refrigerator, he shifted items from one side of the appliance to the other, searching for something quick and easy to prepare for dinner. An assemblage of cut vegetables in a Tupperware container looked appetizing, and he leaned under the counter for the cast-iron wok to stir-fry them in.

The end of Heather's song and Monica James's call sign caught his attention.

"Let's get serious tonight, people. Do you have romance in your life, or has romance left you standing empty-handed by the side of the road? How do you define romance? Give me a call and tell me something good."

A quick spin by Toni Braxton filled the airspace before Monica's voice returned. Preston spooned the cooked vegetables onto a plate, settled himself on a stool at the counter, and listened intently as he slowly consumed his dinner.

"Who's with me tonight?"

"Hi, this is Denise Baines. Romance is dead, Monica. Men have become lazy. Once they have you, they're not willing to put any effort into the relationship."

"Is that what has happened to your relationship, Denise? Has your man just stopped wining and dining you?"

"I'm lucky if he'll take me to McDonald's for a hamburger and fries," the caller said with a laugh.

"Why do you think that is, Denise? Have you stopped being romantic?"

"It's hard to give it, Monica, when no one's willing to return the favor."

"I feel you, Denise. Let me hear from some of you men out there. Give Monica a call and tell me something good. Let me know how you brothers are bringing the romance to your women."

Preston smiled as he placed his dirty dish into the dishwasher, rinsing it under a stream of warm water before he did. He sat back down at the counter, his hands folded against the Corian surface. He wasn't sure how long he sat listening before he reached for the telephone and dialed the numbers Monica repeated every so often. The telephone rang incessantly, and just as Preston was thinking of hanging up, a male voice finally answered.

"This is WLUV."

Preston paused, then cleared his throat. "Yes . . . umm . . . May I please speak to Monica James?"

"Do you have a comment or a question?"

Preston hesitated again. "No, I was just hoping to speak with her for a moment. My name's Preston Walker, and I'm her neighbor."

"Monica's on the air right now, Mr. Walker. Is this an emergency?"

"Oh, no, nothing like that. She just told me to call her. I thought the show might be taped or delayed or something. I'm sorry."

"Hold on." The man's voice disappeared and elevator music chimed in Preston's ear.

From the radio on the counter, Monica's voice spilled into the room. "Let's take our next caller. This is Monica. Tell me something good."

Preston suddenly heard her in both ears, the beguiling tone wafting through his eardrum from the receiver and spilling out into the open air from the radio. "Monica, hello—"

"You'll need to turn your radio down, caller."

He stammered, suddenly aware that he was being heard across the airwaves, his call being transmitted over the radio. He reached for the knob to adjust the volume on his receiver.

Monica teased him. "That's better. All that feedback is gone. So, who wants to talk to me? Tell me something good. Tell me, caller, how do you get romantic with the woman in your life?"

"I'm not involved with anyone at the moment," he finally spewed, the words echoing into the receiver, out of the radio, back across the counter, and through the room.

"And why is that?"

"Don't know that I've met that special lady yet, although there is someone I'm very interested in getting to know better," he answered, deciding to play along.

"And will you be a romantic fool when you do get to know this woman better?" Monica asked.

Preston found himself laughing. "Definitely romantic, but never a fool."

Monica laughed with him. "So, tell us, how romantic will you be? What special skills will you be laying on this woman?"

"Well, if I told you, then it wouldn't be a surprise for her now, would it?"

"But you haven't even given us your name, caller, so how will she know it's you?"

"She'll know."

Monica laughed, a deep, throaty chuckle directed straight at him. "I'm sure she will. So tell us, caller, how did you know this was a woman you wanted to invest your romantic self in?

Preston paused, not sure if he should answer, then decided he had nothing at all to lose. "It was the eye contact. We've shared a few looks that have had my heart beating so fast I could feel it hitting the walls of my chest. They made my head spin and left me breathing heavy. It's just an energy that's difficult to explain."

Monica purred. "Mmmm. That sounds pretty intense."

"It was," he responded, his voice low and deep, sending a cool shiver up the spine of every woman listening intently. "It was as if we were being intimate without touching. I could actually feel the heat from her flesh against my hand. It was one of those gazes that's so deep it leaves you quivering at the knees. I knew right then that whenever we do touch, then that moment will probably change the entire direction of both of our lives."

"And you could tell that from a quick look from this woman?" Monica asked, her tone just a shade away from incredulous.

"Yes," Preston said, his tone hushed, his voice's deep resonance vibrating like thunder. "And it left me breathless."

Monica fanned herself as Bryan stared at her curiously, his interest piqued by the exchange between Monica and her neighbor. The expression across his friend's face was one he'd not seen before. Whoever this man was, he had Monica's full attention.

"You sound very sure of yourself."

"I'm sure of this woman. She's a strong personality and needs a man who can hold his own with her." Preston could feel Monica smiling.

"Sounds like you plan to give this woman a run for her money."

"I don't doubt that she plans to give me a run for mine," Preston said with a grin. "I just hope she's up to the challenge."

"Is there anything else you'd like to tell me tonight, caller?"

"No, ma'am. But if I could ask you for a favor?"

"What can I do for you tonight, Mr. Romantic?"

"If you would, please play me a love song."

Elevator music filled Preston's ear as Monica's voice sang out from the radio. "This is Monica James, and I'm dedicating this one to that last caller. Here's a golden oldie for you, my friend, The Four Tops singing "Are You Man Enough." We wish you much luck, Mr. Romantic."

"Are you still there?" Monica asked, clicking off the elevator tunes.

"Are you man enough? Where's the romance in that?"

Monica laughed. "I guess that will depend on you, Mr. Romantic."

"That wasn't very nice. I wasn't expecting to be put on the air."

Monica laughed again, the warmth of the emotion filling Preston's spirit. "I guess I'll have to make it up to you," she responded.

"What time do you get off?"

"Past your bedtime."

"You sure of that?"

"I'm not sure of anything, Dr. Walker. You're not at all what I expected."

"What did you expect?"

"I figured you for a more conservative type. Maybe even a tad uptight. Bookwormy and a little nerdy, perhaps."

This time Preston laughed. "And that's the type of man you're interested in?"

Monica smiled into the receiver. "I figured it might be interesting to see what it would take to get you to let your hair down a bit."

Preston pondered the comment. "I may be more of a challenge than you can handle, Ms. James."

Monica could feel her heart beating rapidly. Across the way, Bryan was gesturing for her attention, signaling she only had thirty seconds before she'd have to be back on air.

"I take my coffee with cream and two sugars," she said.

"What time can I expect you?"

"The same time you'd be looking for me through the window."

Preston laughed. "I look forward to it."

As she disconnected the call, Preston grinned broadly. Glancing quickly at the clock on the wall, he figured it would take him at least thirty minutes to get to and from the twenty-four-hour Super Wal-Mart. He needed to pick up a can of Folgers and a new automatic coffeepot.

I have every right to be in Wal-Mart, Donata thought as she followed Preston into the store, mindful to keep her distance so that he didn't see her. She watched as he grabbed a shopping cart and pushed it quickly through the grocery aisles and then over to small appliances. As she pulled a baseball cap down low over her face, a tall woman in a blue smock smiled in her direction and welcomed her to the store. Donata returned the greeting with a quick smile, then jumped behind a magazine display, out of Preston's sight. Peeking from behind a copy of *InStyle* magazine, she continued to stare as he studied the display of coffeemakers, finally settling on an inexpensive GE model. With his selections in hand, Preston headed for the checkout counter, and Donata trailed closely behind him.

As he stood in line patiently waiting his turn, Donata eased up behind him, pressing her hands eagerly against the waistband of his pants. When he made an about-face, Donata greeted him warmly, gushing her surprise at running into him at that hour of the night.

"This is Monica James and WLUV-FM radio coming to you from the heart of downtown Raleigh, North Carolina. The violins are playing and I just opened a new box of tissues. Hit me on the phone lines, people! I'm ready and waiting," she sang into the microphone. Bryan tossed his arms up excitedly as the telephones began ringing off the hook. He signaled her to pick up the first line.

"This is Monica. Tell me something good."

"Hey, Miss Monica," a man's deep vibrato echoed over the receiver.

"Who's this on my line?"

"This is Earl, and I'm calling from Mebane."

"Talk to me, Earl. What can I do for you tonight?"

"No, girl. It's what I can do for you."

Monica sat back in her seat, a look of amusement crossing her face.

"Let me get comfortable for this, Earl. It sounds serious. What can you do for me?"

"The problem all you women are having is that you haven't found a real man like myself to bring it to you."

"And what are you bringing, big boy?"

The man chuckled. "A mouthful and then some."

"If that's all you've got, brother, there's no need to waste any more of my time. If you plan on feeding me, you have to come with the whole meal, and I'm talking a five-course feast. You need to kick it off with more hors d'oeuvres than I care to look at. By the time I'm finished, the salad should look like dessert. I need my choice of entrees, some soup, salad, and bread and butter that never stops coming. And when I'm finished, just the right touch of sweet to end the meal. A mouthful won't even begin to whet my appetite."

She disconnected the call, wrapping her hand around the microphone as she pulled it closer to her lips. Her voice dropped low and deep as she spoke to the audience. "Y'all got to do better than that, people. Earl is stepping out like a woman doesn't have anything better to do except make him feel like the man he wishes he could be."

She picked up the next call. "This is Monica. Tell me something good."

"Hey, Monica. My name's Cassandra Elise Thomas Stewart Matthews, and I'm calling from Durham."

"Dang, girl! Where'd you get that long-A name from? You've used up half my time just spitting your name out, girlfriend!"

The woman giggled. "I got a long list of ex-husbands," the woman responded.

Monica laughed. "Tell me something good, Miss

Cassandra Whatever-the-rest-of-your-name-is. What do you want to talk about?"

"Girl, I'm tired of these men stepping to me in the clubs with their broke down clothes and gold teeth."

"Must not be too tired with all those ex-husbands you have."

The woman giggled. "I'm serious, Monica. Girl, these men today need to learn how to present themselves correct."

"When you're out in these clubs, Miss Thang, what are you sporting? Givenchy, Yves St. Laurent? What?"

"Who?"

"That's right. Who designed the dress you wore to the club on Friday? Anyone we know?"

"I was dressed right. My clothes were fierce!"

"I don't doubt it, girl, but let me tell you what my mother used to tell me. If you look like Tuesday's trash, then all you're going to get is Wednesday's leftovers. There's not a man around who's going to step to you if you look like you're out of his league. But if you look and smell like he can pull your chain, then you can bet your last dollar he's gonna give you a tug to see how far he can drag you. You hear what I'm saying?"

The woman sucked her teeth. "Tch."

Monica laughed. "That's right, I went there. We women always want to cut a brother up about something he's doing, but we never stop to examine what we're putting out there. We can't demand caviar when we look like all we want is tuna. And if you're fishing for lobster, girlfriend, stop wasting your time in the cesspools. The big fish play on the big beaches, in *clean* water."

"I hear you, Monica. You preach, girl!" the woman exclaimed with a robust laugh.

"This is Monica James, and I'll be bringing it back after a word from our sponsors, but before that,

here's an old jam from one of your favorite chocolate sons. Here's Maxwell with *Don't Ever Wonder.*"
Monica clicked off the microphone as Bryan joined
her in the booth.

"You're in rare form tonight."

She rolled her eyes. "Who's on the lines?"

"A couple of players on two and three, and a
young girl with a serious question on four. Who do
you want first?"

"Give me the girl. Leave the players holding.
They're bound to hang up if we keep them waiting
long enough."

Bryan laughed. "You are so bad."

"No, Monica has got herself a date tonight, and I
don't want my good mood spoiled by some man who
thinks he's God's gift to the entire female popu-
lation."

Bryan grinned. "The neighbor?"

She nodded her head eagerly, grinning back.

"I thought you were going to make the brother
break out into a sweat for a minute there, but he
held his own. You didn't get the best of him."

"No, I didn't. Did I?"

Bryan eased his way back into the sound booth. "I
bet he won't be so lucky the next time."

The woman laughed. "You've got that right!"

Godfrey still hadn't returned his call, and Preston
felt as if he'd been pacing the floor for hours. Across
the way, Monica's home was dark, the last light having
been extinguished within minutes of her arrival home.
Preston shook his head, mortified by the turn of events
that had ruined their late-night plans. He tapped his
foot anxiously, hitting "redial" on his cordless telephone for the umpteenth time.

Donata's display in the store had been awkward at

best. The few people in line with them and the two cashiers on duty had stared curiously as the young woman had pressed herself against him, cooing suggestively in his ear while winking at her audience over his shoulder. When he'd attempted to push her away, she'd hissed under her breath, promising to cause a major scene. The entire time, a smile had been plastered across her face as if there were nothing wrong with the exchange between them, and the bystanders trying to eavesdrop had been none the wiser. As he'd paid for his purchases, she'd clung to his arm, her hands heavy against his back and side as she'd gushed excitedly about her day.

In the parking lot, Donata had broken down into tears, apologizing profusely for her behavior and asking for his forgiveness. The change in her disposition had been like night and day, a strange perversion of Dr. Jekyll and Miss Hyde. Donata had assured him it would never happen again, professing how a heavy course load and daily anxieties were weighing heavily on her shoulders. As he'd pulled out of the store's parking lot, Donata had still been standing where he'd left her, a strange expression gracing her face.

Preston sighed heavily as the telephone rang in his ear. When Godfrey's answering machine picked up the call, he disconnected, not bothering to wait for the service to tell him the man's mailbox was full and unable to take any additional messages.

The new coffeepot sat on the counter, its box and packing materials strewn across the floor. He'd been reading the operating instructions when the doorbell had rung. Thinking it was Monica, he'd swung the door open excitedly, his enthusiasm falling like cold water on hot coals when Donata stood weeping on the other side. The two had been in heated discussion in the entranceway when Monica made her way up the walking path into the courtyard. Donata's arms had been wrapped possessively around his neck, her grip like a vise against the back of his head. Preston's gaze had met Monica's only briefly as she took in the situation, then shook her head in disgust and continued on into her home, closing the door and the windows behind her. The momentary waver in his attention had been all Donata needed to push herself into his home, settling herself on the sofa as if she were a welcome guest. It had taken an hour of bickering, cajoling, and finally threatening to call the police before she'd finally acquiesced to leaving.

Back in the kitchen, Preston dropped down into a padded chair, putting his head in his hands as he leaned his elbows against the top of his thighs. This mess with Donata had spun totally out of control. Clearly, the girl had some issues that were far more serious than he could have ever imagined. He sighed, tossing his head back to ease some of the tension pulling at his taut muscles.

He had wanted to knock on Monica's door to explain, but he hadn't. He didn't have a clue what he could tell her that would make any sense of the histrionics she'd been witness to. And the expression on her face had shown she clearly didn't want to hear any excuses. He'd stared into her windows, looking for a flicker of acknowledgment, but the blinds and curtains had been drawn tight, only a faint glimmer of light shining through. He'd stood staring for some time before the light faded into darkness, and he knew there was no hope of Monica James sharing anything with him that night. Rising from his seat, Preston turned off the lights and headed up the stairs to his bedroom. He was so lost in his thoughts, he didn't notice the shadow of someone looming in the center of the courtyard, staring straight into his window.

Five

Four-year-old Mariah James-Turner met her at the doorway, pulling open the large wood-clad door as if she personally owned the house.

"It's Mon-ka!" the young child called out toward the older woman walking toward them. "Mon-ka is here!"

"I can see, Mariah. Stop that yelling," Irma James said, reaching to kiss her oldest daughter on the cheek as she closed the door behind them. "Hello, baby. How was the drive?"

Monica nodded at her mirror image, the resemblance between them uncanny. "It was fine, Mom." She leaned down toward her sister, who was pulling excitedly at her elbow. "Hey, Shorty! Where's my sugar?"

Mariah grinned, reaching up to hug her sister's neck as the woman leaned down to lift her off the ground.

"I heard you on the radio," Mariah said, holding tight to Monica as they made their way through the home behind their mother.

"No, you didn't."

"Yes, I did. Didn't I, Mommy? Didn't I hear Mon-ka on the radio?"

"Yes, you did," the matriarch responded as she led them into the small kitchen.

Monica inhaled deeply. "Mmmm. Something smells good," she said, peering over her mother's shoulder down into the pot where the woman was stirring.

"I made a pot of potato-and-cheese soup for lunch. Nothing special. Are you hungry?" Irma asked.

Monica shrugged. "Not yet. Where's Diondre?"

"He not here," Mariah answered, pulling her stubby fingers through the short length of Monica's hair. "He's comin' late."

"I didn't ask you, Miss Know-It-All," Monica said, tickling the little girl's sides as the duo fell to the floor laughing.

Mariah rolled her large, black eyes skyward as she pulled herself to her feet. Her small hands fell to her bony hips as she tossed Monica a look of annoyance. Her lips protruded in a deep pout to reinforce just the right amount of attitude as she responded, "Well, I was talkin' to you!"

Irma shook her head at the child. "Behave, Mariah. Don't be fresh."

As the woman turned her attention back to the pot and its contents, Mariah shook her index finger at her mother, mouthing a silent scolding of her own behind the woman's back. Monica fought back a laugh, pretending to give the child a stern gaze. "You stop," she whispered under her breath, grabbing the child's hand and pushing it down to her side. "You're going to get a spanking if you don't stop."

Mariah grinned, knowing that her sister's threat was idle at best, and that there would be no spanking while Monica was home. Irma lifted the pot from the burner and cut off the stove. Moving toward her daughters, she smiled as she pretended not to know what they'd been doing behind her back. The three were interrupted as Diondre entered the room, Bill Turner close on his heels.

"What's going on in here?" Diondre chimed as he leaned over to kiss his mother. "What are you doing now, Shorty?"

"I not doin' nothin, boy. Hi, Daddy!" Mariah responded, rushing to jump into her father's arms as she stuck her tongue out at her big brother. Diondre returned the gesture as Bill hugged the child tightly, greeting them all warmly.

"Hi, Bill," Monica said, giving him a slight wave of her hand. "How's it going?"

"All's well on this end, Monica. How are you, sweetie?"

Monica nodded at her mother's husband and her baby sister's father. "I can't complain," she answered.

"Won't do you any good," Bill said with a wide smile as he placed the young girl back onto her feet. He leaned down to give Irma a deep kiss on the mouth. Mariah rolled her eyes and twisted her index finger in the air. Both Monica and Diondre laughed out loud, shaking their heads in Mariah's direction.

"You're a mess, Shorty!" Diondre exclaimed.

"No. You are!" Mariah answered.

Irma and Bill joined in the laughter. "All of you need to get out of the way so Monica and I can finish getting lunch ready," Irma said, waving them out the door. "Bill, take that girl outside for a few minutes, please. Diondre, there are two boxes up in the guest bedroom that belong to Monica. Put them in the trunk of her car so she doesn't forget them."

Monica laughed. "Geez, Mom. Are you throwing out the rest of my stuff?"

"No point in that junk taking up space in my house when it can be taking up space in yours," she said matter-of-factly. Irma passed her daughter a stack of plates and gestured toward the kitchen table.

As Monica placed silverware and plates around the table, Bill came racing back into the kitchen to grab one of Mariah's favorite toys. He stopped for one quick second to whisper in Irma's ear, and the two giggled like teenagers. Watching them warmed Monica, and as the door closed behind the man, she said so.

"Mom, you and Bill give me hope."

Her mother eyed her curiously. "How's that?"

"True love does exist."

Irma shrugged, sucking her teeth. "Tch. Child, please." Irma performed the infamous eye roll that both of her daughters had inherited. Monica smiled brightly, rolling her own eyes back at her mother.

Silence filled the air around them as they both fell into their own thoughts. Monica thought about her mother and the course of events that had led her into the arms of Bill Turner. At the age of nineteen, Irma James had been pregnant with her second child when her ex-husband, Monica's father, up and disappeared out of their lives. With little more than a high school education, Irma had found herself being both mother and father to two babies, two-year-old Diondre and infant Monica. With much help from her family, Irma had worked two jobs to support them while attending school part-time to pursue a degree in nursing.

With her career established, she'd put both children through private school; had purchased a small home for them to live in; and had doled out discipline, advice, and love on a daily basis. There had been no time for a man in her life, and if the truth had been told, Irma James didn't think she had any use for one. That all changed the day Monica returned home from Boston's Northeastern University with a degree in communications. The surprise limousine ride from the airport to their Greensboro home had proven to be so much more when Bill Turner stepped out of the driver's seat and introduced himself, asking Monica's mother if she would consider having dinner with him one night.

A man of average height, with the beginnings of a very small beer belly, Bill Turner had been too smooth and exceptionally charming. His eyes, dark orbs that had an eerie incandescence when he stared at you, had riveted their mother. A woman could have easily lost herself in the man's eyes if she had been so inclined. Irma had been appalled by his forwardness and just as intrigued by his confidence. With much cajoling from her children, she had finally conceded to one date.

From that moment on the duo had been inseparable. A quick Los Vegas wedding followed four years later, with Irma refusing to change her name or give up her home, insisting that she was too old for such foolishness and if the man wanted her it would be on her terms. Bill had barely blinked an eye, telling anyone who'd listen that as long as God blew breath into his body, the greatest love of his life could have anything she wanted. Just after Irma's fiftieth birthday, they celebrated their tenth wedding anniversary with the birth of Mariah. Irma called the child her change-of-life baby and still shook her head in surprise at the hand that had been dealt to them.

What Monica loved most was that through it all, Bill still whispered in her mother's ear. He could still make the woman blush and giggle like a teenager despite impending age and a toddler pulling at the two of them. Monica's fantasy's about Prince Charming and dark knights riding atop black stallions were embodied in Bill Turner, with her mother (and best friend) being the damsel beside him. Whatever their connection, it gave Monica hope that one day, her own story might also end happily ever after. The thought pulled her back to reality, and she dropped onto a cushioned seat.

"I met this man," she started, turning to stare up at her mother. "He lives across the courtyard from me."

"Why don't you sound happy about it?"

"I don't know what I am, Mom. I thought he might be interested in me and that maybe we could get something going, but now I get the impression that he's involved with another woman. Apparently it's not going well, and I have to stop and wonder if I'm just rebound entertainment to take his mind off his problems."

"A man with drama, and you're telling me this because . . . ?"

Monica shrugged. "Some advice, maybe?"

Irma laughed. "You can give it to everyone else, but you can't figure it out for yourself?" She dropped into the seat across from her daughter, folding her hands neatly into her lap. The two women studied each other. Then Monica smiled, her eyes spinning toward the ceiling.

"Okay, I already know the answer, I just don't want to face it. But someone else telling me gives it validation."

"So you need me to validate what you already know?"

"I don't know," Monica said with a shrug. "What I do know is that for once in my life I would like to have a relationship that makes me as giddy and as happy as Bill makes you. Jeez, Mom, I'm thirty-four years old. I'm making an incredible salary doing exactly what I love to do. I own a fantastic home. I can afford everything I need, and most things that I want, but I sleep alone every night. I just want to have someone in my life who cares about me, who's interested in things I'm interested in, and who gets excited at the thought of just holding me in his arms. Is that too much for a woman to have?"

"It is if she thinks the entire balance of her life

hinges on her having it. But I know I taught you better than that."

Monica sighed her frustration. "I know I don't *need* a man, Mom. I just *want* one to share my happiness with. I'm tired of being alone and single and dateless every weekend."

Irma slowly nodded her head. "Does this man have a name?"

"Preston. Preston Walker. He's a professor at the university, about Diondre's age, maybe older."

"It's rare for a man these days to come baggage free. Most have some type of drama past or present that they're dealing with. Have you and he even talked about his at all?"

Monica shook her head. "We made plans to have coffee the other night when I got off from work. When I got home, he and his friend were doing battle in the doorway. I didn't wait around to see how it ended."

"And he hasn't said anything since?"

"I haven't given him a chance. I've been ignoring him."

"Pray tell, Monica!" Irma exclaimed, tossing her hands into the air. "What is that supposed to get you? How in the world are you going to know what your options are if you're not willing to ask the hard questions and demand some honest answers from the man?"

Monica hated when her mother was right, and she was grateful for the sudden burst of energy that came bouncing into the room to interrupt the conversation.

"Mon-ka? You want to hear my song? I learned me a new song!" Mariah said breathlessly, running to jump onto Monica's lap. Bill and Diondre followed close on her heels.

"Excuse me," Irma said, her tone scolding. "Mommy was talking to Monica. You don't interrupt grown-ups when they're talking. You know better, Mariah."

The little girl's eyes widened. "I'm sorry. S'cuse me. Can I sing my song for Mon-ka?"

Irma nodded, and the small child grinned broadly from ear to ear.

"Well, excuse us, too," Diondre said with a deep smile. "Mom, when are you going to buy this girl a piano? We have a star in the making," Diondre professed, grabbing the seat next to Monica.

Irma rose. She reached a hand out to squeeze Monica's shoulder, the comforting gesture warming Monica's spirit. Monica leaned to kiss her baby sister's cheek, passing the warmth on. She watched as her mother reached for the pot on the stove to pour the hot liquid it contained into a large, ceramic soup tureen. "Her daddy says she can have a piano when she turns six," Irma finally responded.

Mariah slid out of Monica's lap, twirling to the center of the room. "Watch me," she said, dropping her tiny hands against the lean flesh that would one day be her hips. Her head began to bob rhythmically, a silent tempo beating inside the child's brain. When the lilt of her small voice filled the room, Monica couldn't help but smile as Diondre and Bill moved to be the child's backup singers.

The lyrics to a new Alicia Keys song reverberated through the room as Mariah performed, shaking her head, hands, and body like a well-tuned instrument. Monica was duly impressed.

"You go, Shorty!" Monica said, clapping loudly as the song ended.

"I know some more songs, too. You want me to sing 'em?"

"You can sing later, Mariah. It's time for lunch," Irma said, lifting the young girl into her arms and setting her down onto a kitchen chair. "You need to eat now."

A pout crossed Mariah's face. "I want to sing for Mon-ka," she said, tears rising to her dark eyes.

"Don't you cry," Bill admonished, giving the child a hard gaze. "You know better. You can sing as many songs as you want after we eat, but you have to eat first."

Slowly the child's expression changed, the onslaught of tears replaced with a timid smile. "I wanna say the grace," she said, her gaze flickering from her father's face to her mother's.

Irma nodded as she held hands with her girls, Diondre and Bill completing their family circle. "That's my girl!" she said, smiling down at Mariah. "Bless the table for Mommy."

Six

It had been a good two weeks since Donata had thrown her tantrum in front of Preston's home, willing Monica away from his door. Since that time, the window blinds across the way had remained closed, and Preston had not been able to catch the woman coming or going through the courtyard. As he pulled his car into an empty parking space, he scanned the lot for Monica's vehicle, hopeful that she might be home. Disappointment registered across his face. Glancing down at the watch on his wrist, he realized the time and knew she was already at the radio station.

As he made the walk from the parking lot to his front door, he contemplated the passing of events that had brought him to this point. His workday had gone smoothly, as had the entire week. Today had been the first day Donata had ventured into his classroom since he'd threatened to call the police on her. She'd been quiet, just shy of meek, as she'd stood in the doorway of his European literature course asking permission to speak with him. He'd been nervous when she'd asked to do so in private, noting her intent to drop his class.

As he'd led her into the confines of his small office, he'd been certain to ensure the door remained wide open. She'd been exceptionally cool when she dropped the required documents against his desk, again apologizing for her actions. Her request for his signature had been polite, her eyes avoiding his as he'd scribbled his signature across the university papers. After a quick trip to the department's copy machine, he'd thought he might have had trouble on his hands when Donata had been laughing hysterically to herself as she sat waiting in the overstuffed armchair in front of his desk. When he'd questioned what was so funny, she had only laughed more, explaining her behavior by lifting the school newspaper toward him and gesturing at the day's editorial. The rest of their conversation had been brief, polite chitchat that had ended when Donata needed to get to her next class on time. Preston had heaved a sigh of relief, and did so again as he closed and locked his front door behind him.

In the kitchen he switched on the radio, tuning in the station as he listened intently for Monica's voice. If he hadn't lost his keys fumbling with the mess of papers across his desk, he would have made it home earlier, possibly in time to see Monica in person and attempt to undo some of the damage that had been done. His frantic search had finally uncovered the key ring on the floor of his classroom, beneath the large metal desk that sat front and center in the room.

Ruben Studdard was crooning in the background, a slow, sultry tune that reminded Preston of his college days and the Friday-night dance parties in the basement of the fraternity house. There had always been a line of beautiful, intelligent, chocolate-toned women to draw close to his body and slow dance with beneath the pale blue lightbulb that lit the room. The air had been tinged with the aroma of perfumed soaps and perspiration, the room's temperature raging hot from the wealth of sexual tension and the lack of air-conditioning. There had been some good times in the dark corners of that basement.

The song ended, and Monica's voice filtered into the room. "This is Monica James, and tonight we're talking about credibility, integrity, and the basic principles of right and wrong. One of our brothers was on TV last night being interviewed about his journalistic ethics, or lack thereof. Clearly it was pre-promotion to kick off his new book tour, but of course, I don't think he expected to be hammered by the press the way he was. But let's be for real, people. The man lied. He lied to all of us. It was blatant. It was fraudulent. It was premeditated, and if he hadn't been caught, he'd still be doing it. He's blaming his crazy mother, medication, and the fact that he was a black man in corporate America who wasn't getting a fair shake. And he wants us to drop twenty bucks on his new book so that we can read about how he was wronged. According to him, his word is his bond, and now his word is the truth. I have some issues with this. I mean, once a liar, always a liar. Right? Wrong? Hit me on the phone lines, and tell me something good. I want to know what you're thinking out there, 'cause I'm thinking the brother won't be seeing a dime of my twentydollars."

The next hour of discussion was intense as Monica debated with her callers. The rapport between her and her audience was intense, the dynamics of the give and take quite impressive, and Preston was even more intent on reconnecting with the woman in the window. He reached for the telephone and dialed the radio station.

Bryan pressed a glass of ice water into her hands, nodding his head excitedly. "You are hot tonight. Who's got you all fired up?"

Monica shrugged. "Lines still ringing?"

"They won't stop."

"That should keep us employed then."

The man smiled. "Your neighbor is holding on line four."

Monica cut her eyes in Bryan's direction, lifting her eyebrows skyward. He returned the stare with a wide grin. "He asked that you please not put him on the radio, at least not until he's had a chance to apologize. What did he do?"

Once again, Monica ignored the man's question, glancing toward the clock. "Pay the bills and then spin us into another song. This shouldn't take too long," she said, reaching for the telephone. "Line four?"

Bryan shook his head yes. "No problem. Two minutes of commercials and some Anita Baker coming up."

As the door closed behind him, Monica pushed the line, connecting the call. "This is Monica."

"Monica, hello. It's Preston."

"What can I do for you, Mr. Walker?" Her tone was cool, just a shade away from being icy.

"Give me a chance to make up for the other week. Let me explain."

"You don't owe me an explanation. We just met. We're not even friends, so it's not like I was bothered by what happened."

"Well, I was bothered and I would like to be your friend. I'm hoping you'll give me a chance to prove myself." Preston was ready to beg, and he hoped she could hear it in his voice. Silence filled the space as Monica contemplated what she wanted to do. Across the way, Bryan was signaling that time was running out.

"You owe me a cup of coffee," she said finally.

Preston smiled into the receiver. "Cream and two

sugars. It'll be ready when you get here." His grin widened as elevator tunes sounded in his ears.

She had become comfortable with the voices that danced in her head, teasing her spirit when she least expected them. The last time they'd come with a vengence, welding reign over her energy and leaving her with no control. They whispered softly now, blowing messages into her ear, easy tones that made her feel good about herself and everything around her.

She had wished for the voices and they'd come, louder now, egging her on. Donata lay across her bed, not hearing the heavy rap music spilling out of the CD player. Tijuana and two of their friends were braiding hair, each lined up for one of their monthly wash-and-comb sessions. Despite the noise of the music and the laughter that rang against the walls, Donata heard nothing but the voices in her head, telling her what she needed to do.

Rolling onto her stomach, Donata pulled her fist to her chest, then opened her hand. The newly made house key lay flat against her skin, the lines of the metal etched on her palm. The voices had said it would be easy, swiping his key ring when he'd gone to make her a copy of her withdrawal forms. It had taken her only twenty minutes to run across campus to the local hardware store for a copy, returning the original set of keys to his classroom as he sat in the cafeteria having lunch with Dr. Davis. The two of them had sat smugly, eyeing the female students like fresh meat for the taking. She'd seen their stares, their lewd gazes. She had thought him better than that, but he was just like that fool science teacher. And he had never missed those keys. Tucking them beneath his desk against the furniture leg had been too easy. The voices had guided her, given her strength, and reminded her that he needed to pay for what he had done to her. The voices understood. Pushing the key beneath her pillow, Donata smiled, a malicious grin filling her face.

"Looks like we're having a party up in here!" she exclaimed loudly, joining in the laughter. "Who knows how to do those Goddess braids? That's what I want."

Seven

As Monica turned the last corner toward her home, she was well past the point of no return. Excitement had taken full control of her sensibilities, and she felt herself feeling like a teenager going on her first date. The moment was almost surreal. Pulling into a parking space, she took a quick moment to scan her reflection in the rearview mirror. She'd touched up her makeup before she'd left the station. Bryan had paid her a compliment, and she knew she looked good. She'd had every intention of looking good when she and Preston Walker finally sat down together across a table. She took a deep breath, filling her lungs with the warm night air. As she made her way up the walk, she noted how quiet it was; the wind, a passing car, and the light chirps of summer crickets were the only sounds around her.

His outside lights were on, guiding her to the front door, and just before she knocked, Monica ran a finger against her eyebrows and pursed her lips, moistening the lip color with her tongue. Preston's own excitement greeted her at the door as he pushed open the screen and invited her inside.

"Monica, hi."

"Hi yourself. I'm not interrupting anything, I hope?"

Preston smiled, rolling his eyes slightly. "No. I'm glad you're here."

As he closed the door behind her, Monica took in her surroundings. The decor was minimal and tasteful. The very contemporary furnishings were straightforward and to the point. They suited him, reflective of his nature. Books of every size and shape imaginable lined the walls, filling the built-in bookcases. Monica liked the living space, feeling comfortable in it as she took a seat at the dining room table. He had set the large glass table with a carafe of hot coffee, one large mug, a plate of cookies, and a variety of additions for her to chose from.

"I know you said cream and two sugars, but I figured I'd give you a choice," he said, gesturing toward the sugar bowl and a container of blue and pink sweetener packets.

Monica smiled. "Thank you." She pulled a cookie into her hand. "Did you bake these?" she asked teasingly.

Preston laughed. "I have a side job with the Girl Scouts," he said jokingly. "The thin mints are my specialty."

Monica nodded her head as he filled her cup with hot brew. "Aren't you having coffee?"

He shook his head. "No. I don't drink coffee."

"What kind of man doesn't drink coffee?"

He laughed again. "The same kind who doesn't eat meat, doesn't smoke, and doesn't drink alcohol."

"No meat?"

"None."

"Well, I guess a steak dinner is definitely out of the question then."

"Steak is, but I love lobster."

Monica nodded, nervous energy flooding the air between them.

Glancing across the way, she took notice of her

own condo unit through the living-room window. She'd left her blinds open, and a glimmer of light from the upstairs hallway illuminated the space. Preston turned to where she stared. He grinned broadly.

"Sometimes I sit there," he said, pointing at the recliner across the way, "but then you know that already." His gaze met hers.

Monica smiled, not quite sure how to respond. She was suddenly embarrassed by his blatant acknowledgement of their moments of voyeurism. She changed the subject. "Are you from this area originally, Preston?"

"No. I was an army brat. I was born in Germany, but we lived all over. My father was a military career man."

"Big family?"

Preston shook his head. "I'm an only child. How about you?" he asked.

"My older brother and I were raised in Greensboro. Single parent home. My mother was a nurse."

"Was?"

"She's a stay-at-home mom now. I have a four-year-old sister."

Preston chuckled. "That must be interesting."

Monica laughed with him. "It has its moments. My brother and I have a lot of fun with Mariah."

"Does your brother live close?"

"Durham. He was here the weekend your car was trashed. I should have introduced you."

"That was your brother?" Preston grinned. "I thought he might have been a friend or something."

"Or something?" Monica questioned curiously, noting an edge of jealousy in his voice.

Preston felt himself blush. "I was hoping he was nothing. I mean . . . no one special . . . I mean," he stammered, the color flooding his face. "I think you know what I mean."

Monica grinned at his sudden nervousness. She took a sip of her coffee, then grimaced, the sharp flavor flooding her senses. "I can tell you're not a coffee drinker. This is bad. Really bad."

"I'm sorry. I was afraid I'd used too much, but the amount they suggested didn't look like enough."

She laughed, the warm sound flowing smoothly through the air. "We could remove paint with this brew. I'll have to teach you how to make coffee."

"Can I get you something else?" he offered. "A cup of herbal tea or a flavored water, maybe?"

"No, thank you. I should probably be going. It's late, and I know you have work in the morning. My day doesn't start until the afternoon, so I can sleep in."

He nodded. "You're more than welcome to stay. I really would like to talk with you more," he stated.

Her gaze met his, studying the intensity of his pale eyes. They seemed to swallow her, inhaling every detail, each minute line of her body. Monica could feel her heart beating faster, perspiration rising to the palms of her hands. The nearness of him made her giddy as a sudden flood of heat rushed through her system. To still the sudden wave of lust, she rose from her seat, pushing her coffee mug back onto the table.

"Are you free for dinner this weekend?" she asked, her voice quivering ever so slightly.

Preston grinned. "How's Saturday night?" he asked quickly.

Monica smiled back, nodding her head slowly. She turned toward the foyer, heading to the front door, then spun back around to face him. "I have to ask . . ." she started, her gaze dancing across his face, "what about your girlfriend? Where are you with that relationship?"

Still seated, Preston could feel the smile across his face disappear, thoughts of Donata, and Monica's misinterpretations, tainting his senses. He shook his head. "She's not my girlfriend. I have never been involved with that woman. She was one of my students only, and she has some serious emotional issues that she's trying to work through." He came to his feet, moving to stand beside Monica. "I would not be trying to start a relationship before I ended one. I'm not that kind of man."

The heat around them was steadily rising. Monica took a step back, wishing for cooler air to come between them.

Preston closed the space, stepping in toward her for the second time. He pulled her hand into his, his gaze still locked with hers. "Thank you for stopping by," he said softly, his voice barely a loud whisper. "Maybe we can do it again tomorrow?"

Monica nodded, acutely aware of his fingers pressing against hers. His hand was large, his palm covering hers completely. His skin was like silk, soft against hers. "Maybe again, but not tomorrow. And next time, I'll make the coffee," she said with a smile, trying to regain control of her senses. She pulled her hand from his as she reached for the doorknob. "Goodnight, Preston."

"Goodnight, Monica. Sleep well."

Preston stared after her as she crossed the courtyard to her front door, sliding her key into the lock. A full moon, resplendent against the dark sky, illuminated her path, shining brightly upon them. He waved as she turned and called out goodnight, closing the door evenly behind her. The moon seemed to want to say goodbye also, fading behind a wreath of clouds that passed overhead.

Behind his own locked door, he cleared the dishes off the dining table, emptying the container of coffee down the sink. With the kitchen clean, Preston turned off the lights, then headed up the stairs to his bedroom. As he glanced out the window, he realized that Monica's blinds were still open, the full view tempting. Behind the veil of night, he stood staring down into her living room. He smiled as she sat on her sofa, sipping the last drops from a large ceramic mug. He imagined she'd wanted a good cup of coffee after the thick paste he'd tried to pass off on her. As she disappeared out of sight, he chuckled softly, remembering her expression as she'd sipped the foul drink.

Her downstairs lights darkened, and he could see the faint outline of her body moving toward the stairwell. A brief minute passed, and the line of her figure appeared on the second level, entering the room across from his. The temptation to watch was overpowering. He wanted to stay where he stood, hopeful that Monica might tease him, offer him a touch more to see than she'd given him before. An acute awareness that she might be unnerved by his presence suddenly slapped his senses, and he pushed what he wanted back into the dark recesses of his mind. Averting his gaze, he crossed over to the window and closed the blinds.

Monica stood still in the doorway, knowing that Preston was there, watching. The reminder of his hand against hers still burned hot, and she brushed her left fingers against the palm of her right hand. As she watched him close his windows she heaved a deep sigh and moved to close her own.

Without turning on the lights, Monica slipped her silk T-shirt over her head and stepped out of her linen slacks. Tossing the garments onto the end of the bed, she crossed the room, heading into the bathroom. The master bathroom was one of her favorite rooms. It had been a major selling point when

she'd first seen the home, drawn to the oversized
Jacuzzi tub that sat pristinely in the corner. The Old
World cabinetry, marble counters, and gold fixtures
accentuated the peach-toned walls. The room was
warm, inviting, and quietly seductive. The decor
throughout the entire house was very European,
reminiscent of a Tuscan village, with its abundance
of natural flooring, warm colorations, and very romantic air.

Monica moved to light the many candles that lay
against the edge of the tub and the countertops.
Pulling at the length of hair atop her head, she made
a mental note to schedule an appointment for a haircut. She liked her shorter style. The contemporary
lines were just soft and feminine enough, but with an
edge that spoke volumes about her personality.

Staring at her reflection in the mirror, she smiled.
The day had gone well. The evening had gone even
better. She was excited at the prospect of getting to
know Preston. There was something about him that
she couldn't quite put her finger on. He had a presence that was both angelic and devilish. She was starting to obsess, wanting to delve deeper, to know more.
Preston Walker intrigued her.

After a quick shower, Monica slipped into her
bed, sliding naked between the freshly washed bed-
sheets. Thoughts of Preston were still on her mind
as she lost herself in reflection, remembering the
warmth of his touch against her skin. She giggled
softly as she thought about her reaction to the nearness of him. The mere prospect of his presence
made her quiver with anticipation, sweat trickling
along her inner thighs and between the cleavage of
her breasts. Just the mere mention of his name was
making her breathe heavy with wanting. Preston
Walker excited her.

It had been a very long time since any man had

stimulated her the way Preston did. As she marveled at the possibilities of the two of them together, her fingers traced a slow trail against her flesh, running a slow race against her arms, over her shoulders, down to her breasts. She cupped the melon-shaped tissue in the palms of her hands and imagined that it was the heat from Preston Walker's large appendages burning against her chest. Her nipples blossomed full against her fingers at the thought. and the sensation shimmered down to her pelvis. She pressed a palm between her thighs, wanting to still the rise of wanting between her legs. Monica closed her eyes and wished for sleep, whispering Preston's name into the darkness.

Eight

Faint wisps of smoke filtered through the room, dulling Preston's senses. The Corner Pocket, an upscale pool hall and full-service restaurant, was not one of his favorite places, but Godfrey enjoyed the classic ambiance with its upscale furnishings. The spacious room was tastefully decorated with tufted leather spectator chairs and late eighteenth century French reproduction pool tables. With its well-stocked bar, humidor cigar room, and waitstaff of buxom, sweater-wearing college students, his fraternity brother was as content as any one man could be.

Although the expensive decor beckoned to an elite clientele, the eclectic mix of people present was a hodgepodge. In addition to Godfrey and Preston, there was only one other black male present, a short, bronze-toned brother in an expensive navy blue suit. It was obvious that the man was playing socially with colleagues from work, their conversation nothing but high-tech, sales-based talk not worth eavesdropping on.

The rear tables were being played by a gathering of Latino workers still dressed in the gray khakis and dull blue work shirts required by the cement and brick company that sat across the street. Between rounds of pool, they were downing a quick lunch of buffalo wings, and chili-and-cheese fries.

Four couples cuddled against the bar, the barely legal, blue-eyed blondes dressed in Southern-belle polyester next to slow-moving, slow-talking young men with deep, guttural Southern drawls.

When a tall brunette leaned over unnecessarily, her breasts brushing against Godfrey's arm, Preston could only roll his eyes in annoyance. He made a mental note to never let Godfrey con him into playing pool at lunchtime again. The young woman winked in Godfrey's direction, feigning an apology as she gathered the empty glasses and tempted him to order another round of drinks. Preston's irritation at the display between the girl and his friend was painted across his face.

"Rack 'em," Preston said, gesturing toward the rosewood table with its cast-iron legs and gold leaf embellishments. So intent was he on his flirtation, Godfrey barely noticed until Preston reached to return his cue stick to the hanger against the wall.

"What's your problem?" Godfrey asked, still staring after the waitress as she sauntered to the kitchen.

"You. Don't you ever get tired?"

"As long as there is still a woman with long legs, a full behind, and breasts like beach balls that I haven't caught, I am not tired. I'm not even winded."

Preston shook his head. "One day. Mark my words. One day your womanizing ways are going to come back to bite you right on the ass."

Godfrey laughed. "Maybe, but it won't be happening on this day. So, what's up with you? Donata still giving you a hard time?"

"No, thank goodness. That fiasco seems to have finally calmed down."

"Told you. Our girl has probably set her sights on bigger and better."

"As long as she's moved on. She was starting to cause trouble in my new relationship before I could get it started good."

Godfrey raised an eyebrow. "What new relationship?"

Preston paused as he selected a new cue stick and leaned across the table's green surface to shoot. He moved two balls into a side pocket, then walked around the table to scope his next shot.

"Well?" Godfrey questioned again.

"I called Monica James. We're having dinner this weekend."

Godfrey burst out laughing, the sound resonating loudly and causing many in the room to turn and stare at the two of them. Catching his breath, he waved a hand in Preston's direction. "Yeah. Right. Monica James. You are too funny," he said, still chuckling loudly.

Preston cut an eye toward his friend. "Why is that so humorous?"

"'Cause you know you don't have a date with Monica James. You don't even know the woman."

Preston laughed as he scratched the shot, sending the white cue ball into a corner pocket. "I know things about Ms. James that would make you blush, boy!" he exclaimed, memories of Monica in her window flashing across his mind.

Godfrey was still laughing as he cleared the table, sinking a steady stream of brightly colored balls. He stood up straight, staring hard at his friend. His hands were wrapped around the cue stick, the length of wood braced against the floor between his feet. The man shook his head in earnest. "What you know wouldn't fill a ten-cent thimble," he said still chortling under his breath. "But you keep dreaming big. You just might get lucky one day."

"Thanks," Preston replied sarcastically.

"You're welcome." Godfrey shook his head. "Hell, if you ever come close to hitting that kitty, I'd give up women altogether. Celibacy would be my middle name," he said, still shaking his head in disbelief.

Preston grinned as he racked up the balls for another round. "Well, you better go on and sell that Trojan stock you own, 'cause brother, you won't be needing them any time soon."

Monica cooed into the microphone, "Let's talk about first dates, people. Good ones and bad ones. Call and tell me something good. Who's on the line tonight?"

"Monica, Monica! Do I have a story for you. This is Kelly."

"Hey, Kelly. Tell us your first date story, girl."

"Well, it was actually a last date that turned into a first date."

"How'd you do that, girlfriend?"

"My ex-husband and I had gone to dinner at Red Lobster for that all-you-can-eat shrimp special."

Monica laughed into the receiver. "Did you get all you could eat, Kelly?"

"And then some, girl! The place was packed that night, so we took a seat at the bar and ordered a few drinks to wait until they had a table. Well, to make a long story short, the situation was bad. The man and I barely spoke two words to each other the whole time. We might as well have been strangers. He gets up to go to the restroom and when he does, the woman sitting on the other side of me turns and says, 'Really bad first date, huh?' Well, I just fell out laughing. Girlfriend and I started talking, and we've been together ever since."

"No, you didn't!"

"Yes, I did. Got me more than a plate full that night!"

"Kelly, you are too nasty for me! You go, girl!"

"Keep doing what you're doing, Monica. We love you, girl!"

"This is Monica James and WLUV radio. Call and tell me something good!"

Donata thought about calling the woman on the radio. She had a story to tell. A good one. She turned up the volume, trying to drown out the voices in her head. The voices were ugly that day, pushing and pulling at her spirit like vultures attacking raw meat. It was late. She wasn't quite sure how late, though. She'd missed all of her classes, not bothering to pull herself up and out of the bed that morning. She'd feigned illness, fueling concern from Tijuana.

As she rolled across the bed, turning her body toward the salmon-colored walls, she reached a hand beneath the flattened pillow under her head. His house key was where she'd left it, safe and secure, waiting for just the right moment. But it wasn't time yet. She wanted him to think she wasn't interested. It was important that he didn't think about her at all. The voices would let her know when the moment was right. Then she could call the woman on the radio and tell her story, about their first date and the English teacher who loved her. It was a good story.

Nine

Monica watched as her big brother entered the restaurant, his long strides capturing much female attention as he made his way to the table. As family photos proved, the man was a carbon copy of the father that neither of them had known, his dark features and strong masculine lines rising from the paternal side of their family. Monica had often wondered if this bothered her mother, or if she had ever harbored any bitterness toward the son who looked so much like the man who'd left them all behind. The striking resemblance had often given rise to many questions in Monica's young mind, even a touch of jealousy, but her brother's quiet spirit had always diffused any ugliness Monica might have thought to show. She smiled as he took the seat beside her, draping the jacket to his Armani suit around the back of his chair. He winked, not bothering to give her a hug or a kiss.

"What's up?" Diondre exclaimed cheerfully, pulling a cloth napkin into his lap.

"What? I don't rate a hug at least?"

"Don't want any of the sisters to get the wrong idea. There are some nice-looking women in here," he said, smiling widely as he glanced around the room.

Monica laughed, slapping lightly at his shoulder.

"You're a fool." She leaned to kiss her brother's cheek, stopping to rub the smudge of lipstick left behind after she did.

"See, that's what I'm talking about," Diondre said playfully. "What woman is going to want to give me some play with your lipstick all over me? I look cheap."

"You are cheap."

"Who are you to talk?"

"Hoochie."

"Takes one to know one."

Their teasing banter was interrupted by a waiter anxious to take their lunch order. "What can I get you this afternoon?" the young man asked, his blond hair waving against his shoulders.

"I'll have a Reuben," Monica responded, ordering one of her favorite sandwiches. "I'll also have a sweet tea," she added as she passed the waiter her menu.

"The Philly cheesesteak for me," Diondre said, "and a coke with a twist of lemon."

The man jotted the orders onto an unlined notepad, then turned toward the kitchen. Monica watched him as he walked away, then turned her attention back to her brother.

"So, what's new with you?" she asked.

Diondre shrugged. "Not much. Busy as ever. My pro bono work is taking up all of my free time."

"How many cases do you have now?"

"Six, and all of them in family court. Something is always wrong with somebody's child, parent, teacher, or friend. Doesn't make any sense."

Monica laughed. "You're the one who wanted to be a lawyer. What's the saying? Be careful what you wish for?"

"Well, now I just wish I could get paid, but that doesn't seem to happen often."

"Like you're really hurting for money."

Diondre's attention was diverted toward a striking Asian woman who walked past their table, taking a seat at her own. "I'm hurting all right," he managed to say, his eyes still focused elsewhere.

Monica laughed, tapping him against the shoulder for a second time. "So, have you spoken to Mommy?"

He nodded, turning to stare back at his sister. "I hear you finally have a date. Who is he?"

Monica rolled her eyes, spinning them way back in her head and around again. "Did you speak to Mommy about keeping Mariah at the end of the month so she and Bill can go to the mountains?"

"Yes, I did. I will pick her up the day they plan on leaving, and between us, we get to keep Little Shorty occupied until they get back that following Sunday. You get the day shift. Now, don't change the subject. Who's the guy?"

Monica sighed, then answered. "My neighbor."

"The one with the messed-up car?"

She nodded her head yes. "His name's Preston."

"What about Preston's wife?"

"He doesn't have a wife."

"He's got something, a woman trashing his ride like that. I hope you're not getting yourself in the middle of some mess. You know spouses can still sue for alienation of affection in this state. I'm not representing you if you get in trouble. You won't be ruining my reputation," he said with a smirk.

"I'm not, but thank you for being concerned," Monica responded, an air of defensiveness rising in her voice.

The duo paused as a second waiter placed their orders on the table, then questioned if he could get them anything else.

"No. Thank you," Diondre responded as Monica shook her head.

She returned them to their conversation. "He says he's never been involved with the woman. She's one of his students who's going through a bad time."

"And you believe that?" Diondre questioned, his expression skeptical.

Monica took a bite out of her sandwich, chewed, and swallowed before answering. "Why shouldn't I?"

"Because no woman ruins a man's car like that, or gets in his face the way she has, unless there's been something between them. It might not have been serious, but he had to have done something to make her think she had a right to act stupid. I don't doubt he gave her some hope that there might be a chance for them and then dropped her like a hot potato. Some brothers can be like that," he concluded.

"Some brothers?"

Diondre shrugged, pushing his wide shoulders upward as he raised his eyebrows. Monica couldn't help but laugh at the silly expression that graced her brother's face.

"Well, I believe him when he says there was nothing between them."

Diondre shrugged again. "Like I said. He had to have done something. Just don't get caught up in something you don't need to be dealing with."

He rolled his eyes as she rolled hers, and Monica laughed, wanting to infuse some levity into the conversation to ease the sudden rise of doubt she felt about Preston Walker.

As Monica made her way back to Raleigh, her brother's comments were weighing heavily on her mind. He had made a valid point, and she couldn't discredit what he'd been trying to say. Realistically, something had to have happened between Preston and that girl to warrant the woman's anger. Clearly, for her to show up on his doorstep, not once, but twice, had to be indicative of some form of relationship between them. What woman in her right mind shows up half naked at a man's home unless she's been given reason to believe that her presence might be welcomed? Preston's attitude was also mystifying. It was almost as if he'd shrugged the event off, wishing it away as if it had never happened. That he seemed to have any understanding for this woman raised questions Monica had no answers for.

She heaved a deep sigh, glancing in her rearview mirror before easing onto Interstate 70 toward her home. As she drove the thirty-plus minutes to her housing complex, she mulled over every conceivable scenerio about Preston and his friend that she could dream of. By the time she pulled into the parking lot, easing her vehicle into a vacant spot, she was more determined than ever to learn as much as she could about this man who made butterflies flutter in the pit of her stomach.

As she knocked on his door, waiting for him to answer, nervous excitement flooded over her. Preston pulled the door open, his cautious expression changing to one of complete surprise. The gaze that swept over her was like a warm breeze, or that wave of heat that licks your face when you pull fresh-baked cookies from a hot oven.

"Monica! How are you?"

"Am I interrupting?" she responded, leaning against his front door for support as her knees melted into jelly. "I know it's late."

"No, not at all. I was just watching a movie."

Monica glanced over his shoulder toward the widescreen television behind them. "Oh, which one?"

The Defiant Ones. It's an oldie."

Monica grinned. "Sidney Poitier and Tony Curtis making a break from the chain gang. It's a good film."

"You know old movies?"

"I know Sidney Poitier. I also know how to make a better cup of coffee than you do, and I could use one right about now. Are you up to watching the rest of the movie over at my place?"

Preston smiled. "I can do that."

Monica smiled back. "Give me a few minutes to get myself settled, then come on over."

The man beamed, nodding his head as she turned and crossed the yard to her front door. By the time Preston found his way to her entrance, Monica had changed into a pair of grey sweatpants and a Carolina Panthers T-shirt. The aroma of freshly brewed coffee greeted him in the entrance-way, and he inhaled the fragrant aroma.

"That does smell better than mine," he professed, nodding toward the cup of java pressed between her palms.

Monica chuckled. "What can I get you?" she asked, heading into the kitchen. "I have water, tea, apple juice . . ."

"Apple juice, thank you. I bought us some snacks," he said, lifting a bag of goodies in front of him. "Popcorn and candy."

"What kind of candy?" Monica asked, one hand dropping to her hip. The look she tossed him was spellbinding, fueled by an aura of pure passion emanating from the perfect lines and curves of her body.

Preston could feel his cheeks becoming flush, the beautiful woman causing his temperature to rise. He cleared his throat before responding. "Movie-theater candy. All the stuff you want and know you have no business eating."

Monica laughed, pulling a carton of juice from the refrigerator and pouring it into a glass. Preston eased down onto the chenille love seat, making himself comfortable. As she dimmed the room lights, she gestured toward the television and the remote control on the mahogany coffee table before him.

"Make yourself at home," she said, joining him on the love seat. She sat down on the opposite end, making herself comfortable against the plush cushions. Curling up in the corner, she turned her body in his direction, pulling her legs and bare feet beneath her as she did. She reached for a throw pillow that lay between them, pulling the stuffed cushion to her breasts, her arms crossed evenly over her chest. On the television screen, Sidney Poitier and Tony Curtis were engaged in deep conversation.

The two sat in silence until the flow of the movie was interrupted by a sequence of commercials for toothpaste, a Cadillac, and a trip to Disneyland.

Preston smiled, shifting his body to face hers, his hands twisting nervously in his lap. "Thanks for inviting me over. It's nice to have some company for a change."

A pregnant pause filled the space between them as her gaze locked with his. For a brief minute rational thought seemed to escape her, and she felt herself falling deep into the sensuous valley of his stare. The sound of her own heart was beating a drum line in her ears, and her flesh burned, the acute sensation of him having grabbed her hand beneath his inundating her senses. She struggled to find her words, nodding her head foolishly in his direction as she sat speechless before him.

"Thank you for coming," she finally sputtered, the tone of her voice strange to her own ears.

Preston could feel the rise of perspiration on his forehead. The sudden rush of tension across his lower extremities was consuming. He bit down against his lip, trying to will the sudden sensation away.

"How about some of that candy?" he said finally, reaching for the contents of the brown paper bag.

Monica took a deep breath. "What 'cha got?"

Pulling an oversized bag of M&M's from the bottom of the sack, he smiled. "Now, this is real movie candy," he said, sliding to sit closer beside her.

"One of my favorites," Monica said with a light laugh.

He slowly tore open the bag of bite-sized, candy-coated chocolate pieces, pouring the multicolored contents into the palm of his hand. Monica's eyes widened with intrigue as he selected a red candy between his fingertips and eased it past his lips. His eyes never left hers as he rolled the confection in his mouth, allowing it to linger and melt against his tongue. Monica's heart skipped a beat, then two, and she felt herself gasp lightly. She took a deep breath, filling her lungs with air. The sweet aroma of chocolate swam up her nostrils.

Preston pulled another candy between his fingers, a yellow one, then guided it to Monica's mouth. His finger gently brushed against her lower lip as he placed the chocolate into her mouth, following with a brown one, and then another red. Monica smiled ever so slightly as he brushed her flesh with each pass of his hand, tempting her. He shuffled the mix of sugar-coated pieces in the palm of his hand, playing an erotic game.

Her smile widened as he reached for another, slowly easing it in her direction. Her tongue protruded ever so lightly as she took both the candy and his fingertip into her mouth, pressing each against her taste buds. Unable to resist, she wrapped her lips around his finger and suckled like an infant, her palm clasped around the back of his hand. Preston felt a raging surge of excitement filling his cotton briefs. The sensation was electric, and it made him want to lean her back against the chair to cradle that wave of energy between her thighs. He pulled his hand away, popping a fistful of candy into his mouth, hoping to dispel the sudden rise of wanting that had consumed him. The woman had taken his breath away. Monica smiled, a smug expression crossing her face.

"You're a tease," she said, shifting her body even closer to his. "You're teasing me."

"You're one to talk," Preston said with just an edge of sarcasm. He grinned. "We're supposed to be watching the movie."

"The movie's over," she responded, gesturing toward the credits as they ran across the screen.

Preston nodded slowly. "It is, isn't it?"

Silence again filled the air around them. Monica took a deep breath, inhaling the scent of his cologne. The expensive aroma was a spicy blend of fresh air, ginger, and succulent flora. He smelled wonderful, she thought, wanting to lean in and press her nose against his neck and chest. She tried to focus on the television, an infomercial for a popular diet program playing. Anxiety was walking a seductive tightrope between them. Monica could feel Preston sneaking glances in her direction, fighting to focus on the program that neither one was interested in. When the chore became to difficult, he simply reached for her hand, entwining her fingers between his own.

"You make me nervous," he said, his voice barely a loud whisper.

Monica smiled, her gaze dancing with his. "Why?"

Preston shrugged. "I'm not sure. This is foreign territory for me. I'm much better at analyzing poetic structure than seductive overtures."

"But I hear you're such a romantic," Monica teased, just the faintest hint of sarcasm in her voice.

Preston laughed, tossing his head back against the cushioned seat. "I guess you did, didn't you?" he chuckled.

Warm laughter embraced them. With her hand still clasped in his, Monica shifted her body even closer to his, dropping neatly into the crevice of his arm. The invitation had been unspoken, and Monica had responded without saying a word. The energy dancing between them was shouting anything that needed to be said. The side of her leg pressed against his, and their bodies curved one into the other. Preston adjusted his body against hers, his arms reaching around to hug her tightly. He pressed his face into her hair, the sweet scent of rosewater tickling his nostrils. As Monica slowly twisted her fingers between his, pressing her palm to his palm, he pressed a delicate kiss to her cheek, allowing his lips to linger gently against her flesh.

The duo settled themselves comfortably against each other. Across the room, an old Shirley Temple movie had replaced the infomercial. Monica couldn't help but think of her little sister as the little blonde girl sang and danced across the screen. Beside her, Preston continued to stroke her hands, her hair, the length of her arms, never once attempting to manuever for more.

"I should be going," he whispered softly, brushing his cheek against hers.

Monica nodded slowly, savoring the sweet sensations that were skating across her nerve endings. She felt like putty: a soft, mushy, puddle of a woman who was completely out of control. She forced herself to open her eyes, to regain some semblance of composure. Preston still held her tight, as lost in the moment as she was.

They both inhaled simultaneously, sharing the oxygen between them. Time ticked by slowly. Preston found himself wanting to whisper her name against the round of her mouth, to taste her lips with his own. As he fathomed where that one kiss would

lead him, he suddenly willed his mind to draw back,
to pull away from the temptation his body was yearn-
ing for. Tension washed over his expression, hard-
ening the lines of his face. The gesture was not lost
on Monica, the man's obvious uneasiness stalling
her own arousal.

"What time would you like to meet for dinner tomorrow?" she asked as Preston rose to his feet,
pulling her up to stand beside him.

Still holding onto her hands, he shrugged.
"Would you like to make an afternoon of it?" he
asked. "We could leave here around one o'clock and
spend the day together."

"I'd like that." Monica walked him to the door,
frustration washing over her spirit. "Thank you," she
whispered, pressing her palm to his cheek.

Planting one last kiss against the palm of her
hand, Preston smiled, nodded, then made a swift
exit, wishing for the cool evening air to bring his
body some relief.

Beneath the comfort of his covers, Preston stared
toward the ceiling, his vision lost in the darkness.
Both arms lay against the pillow, crossed neatly beneath his head. He had craved her, and it had been
clear that she wanted him just as much. It would
have been easy, he thought. It would have been too
easy to lose himself in Monica's arms and never
think about returning. If he had kissed her mouth,
her full lips beckoning his, it would have been over.
He had no doubts that he would have fallen asleep
in Monica's bed and not his own, his body wrapped
sweetly around hers.

He would have to share his secret tomorrow, he
thought. He would have to open his heart and let
Monica inside. He wanted her to know him, to

understand the man he was and why. He could see it in her eyes that she was interested in who he was and how they might fit together. He felt himself smiling.

He had rushed out of her home, and now he worried that she might have been offended. He should have taken the time to tell her then, but the moment had been too much for him. His desire had been tenacious, and he had needed to regain control. He would have tomorrow to explain. Tomorrow he would tell her, and he prayed that she would understand.

Monica had replayed every detail of the experience between them until each and every innuendo was carved into her brain. Being with Preston had been too comfortable, as easy an exchange as breathing. When she'd anticipated more, he'd left instead, almost running from her presence, leaving her with a dull ache in those places that defined her femaleness. A strange expression had briefly crossed his face, but she had still been witness to the longing that lingered beneath his gaze. It had matched her own, spreading like brushfire between them. Monica suddenly marveled that she still knew very little about the man, other than he'd left her hungry for him, the sweet craving growing into a delirious itch.

She had stared after him as he'd gone home, her gaze following him through his house. It quickly became clear that something was on his mind when he'd ascended to his second floor bedroom without bothering to close his window treatments. There had been no glimmer of flirtation as he'd stripped out of his clothes, throwing himself into his bed with the blinds still open. It was as if he'd forgotten that she might be there.

Monica had salivated at the sight of him as he pulled his shirt from his broad chest, exposing a wealth of café au lait skin. Lean flesh pulled tight against the thick line of solid muscle. She had needed to take a seat, falling back against the corner of her bed when he pulled at his belt buckle. When he stepped out of his 501 denim jeans, posing in the briefest pair of black silk boxers, her muscles had spasmed in pure ecstasy, sending her to the door of a climactic convulsion. No man had ever before sent her that close to the edge of seduction without laying a hand upon her. When he'd crawled beneath the covers, drawing his blankets and the dark night around him, Monica lay sprawled across her own bed, reflecting back on the details of the evening.

Ten

The telephone ringing startled Monica from a deep sleep. She'd been dreaming about the ocean, a vast expanse of deep blue water cushioning her body. She'd been floating contently, exploring the open waves beneath a rising sun that cascaded over her in shades of red and gold. Then the phone rang, spinning her into the pool of salt water. She awoke with a start, feeling as if she had really been choking on saline, just mere seconds away from drowning.

"Hello?" she sputtered, coughing to clear her lungs and throat.

"What's wrong? Are you okay?" Irma asked, concern rising in her voice.

"Yes, sorry, Mom. I'm fine," Monica responded, pulling her body up against the pillows.

"Were you still asleep?"

"Yes, ma'am. I went to bed later than usual last night. What time is it anyway?"

Monica could sense her mother shaking her head. "It's almost eleven o'clock. Why did you go to bed so late?"

"I had company after I got home."

"That late!" Who came over that time of the night?"

"Preston."

Monica could feel her mother's silence. It was tangible, teeming with an opinion that filled the space between the telephone lines. Monica could feel it growing, swelling thick and full, just shy of exploding into something ugly.

Irma tempered her response, treading cautiously in territory between a mother and daughter that was potentially volatile. "He's not still there, is he?" she asked.

Monica heaved a deep sigh. "No, he did not stay the night and I did not sleep with or have sex with him."

"Well, thank goodness for something," her mother responded.

"But it's not like I didn't want to or wouldn't have if the opportunity had been there, either," Monica said nonchalantly.

Irma chuckled softly. "You had to slip that in, didn't you? I don't always want to know what you're thinking, Monica. I know you too well. I raised you, remember?"

"I wanted to make sure I answered all your questions."

"I didn't ask that question."

"But you wanted to ask it. I know you, too."

Irma nodded into the receiver, a wry smile gracing her face. "Did you resolve your concerns about his girlfriend?" she asked, moving the conversation in another direction.

Monica hesitated briefly before responding. "Yes. He says there's nothing between them, and I believe him. We're spending the afternoon together."

Irma's head continued to bob up and down. "Be smart, Monica. I don't want you to get hurt."

"I won't, Mom. I promise. So," she asked, changing the subject, "how's Mariah?"

"The baby's good. She can't wait to come stay with you and Diondre."

"We'll have a lot of fun. Diondre is going to stay

here so we won't have to shuttle her back and forth. She and I will hang out during the day and big brother will get the night shift when I go to work."

"I'm not worried. I know she'll be in good hands."

"How's Bill?"

"Getting on my last nerve. We're not speaking at the moment."

Monica laughed. "What did he do now?"

"I just don't have any patience for some of his mess. He's been crying and whining for weeks now about his back hurting him. Every time I want to do something he can't because his back hurts. I've made two appointments for him to see the doctor and he's canceled each one, saying he can't take the time off from work. I told him last night that I have had enough. Obviously his back isn't hurting him that much since he won't take time out to go see the doctor."

"You know how Bill is about his job. That man has never taken a sick day in fifteen years, and he will go in early and leave late. He's got serious dedication."

"He can have all the dedication he wants, but let me hear one more word about his back pain. He won't like what I tell him to do about it."

Monica laughed as she stretched her body along the length of the bed and then yawned, willing the last of her muscles to wake up. "Well, I guess I need to get up and get dressed. Preston and I are leaving at one."

"Are you coming for dinner tomorrow?"

"I think so."

"Well, you can tell me all about your date then. You have a good time, and stay safe."

"Yes, ma'am. I love you, Mom."

"I love you too, Monica. Give me a quick call when you get back home so that I know you're well."

"I will. Bye, Mom."

As she headed into the shower, Monica switched on her CD player and pushed the play button. *The Preacher's Son* by Wyclef Jean had been left in the CD player and "Party to Damascus" filled the room. Monica suddenly felt like dancing. A wide grin filled her face as she gyrated to the music, the beat intoxicating, spinning her into a drunken state of bliss. The Wyclef CD had been a gift from her mother. "He sure can make some music with his sexy self," Irma had gushed as the two of them had danced around Monica's living room, Mariah trying to mimic the words with a pretend microphone.

Irma was her best friend, and Monica knew her mother's intentions were good. She knew that any doubts Irma had were out of concern for Monica. The two knew which buttons to push and which to avoid, and as always, neither ever had any problems with coming straight to the point on issues. Monica had inherited that straightforwardness from her mother, a personality trait she most appreciated having.

Stepping into the flow of hot water, thoughts of Preston crossed her mind. The man had clearly made an impression. It had been some time since a man had captured her attention the way Preston had. Monica had changed men the way people changed cars, trading up when it suited her or abandoning the suitors that just didn't meet her needs any longer. Her long-term relationships had been few and far between. Jessie had been the first, the college boyfriend she'd dropped as quickly as she'd picked him up. She'd given him her virginity, and he'd given her the keys to his Ford Escort for the one year they were together. The day after graduation, she said good-bye and gave him his keys back. Then came Tyrone, the blue-eyed sports agent she'd met during her brief residence in New York. Tyrone had taught her what she clearly didn't want in a

man. He'd lasted just over five months, exactly four
months and two weeks longer than he should have.
Her last fling, and the longest commitment she'd
made to any one man, was the relationship that still
made her cringe when she thought about him. King-
John Vega had been her first real love, and now, the
dark stallion was making her work harder than she
should have had to. King-John had been the one
man that had left her giddy and foolish, and feeling
completely out of control when it was finally over.

Monica stroked a line just beneath her breasts,
rubbing at the dull ache that rose so mysteriously
each time she thought about King-John. They'd met
at a national convention for black radio broadcasters six years earlier. His impeccable reputation had
preceded him, and when she'd found herself seated
at the same table, Monica had been enamored. One
month later, she had moved from New York to
Chicago to work with the man. King-John had taught
her how to grab an audience and hold tight, to make
them feel that you were speaking to each and every
one of them personally, to make everyone listening
believe you were their best friend. He'd taught her
well, and Monica had taken each lesson and im-
proved upon it.

The two had become inseparable, and when she'd
fallen willingly into the man's bed the following
Christmas Eve, she'd been convinced that if love was
corporeal, its name would have been King-John.
Monica had believed the connection between them
to be like a rare wine: expensive, precious, and intoxicating. The man had been able to soothe her,
mesmerize her, and enthrall her by doing nothing
more than walking into a room and letting his intense gaze grace her body.

Their electricity had been explosive. King-John's
skills between the sheets had far exceeded his on-air

talents. The man had been the smoothest, most attentive lover Monica had ever known, and the fireworks between them made the New Year's Eve display in the New York Harbor look like fireflies on low batteries.

But good sex and the man's zest for mentoring did nothing to squelch his competitive nature. King-John had wanted Monica to take a backseat to his domineering spirit, and Monica wasn't a woman who took a backseat to anyone. When Monica's talents began garnering national attention, it became too much for the man. As president and headman in charge of his own personal pity party, King-John became manipulative, condescending, and just plain ugly. By the time Monica had decided she'd had enough, King-John left her for a job in Atlanta, marrying his program director one year later.

Monica's dull ache was throbbing incessantly, and she sighed deeply, shaking the memory from her mind. The hot water had cooled considerably, and she rushed to rinse the wealth of soap from her body before the flow turned cold altogether. Steeping out from behind the glass enclosure, she reached for an oversized towel and wrapped it around her body. The plush terry cloth warded off the room's chill.

After King-John, a relationship had been the last thing on Monica's mind until now. Since meeting Preston Walker, Monica was suddenly open to the possibilities that whispered beneath the pale amber of the man's eyes. Relishing the thought, Monica could suddenly feel the room's temperature rising.

Eleven

The clock had barely struck one when Monica locked the door of her home, then turned to watch Preston as he packed items in the back of his car and closed the hood. She smiled widely, raising her hand in greeting.

"Hello. How are you?" she asked as she sauntered down the walkway to meet him.

"I'm well. How are you?" Preston said, blushing ever so slightly.

She nodded, shifting a leather sports bag against her shoulder. Preston extended a hand to take the satchel from her.

"I took the liberty of making some plans for us. I hope you don't mind," he said, unlocking the car doors and placing her bag onto the backseat. He opened the front passenger door and gestured for her to get inside, closing the door easily after she'd taken a seat. Monica watched as he made his way around the front of the vehicle and slid into the driver's seat.

"So, where are we headed?" Monica asked as she pulled the seat belt across her chest and latched it at her hip. "What plans did you make?"

As Preston started the engine, somebody's symphony of string instruments filled the car's interior, the radio set on the local college's jazz station. The music was soft, easy, and just a touch short of boring. As if reading her mind, Preston reached to change the radio station, then finally pushed a CD into the player. The Temptations filled the interior space, and as Eddie Kendrick's sang "The Way You Do the Things You Do," Monica felt herself bobbing in time to the music.

"I thought I'd surprise you," he finally answered. "Show you I'm not the dull professor type that you had me pegged for," he said, a wide grin filling his face and his gaze sweeping over Monica.

The look he gave her sparked a rise in her temperature, and Monica could feel the heat flooding her face and shimmering through every nerve ending in her body. She cleared her throat before speaking. "Did I have you pegged for dull?"

"You know you did."

Monica grinned back, settling into her seat. "I hope I'm dressed appropriately," she said, gesturing to the printed capri pants and blue cotton sweater she wore. "I bought a change of clothing just in case."

"Not to worry. I packed everything I thought you'd need."

"Let me guess. You were a Boy Scout, weren't you? It's that 'always be prepared' motto, right?"

Preston laughed. "And I'm trustworthy, loyal, courteous, kind, brave—"

Monica held up her hand, giggling loudly as she interrupted him. "Okay, okay." She shook her head. "So, how far in rank did you get?"

"Star scout. I'm also an assistant scout leader now for a troop of boys in Durham."

"Impressive. My brother only made it to Second Class. He didn't like his troop leader."

"What about you? Did you do Girl Scouts?"

"Oh, please!" Monica said with an eye roll. "I've always rebelled against structured activities that forced me to be in the company of more than one other female at any given time."

"Why is that?"

"Women don't play fair."

Preston raised an eyebrow. "You really believe that?"

"You haven't had much experience with the female sex, have you? We can be our own worst enemy without even putting our minds to it."

"Why is that?"

"The laws of nature."

Preston looked at her questioningly.

"The statisticians says that there are approximately four women to every man. That means competition is fierce, and with there being a shortage of eligible males to begin with, since half are gay or already committed, it doesn't leave the door open for anything but foul play between us girls."

"You just haven't met the right female friends, obviously."

"That might be true. Growing up, I had to spend most of my time with my brother. Since Mom worked, he was my primary caretaker after school and on weekends. I hung out with the boys a lot. So, suffice to say, my closest friends have always been male."

Preston nodded, checking his mirrors before he pulled onto the interstate. "Since we moved a lot when I was growing up, Scouts was a way for me to stay grounded with my peers. Most troops are exactly the same, teaching the same principles. The rules and activities never differed. It was easy making friends because we all had one major thing in common. Scouting was one of the more stable factors for me when I was growing up. A scout troop was like home no matter what army base we were living on."

"What were your parents like?" Monica asked.

"Dad was strictly military. He was very hard edged, a stern disciplinarian. My mother was the exact opposite. It made for an interesting balance in our house."

"Are they still living?"

"My father died four years ago. He never recovered from open-heart surgery. Mom lives in Florida with her two sisters. The ladies share a beach house and run an antique shop. I hope that I have a chance to introduce you two one day." Preston gave her a quick glance and a deep smile.

She nodded, not responding as she focused her attention on the drive, trying to distract herself from the heat rising off her body. As Preston pulled off the interstate toward Cedar Grove, Monica's curiosity was raging. Outside the vehicle, the countryside glided by them, large open fields, an occasional herd of cows, and an intermittent trailer home dotting their path. They could not have picked a more perfect day to spend together, with the sun shining brightly as the warm temperature caressed their bodies.

As Preston pulled off the main highway, onto a dirt road, Monica's expression changed from calm curiosity to amusement. The signs for Predator Paintball were pointed in the same direction they were headed. Preston laughed as he caught her gaze.

"Paintball?" Monica queried, turning to face him.

"What? Too tame for you?"

"You must have me pegged for a real adventurer."

""Are you saying you're not up for the task?" Preston asked as he pulled into a parking space and turned off the engine.

Monica's wide smile was warming, sending a wave of sensation through Preston's body. "I'm saying," she answered, her tone challenging, "that I hope you're ready to take a butt whipping. You're playing in the big leagues now, Mr. Romantic."

Preston grinned. "Let the games begin, Ms. James."

* * *

An hour later, Monica sat perched in an old oak tree, the large limbs supporting her body beneath a covering of vivid green foliage. Crouched low, her back pressed tight against the massive trunk, she signaled to the guide who sat in the tree opposite her, pointing toward Preston and his own companion below. They both smiled in unison, silently noting the stealthy movements of their opponents.

Monica pointed in the direction of Preston's red flag, which sat in wait just yards away, ready for the taking. When her partner, Tuck, a large white man with the beginnings of a rotund belly and the tail end of a full beard, nodded in agreement, Monica pointed her semiautomatic paintball gun toward her adversary and pulled the trigger. A plethora of water-soluble paint pellets rained down on the two men below, spattering bright shades of blue paint against their helmets and clothes. As Tuck dropped to the ground, racing to retrieve the flag, Monica gave a loud Tarzan yell, her smug gaze meeting Preston's.

"I think that means you done got beat good, Mr. Romantic. That makes five games to two," Monica said, easing her way out of the tree to go stand by Preston's side. He reached out to hug her warmly, and when his body brushed against hers, Monica felt her knees quiver. She stepped out of his arms, not wanting him to notice that he'd unnerved her.

"That wasn't fair," Preston said as he pulled off his helmet. He shook his head, laughing. "That wasn't fair at all."

"All's fair in love and war," Monica responded, her eyes meeting his, then darting quickly away. She fought to focus on the man who was quickly approaching.

"That's some nice field action, little lady," Preston's guide, a lean young man said, joining them. "You done good. You done real good for a woman."

"What's being a woman have to do with it?" Monica asked, still grinning. "I mean, if it was a man thing, then I'd be the one boo-hooing about being beat right now and not you."

"That's right," Tuck said, joining them. He passed the red flag to Monica. "I think this belongs to you. Earned it fair and square, you did."

Preston was still shaking his head. "I've had enough. We need to go do something I'm good at so I can redeem myself." He grabbed Monica's hand as they all made their way back to the log hut that housed the office. Once inside, Monica pulled off the old sweatclothes that Preston had given her when they arrived. The garments had covered her clothes nicely, sparing her from having to wash paint out of them later.

Preston watched her out of the corner of his eye as she bent over and reached to untie her work boots. Monica had a backside that could make a grown man cry with anticipation, he thought. The sudden thought of her buttocks pressed against his groin made his muscles harden with desire. When he noticed his eyes were not the only pair focused on her rear end, he moved to step in front of her, blocking the view Tuck and his partner were taking far too much enjoyment from. As she stood, adjusting the waistband of her pants, he moved against her, his hands pressing against her shoulders as he planted a kiss against her neck, his lips lightly brushing against her flesh. The motion was possessive as he marked his territory, wanting the two watching to understand this exquisite woman was already taken. Monica felt herself gasp as her gaze met his. When Preston grinned, she smiled back, suddenly wondereing what his lips would feel like against the rest of her flesh.

As they said their good-byes, Preston clasped her hand in his. Side by side, they made their way back to the car, their arms swinging in unison between them. Preston was still amazed at her prowess and said so. "Where did you learn to climb a tree like that?"

"You forget, I had a big brother. You'd be amazed at some of the things he taught me. You ever race go-carts?"

Preston shook his head no.

"I've won two trophies. If Diondre did it, thought it, wanted it, or attempted it, I was right there beside him doing it, too."

"I should be embarrassed to be beaten so badly."

"Why?"

"It's a man thing. Let's just keep this to ourselves," he said, pulling onto the main road back toward Raleigh. "It can be our little secret."

Monica laughed. "I'm a woman with a radio program, and you want me to keep a victory like this a secret." She rolled her eyes.

Preston grinned, reaching for her hand. "I'll pay you," he said, pulling her palm to his lips and planting a soft kiss in the center of it. "Whatever it takes. You can't ruin a brother's reputation like that. I'd lose my membership to the he-man club."

Monica felt the muscles in her stomach somersault, spinning lust throughout her system. Her hand burned where he'd touched her, and the rush of heat was suddenly intoxicating. She struggled to speak, trying to ease the tension that had swelled within her. "Well, I think it's going to depend on what else you have planned for us this afternoon," she said, her voice coming low and husky.

He shook his head, a deep chuckle rising from his midsection. "Trust me, it's something I know and know well. I think it'll convince you to forget all about that debacle back there."

The ride was pleasant, a cool breeze wafting through the open windows. Monica welcomed the relief that blew over her body, and she settled back in her seat, enjoying the flow of music that danced in the space. The conversation between them was casual as they shared likes and dislikes, discovering a shared passion for Thai food, ethnic art, Southern architecture, and political activism. As they maneuvered down the highway, the conversation turned serious.

"I think what I respect most about Angela Davis was her unwavering commitment in her beliefs. I don't agree with all of her politics, but who says I have to? I can agree to disagree with her, and still respect what she has to say," Monica stated, moving herself into intense debate mode.

"So what do you think are the issues we as a people need to be focused on?" Preston asked. "Some of my fellow colleagues and I had an interesting conversation about the plight of black America recently."

"What was the general consensus?"

Preston shrugged, raising his eyebrows slightly. "I think we agreed to disagree."

Monica paused, collecting her thoughts. "There is so little solidarity among us that I think we waste far too much time and energy ranting about asinine issues. We're investing so much of our attention on nonsense, it distracts us from discerning the more relevant topics."

"What are the asinine issues?"

"Where do I start? The Confederate flag is one that always burns me. While we're throwing tantrums over where it does or doesn't hang, our children are arguably the most undereducated. A black woman shakes a breast on public television, and suddenly we're rewriting what we should and shouldn't censor over the airwaves. In the meantime, black families are impoverished and black men are underemployed, and no one is interested in formulating strategies hat will effectively address and irradicate those problems."

"I think not supporting the Confederate flag hanging in public arenas is relevant. It's symbolic of an era of treatment that we as a people shouldn't have to be continually reminded of."

"Maybe we need to be reminded. Maybe that reminder is what will force us to get off our butts and fight harder for what we deserve. Right now, the energy invested in fighting it is energy wasted, because any man who wants to stand behind the hatred and bigotry that flag represents will. That's something you can never stop, whether you remove the symbol of it or not. What I question is, why are there so many allowing its presence to have such a significant impact over them? Why are they giving it and what it represents so much power?

"What we need to be investing our energy in is the obvious downfall of our young people. Our young women can't seem to remember what self-respect is. Dancing half-naked in gangster videos seems to be the career goal of choice for girls these days. And don't even get me started about our young black men. Besides not having an ounce of fashion sense, with those pants that hang half off their backsides, the majority are headed straight for incarceration over stupid stuff."

Preston chuckled. "But the black male has always had a hard way to go. We can't begin to count the number of black males sitting in prison for crimes they didn't commit."

"I agree, but history has already shown that if a black man wasn't willing to walk the straight and narrow, then he had to be ready to face the consequences, because sooner or later they were going to catch up with him. So not only won't these young boys be the first to pay for misdeeds they may or may not have committed, but they won't be the last. Bottom line, though, black mothers have been teaching us since before we were born that we had to do better, be better, try harder, and not get pulled into situations that we know we had no business in. Our integrity would either make us, or the lack thereof would break us. Like it or not, those were the rules tattooed in the color of our skin. But these young boys haven't been paying a bit of attention. They don't care."

Preston shrugged. "I don't know that I agree with that. I think there are plenty who care but don't know where to turn."

"That's because most of our sons are chasing the wrong dreams. The role models they're emulating are men running after that almighty dollar, pretending they can sing just because they can keep a beat, or spinning a basketball on their finger."

"At least they have dreams they can chase. There was a time a black man couldn't even have that."

"Sooner or later these kids will need to understand that there is no difference between them and every other Joe locked up if they're not intelligent enough to fight a respectable fight that allows their voice to not only be heard, but also respected. Sadly, too many black men with unlimited potential are behind bars, and we will never know the good they could have been doing on the outside because they made stupid choices. And whether we're willing to admit it or not, not many people are interested in hearing what an incarcerated felon, doing a life sentence, or worse, on death row, has to say."

"The lady speaks her mind. I'm glad you don't hold back," Preston said, glancing in her direction. He smiled, then refocused his gaze back onto the road.

"I never hold anything back, Preston. I don't bite

my tongue or sugarcoat my opinions. People either take me as I am or they don't."

He nodded. "I like that. I'll always know where I stand with you."

Monica smiled back. "Have no doubts, my friend, you always will."

As Preston turned off the main road, manuevering throught the streets of historic Rougemont, North Carolina, Monica focused her attention on the sights around her. As he pulled the car into the parking lot for an exquisite, Italianate-style mansion, her curiosity was piqued. Monica couldn't help but admire the lush surroundings, situated on a beautifully landscaped knoll. As she stepped out of the car, she was instantly drawn to the expansive length of the front porch. Groupings of white rocking chairs beckoned her to sit down and allow her mind to flow free of any concern, to leave all hints of anxiety back down at the end of the circular driveway. A small sign on the door welcomed them to Bellvue House.

"What is this place?" Monica asked, her excitement spilling out of her wide eyes.

"It used to be a bed and breakfast, but they closed it a few years ago. The owners are old friends, and occasionally, they let me borrow space to work in."

"What kind of work?"

"Writing mostly. Some poetry, and when I'm motivated, a book of fiction I'm working on." He extended a hand in her direction. "Come on," he said, "let's go around back."

As she clutched his hand and he hers, Monica followed him around to the side of the house and down the short flight of stairs that extended into the gardens. Around the perimeter of a small lap pool, explosive summer color filled the space, a wide assortment of bright flora in full bloom. Monica

leaned to smell a bush of red roses before they
headed to the entrance of a small brick structure
that bordered the opposite end of the cultivated
plot. Reaching into his pocket, he pulled out a small,
brass key and unlocked the door.

Intrigue pulled her through the door, and as Preston closed it firmly behind them, Monica's mouth
dropped in awe. As her eyes flickered back and
forth, trying to take in the entire view at one time,
Preston dropped down onto a large bed that sat in
the center of the room. A large ceiling fan spun cool
air through the small space. The bedcoverings were
exquisite, a blend of silk and satin reminiscent of vintage Victorian decor. Freshly cut hydrangea sat on
top of a small bedside wooden table. A partial wall
acted as a headboard, and on the opposite side, a
large whirlpool tub built for two filled the space.
Candles in varying heights occupied the space
around the tub. Across from the bedside, a fireplace
filled the wall, its darkened interior filled with a collection of plants and cacti in varying shades of green.
In the far corner, there appeared to be a flight of
stairs that extended upward, and as Monica peered
up curiously, Preston laughed.

"This was the old slave quarters," he said, answering the question running through her mind. "This
area was the original kitchen to the main house, and
the house servants slept upstairs. It was renovated
into a bridal suite a few years back."

"It's beautiful."

"It has incredible atmosphere. I like to write here.
I feel as if the spirits are telling me their stories, helping me to get the words onto paper."

Monica walked around the room, studying the
trinkets and keepsakes that adorned the small space.

"Are you hungry?" Preston asked. He lifted himself from the bed and reached for a large picnic

basket that sat on the top of another small table in the corner of the room. Lifting the lid, he pulled at the contents, placing each item neatly onto the table. Someone had packed an appetizing mix of assorted cheese and crackers, pasta salad, a loaf of fresh bread, chocolate-covered strawberries, and bunches of seedless, green grapes. A bottle of sparkling white grape juice completed the meal.

Monica watched as Preston spread a large checkered blanket across the bedding before setting the food in the center. He gestured for her to join him as he filled two wine goblets with drink and passed one to her. As she pulled herself up onto the large mattress, she couldn't help but laugh, the warmth of her glee adding to the ambiance of the space.

"What's so funny?" Preston asked, swallowing a bite of peppered water cracker and Havarti cheese infused with jalapeno. He slid another slice of cheese onto a second cracker and passed it to Monica. "Careful," he said, digressing for a quick moment. "It has a mild bite. So, what's so funny?"

"I was just thinking that this probably has to be the most creative move any man has ever made to get me into bed with him."

Color flushed Preston's face. "I'm sorry," he said, apologizing profusely, "I didn't mean . . . It's not like that. . . ." he stammered, suddenly embarrassed.

His reaction was so sincere, his unease washing over his expression, that Monica wanted to reach out and hug him, to assure him that all really was well. She giggled softly. "It's okay, Preston. I know you weren't trying to seduce me," she said, a faint touch of sarcasm dripping from her voice.

He dropped his chin against his chest, shaking his head, then glanced back up at her, joining in her laughter. "It does seem a bit contrived, doesn't it?"

Monica shrugged. She reached for a grape and

pulled it into her mouth, allowing the fruit to roll slowly against her tongue. "I don't know. If you bring a woman to a private estate, take her to an intimate honeymoon suite, feed her an incredible picnic lunch, and get her totally relaxed, why should she think she's being seduced? What would give her that idea?"

Preston bit down against his bottom lip, chewing nervously. He inhaled, forcing oxygen into his lungs. He chose his words carefully before speaking, knowing that a moment of truth had arrived for them both. "Would knowing that the man she's with is a virgin ease her thoughts in that direction?"

The statement caught her off guard, the shock registering on her expression as she stared directly into his eyes. For the first time since she and Preston had left home, Monica was at a loss for words. She opened her mouth to speak, then shut it, sound failing her. Preston studied her, his gaze absorbing the intensity behind her eyes, the swell of her throat as she swallowed, the wave of confusion that filled her face.

"I wasn't prepared for that one," she finally said, pulling a spoonful of salad into her mouth. "Are you really a virgin?"

Preston nodded. "I am. I know it sounds strange, but I made a vow to myself that I would wait until I was married, and so far I've been able to keep it. I wanted my first time to be with a woman I planned to spend the rest of my life with. Unfortunately, I've not had much success finding that woman." He could see the questions risng in her eyes.

"How old are you?" Monica asked, skepticism floating in her voice.

Preston chuckled. "Thirty-seven. I'll turn thirty-eight next month."

"And you have *never* made love to a woman before?"

He shook his head. "Never. I admit I've come very close a time or two, but I have never completed the act."

"You've not been getting it on with any men, have you?"

He laughed. "No. I'm definitely heterosexual. I like women. In fact," he said, smiling coyly, "I like one woman in particular, and I have to tell you, Monica, watching you, then spending time with you, has really been a challenge for me." His voice dropped low as he reached a hand out and drew his fingers against the length of her profile. "I think you know how I was feeling about you the other night. It was why I rushed out the way I did. I should have told you then, but I couldn't think clearly. You had my head spinning."

Monica smiled as she processed everything he'd just said. As they ate the balance of the meal, cleaning their plates, questions were still spinning through Monica's mind. "So tell me," she said, "what motivated you to make such a decision? And how have you been able to resist temptation for thirty-seven years?"

Preston laughed again. "Well, the first eighteen or so weren't a real problem."

Monica smiled at his attempt at humor. Holding her gaze, Preston felt himself holding his breath as he reflected back on memories that had shaped his existence. The story unfolded slowly.

"We were living in Korea. My father was stationed at Osan Air Base. My best friend was this kid named Robert Miller. We were both seventeen, and you know how it is at that age—hormones were raging and all we could ever think about was how we might get laid." He smiled, stroking his brow, then continued. "Robert lost his virginity to a prostitute named Pearl. He paid her twenty dollars, and she gave him exactly ten minutes of her time. When it was my turn, I couldn't do it. I just didn't feel right. Besides that, I had a huge crush on this girl in my history class. I had my mind set on her being my first, but she wouldn't give me the time of day. I was a little too geeky for her."

Monica smiled, shaking her head as he went on.

""Well, it just never happened for me, although Pearl kept offering her services. Then right before graduation, Robert got sick. His parents sent him back here to the States because they couldn't figure out what was wrong with him. I found out later that he was diagnosed with AIDS. This was before we really knew anything about the disease. When Robert died the following year from pneumonia-related complications, I just decided it wasn't worth the risk. I didn't want a casual relationship, and between obtaining my doctorate and working toward tenure at the university, I've not had a whole lot of time to build a long-term relationship with a woman. Besides, not surprisingly, most of my dates run the minute I tell them I'm a virgin." He chuckled softly and Monica laughed with him, the gesture warming.

"What do you do when you get aroused?"

Preston cut an eye in her direction as he cleared away the empty dishes, dropping them back into the large basket. He raised his eyebrows, not bothering to respond.

"Okay, dumb question," Monica said, embarrassment creeping over her at the sudden thought of Preston self-pleasuring himself. "Duh!"

Preston laughed again, then returned to the bed, dropping his body down beside her. As Monica pulled herself back against the wealth of pillows, he stretched the length of his frame alongside hers, leaning on his side as he propped his head against his hand, his elbow tucked beneath him for support. He stared into her face. "Does it bother you?" Preston asked.

Monica pondered her response before answering. The brief silence caused Preston's heart to skip with anxiety. He felt a wave of sweat rolling across his brow. When she finally answered, he breathed a sigh of relief.

"It doesn't bother me because I understand now where our boundaries are, but I think it raises a larger issue."

"What's that?"

"I'm not a virgin. I can't pretend to be a virgin, nor would I want to. I've not been promiscuous, but I've had a few intimate relationships that were extremely satisfying. Can you handle being with a woman who's had her share of experiences and doesn't mind admitting that she enjoys sex, particularly great sex?"

"I can if she's willing to put aside her own desires as we try to build a relationship between us. I also understand that such a request may be too much to expect from some women. We may never consummate what we share, but I have to hope that with whatever happens you'll respect me enough to not look to another man for that relief while we're together. We might not have intercourse, but there are other ways to still be intimate with a person."

"Mmmm," Monica purred softly. "That sounds interesting, Mr. Romantic."

Preston grinned. "I'm hoping you'll hang around long enough to find out."

She nodded. "I guess we won't know until we try, will we?"

The man grinned, a mile-wide smile filling the beauty of his face. His breathing was easy, and Monica felt comfortable when she reached out her palm, placing it against his chest. She could feel his heart beating against her fingertips. Reaching for her hand, he wrapped his fingers around hers, his head bobbing up and down with joy.

Taking another deep breath, he opened himself further, feeling that there was no reason for him to hold anything back from this woman who made him feel giddy and vulnerable, and masculine and secure all at the same time. Her eyes were teasing, mulling over the dynamics of where her newfound knowledge might very well lead them. His voice came low, a deep whisper that sent heat waves washing over her.

"I wrote a poem for you," he said, nervous energy shimmering in his speech. He leaned off the side of the bed and pulled a sheet of yellow-lined paper from a drawer in the nightstand. His gaze danced everywhere but on her face as a sudden surge of anxiety affected his spirit. It reminded him of that time in his past, when he was only eighteen, asking Cynthia Holeman, class brain and beauty, to go to the senior prom. He was reminded that she had turned him down. He looked up hesitantly, half expecting Monica to laugh in his face as she told him what to do with his poem. Instead, her stare was a winsome caress, gracious and receiving, filling his spirit like a satisfying meal.

Monica listened as his words swirled and swayed around them. They teased her, took her to the edge of temptation, and held her close, refusing to let her fall. Dropping the paper to the floor, he waited for her reaction, searching out her emotions. His gaze brushed against her skin like a feather falling against silk. Monica inhaled his presence, filling her lungs with the essence of his spirit. He had left her content, satisfied, and complete. And in that ancestral space, their being together felt amazingly right. The connection was overwhelming, and when Preston leaned up to press his mouth against her mouth, allowing his lips to skate lightly across hers, Monica swore she could hear her name beating within the folds of his heart.

Twelve

Diondre's voice was calling out to her from the answering machine. Rolling onto her side, Monica struggled to find the telephone, knocking an empty water glass, a box of tissues, and her leather-bound Bible from the nightstand.

"What?" she answered, sleep muffling her voice as she spoke into the receiver.

"Why are you still in bed? I thought we were going to church this morning?" her brother asked, irritation creeping into his tone.

"What time is it?"

"Almost ten o'clock. What time did you get in last night?"

Monica still lay with her eyes closed and her naked body pressed against the mattress. "I don't know," she muttered, yawning widely.

"Wake up, girl!" Diondre exclaimed, shaking his head into the receiver. "You need to get dressed. I'll be there in thirty minutes."

"Why so soon? Service doesn't start until eleven, and I only live two minutes from church."

"Just be ready," her brother said, authority rising in his tone.

Dropping the receiver back onto the hook, Monica forced her eyes open, scowling at the bright sunshine that peeked through the windows. She sighed, pulling herself up and toward the shower. At precisely ten-thirty, she stood dressed and ready when Diondre rang the doorbell. As he entered her home, she handed him a mug of hot coffee, kissing his cheek as he greeted her.

"You actually look pretty good this morning," he said, welcoming the morning brew. "Better than you sounded, at least."

Monica stuck her tongue out at him, then turned to appraise herself in the ornate mirror that hung in her hallway. The navy suit she wore was classic, a vintage Anne Klein silk purchased almost eight years earlier. Despite having had a long day and evening with Preston, she looked rested, radiating a natural energy. She nodded approvingly.

"You look pretty swell yourself," she said turning her attention back to Diondre.

The man grinned, pulling at the lapels of his suit as he tapped the toe of his alligator shoes in her direction. Monica flipped her hand at him, rolling her eyes as the two broke out into laughter.

"So, how was that date?" Diondre asked, taking a seat against the oversized ottoman at the foot of her recliner.

Monica grinned. "It was great. I had a very nice time."

"Where did he take you?"

"We went to Cedar Grove to play paintball and then for a very romantic picnic lunch. Afterwards, we spent the rest of the evening talking. Before I knew it, the time had blown by."

"Paintball?" Diondre said, shaking his head. "Brother couldn't do any better than that?"

"Brother did just fine. We had a lot of fun together."

"The wife didn't come after you, did she?"

"He doesn't have a wife, Diondre."

"Sure," her brother responded, sarcasm oozing out of his pores. "Girlfriend, then."

Monica took a deep breath. "I need your take on something, and if you repeat this to anyone, I will kill you."

Diondre reached for the coffee cup he had set on a cocktail table. "This sounds interesting. Spill it. What don't you want me to tell anyone?" he asked, taking a sip of the hot brew.

"Preston told me that he's a virgin. He's never been with a woman before. He's saving himself for marriage."

Diondre spewed a mouthful of coffee across the room as he reacted to the statement his sister had just uttered. He fought the laughter of mirth that suddenly consumed him. "Lord have mercy," he finally sputtered, wiping at his mouth with a paper napkin that Monica had passed to him.

"Are you through yet?" she asked, annoyance coating her words.

"Give me a break," Diondre said, still chuckling. "How often does a guy get to hear a joke as good as that one?"

"I'm not joking. He's a virgin."

"Just like that woman isn't his girlfriend. When did you get so naïve? Irma James sure didn't raise you like that! You'll believe anything if you believe that."

"Why do you think he's lying? You don't even know the man, and you're not bothering to give him the benefit of the doubt."

"I'm a man, that's why. I know better."

"Just because you're a dog, then he must be also, just because he's a man?"

"Who are you calling a dog?" Diondre said, pretending to be offended. Monica rolled her eyes at him. He continued, ignoring her annoyance. "I just know that if he's, what, thirty-five, forty, and he's claiming that he's never had sex with a female, then he's either gay, impotent, or suffering from some serious mama's-boy complex. In any case, you need to run, and run as far from the man as you can get."

"I like him, Diondre. I like him a lot," Monica said, dropping down onto the seat beside her brother. "In fact, I haven't felt like this about anyone since King-John."

Diondre studied his sister's posture, noting the look of confusion on her face. He could see it in her eyes that she was in want of his advice, that she was seeking his support as she contemplated pursuing this new relationship. He wrapped an arm around her shoulder, pulling her to his chest. He dropped the jokes, turning serious.

"Okay, so maybe he is still pure. What do you think about it? I mean, it's not like I'm interested in sleeping with him."

Monica shrugged, her eyes searching. "Honest?"

Diondre nodded his head. "Nothing but. You know that."

She sighed, blowing warm breath past her lipstick-lined lips. "I don't think it's a bad thing at all. In fact, it takes the pressure off. I like the prospect of our building a relationship without lust messing things up. Besides, I've been celibate for so long now . . . " Her gaze met his.

Her brother smiled. "Not like it's been by choice." Looking down at the watch on his wrist, Diondre rose from his seat, pulling her up by the hands. He cupped his large palm beneath her chin, lifting her gaze to meet his. "Monica, you're one of the most intelligent women I know. Trust your instincts. They have never steered you wrong. If you like this guy, then I'll love him. What anyone else might think doesn't matter as long as he's making you happy. But let him hurt you, and then I'll have to put on my big brother–superhero gear and make him cry."

Monica wrapped her arms around Diondre's waist, hugging him tightly. "Thank you," she whispered. "You're a great big brother, even if you are a dog."

"Woof, woof," he answered, hugging her back. "We're going to be late for church. Let's go. After this conversation it sounds like I need to pray for you."

Monica laughed, racing behind him as he made his way out the front door.

Donata had parked her car in the parking lot of Preston's complex, leaving it in a space some distance from his. The woman who lived across the courtyard from him had been driving out just as Donata'd shifted her Hyundai Accent into park and shut down the engine. The woman and the man she was with were chatting animatedly, sharing some joke between them as they laughed easily together. Neither had noticed her sitting by herself in the corner space, obscured by an oversized Ford Expedition parked next to her.

As she stepped out of the vehicle, she debated her options, the voices in disagreement over what she should do. She could surprise him, she thought, letting herself into his home and crawling into bed beside him as he slept. She could ring the bell and pretend to need his help when he answered the door. She'd apologize again for disturbing him and he would forgive her, telling her that he'd not minded. She could just barge in and demand he tell her the truth. She'd make him admit how much he wanted her, and when he did, she would tell him that everything was okay. She would show him, that she understood his previous confusion. With any scenario, she was confident that he would welcome her

warmly, opening his arms and eventually his heart to
her. She would let the trench coat fall to the floor
then, and he'd be overwhelmed by the beauty of her
nakedness beneath, wanting to hold her close
against his body.

Donata smiled, as she stood frozen behind a
statue, peering into the shadows of the darkened
glass. If it were night, she would be able to see him,
the lights from inside illuminating her gaze. Daylight
kept him from view and threatened to ruin her surprise for the two of them. Donata eased her way back
to her car, stopping to say good morning to the elderly white couple that had been so nice to her the
night before.

She had waited for hours for him to return home
so that they could share some time. The couple had
been returning from dinner, holding hands as they
headed toward their own town house. The old
woman had told her that Dr. Walker had been gone
since just after lunch. "Rode off with that lovely
woman, Monica James, from next door," she'd said,
supplying Donata with much-needed information. "I
think they were headed out to lunch," the woman
had volunteered, nodding her silvery head enthusi-
astically.

"Is Dr. Walker expecting you?" the husband had
questioned, appraising her in her newly purchased
trench coat and the black fishnet stockings that
peeked out from below.

Donata had smiled sweetly. "No," she'd responded.
"I'm his fiancée. I've been out of town, and he wasn't
expecting me. It's his birthday, and I thought I'd drop
by to surprise him. I'll just have to try to reach him
later," she'd said, waving easily as she'd turned to
leave.

"Would you like us to tell him you were looking
for him?" the woman had asked, making it necessary

for her to turn back to them, and to smile sweetly
one last time.

"No, thank you. I really want to surprise him. He
loves surprises," she'd gushed, soliciting their du-
plicity in her plans.

The couple had nodded agreeably, wishing her
good luck.

"We don't need luck," Donata had muttered to
herself as she pulled out of the drive. "We just need
him to do right," she'd chanted as she drove back toward campus and her dorm room. "We just need Dr.
Walker to do right."

That was last night, and the couple seemed de-
lighted to see her again, asking if she'd ever caught
up with the professor.

"I did," Donata answered. "Thank you both so
much. It was good to see him. He was thrilled. We
missed each other so much."

The older woman smiled, patting Donata gently
against the shoulder. "You take care, dear. It's supposed to be very hot today, and that coat might make
you sick. Wouldn't want to see you get heatstroke."

"No, ma'am. I'm headed home to change right
now. It had looked like rain earlier, and I just wanted
to be prepared. Just in case."

The couple smiled, nodding their understanding,
and then waved as they headed to their car and Donata returned to her own.

Preston was stepping out of his own car as Monica
and Diondre returned from Sunday services. He
smiled widely, waving his hand excitedly as he waited
for the duo to reach his side.

"Monica, hi," he said before leaning to give her a
quick kiss on the cheek. He squeezed her arm gently, suddenly self-conscious in Diondre's presence.

Diondre extended his hand in greeting. "Hello, you must be Preston. I'm Monica's brother, Diondre James."

"It's nice to meet you. Your sister has told me a lot about you."

"Don't believe a word of it," Diondre responded with a quick laugh.

"Where were you headed?" Monica asked, slipping her hand into Preston's as the three of them strolled toward the center courtyard.

"I had some paperwork to do in my office so I made a quick run to campus. How about you?"

"Church. I was just about to change. We're headed to Greensboro to have dinner with the family. Do you have any plans? I would love for you to join us," Monica said with a shy smile that caused her brother to give her a second glance.

Preston shook his head. "I don't. Just thought I'd watch golf on television this afternoon. Tiger's leading the tournament."

"You golf?" Diondre asked as Monica slipped her key into her door.

Preston nodded. "Avidly. How about yourself?"

"I'd spend all my free time on the golf course if I could. We should play some time."

"Just say when."

"How about now? Our stepfather and I were planning on going to the driving range to hit some balls this afternoon. You could join us."

Preston looked at Monica questioningly. "Would you mind? I mean, I wouldn't want to be rude since I'd be meeting your mother for the first time."

Monica shook her head as Diondre spoke for her. "Trust me, Mom won't think you're rude. Besides, Monica doesn't play. It'll give us men a chance to get acquainted."

Preston grinned in her direction. "You mean there's something you don't do?"

She cut an eye at him. "Chasing a small ball around a large plot of green grass is not my idea of entertainment. But help yourself."

"I need to change," Diondre said, excusing himself as he headed up the stairs to Monica's guest room.

"So do I," Monica said as Preston reached to hug her around her waist. "It shouldn't take too long."

He nodded, brushing his lips against her forehead, planting a light kiss against her eyes, her cheek, and then her lips. Monica melted into the embrace. His mouth was a soft, velvet pillow easy to fall into. Reluctantly, she pulled away, holding him at arm's length as he inhaled her essence, her vanilla-scented perfume caressing his taste buds.

"I had a great time yesterday," he said, his tone low, his voice deep. "I'm looking forward to many more with you."

Monica wrapped her arms around his neck, leaning her body close to his. "Me too," she responded, kissing him quickly. "I'll be right back."

"I'm going to run home and change, too. I'll meet you both back outside in a few minutes," Preston said as he headed toward the door.

From the guest room window, Diondre watched as Preston eased his way across the courtyard. As he stood watching, he could hear Monica humming softly as she made her way up the stairs into her own bedroom. It was obvious that there was something happening between his sister and her neighbor. Something that was clearly making his sister a very happy woman. As he reflected on the two of them and what their relationship could mean, he never noticed the young woman with burgundy Goddess braids pulling her car out of the parking lot, burning rubber as she sped out of sight.

* * *

As the trio stepped into the foyer of the James family home, Mariah came running excitedly down the hallway. She stopped short when she caught sight of the unfamiliar man standing beside her big sister.

"Hey, Shorty," Diondre said, greeting her warmly.

"Hey, boy," the child replied, slowing her pace as she eased herself over to say hello. She grabbed Diondre's leg and peeked out curiously from behind him. "Who are you?" she asked, as she looked Preston up and down.

"Mariah James-Turner! That was downright rude," her mother chastised as she came to greet them. "You're supposed to say hello and introduce yourself."

Mariah glanced quickly at her mother, then turned back to stare at Preston. Instead of saying hello, she pulled a thumb into her mouth, gaining a tighter grip on her brother's leg.

"This is my friend, Preston. He's going to have dinner with us tonight. Can you say hello, Mariah?" Monica asked, dropping down to the little girl's eye level.

Mariah cut her eye from Monica to Preston and back again. "He your boyfriend?" she asked, releasing her grip on Diondre to wrap her arms around Monica's neck.

Monica laughed. "He's my friend, but he's a man, not a boy."

Mariah rolled her eyes and giggled at her sister. "That's silly," she said, the initial wave of shyness subsiding. She turned to stare at Preston, grinning widely in his direction. "Hello. My name's Mariah James-Turner," she said quickly, the words running together.

"Hello, Mariah. It's very nice to meet you," Preston said.

"Welcome to our home, Preston. I'm Irma," the

matriarch said, reaching to shake Preston's hand. "You kids come on in. We were just back here in the kitchen."

"Is Bill ready?" Diondre asked.

Irma nodded as she led them toward the back of the house. "He's in the garage. He said to come get him when you get here." Irma gestured to a wooden chair at the table. "Have a seat, Preston. Make yourself at home."

"Thank you for having me. I hope I'm not intruding?"

"No, not at all. There is always plenty of food to go around in this house." Irma leaned to give Monica a quick kiss, waving a hand at Diondre as he excused himself to search out Irma's husband. Mariah sat quietly in her sister's lap, staring inquisitively at the stranger who was making funny faces at her.

"So, did you two have a good time on your date yesterday?" Irma asked, looking from Monica to Preston as she leaned against the kitchen counter.

Monica grinned. "We did. We had a great time."

Preston nodded his agreement. "Your daughter beat me at paintball, Mrs. James."

Irma laughed. "I heard. And please, it's Irma. We're very casual around here."

"Yes, ma'am." He shook a finger at Monica. "You said you weren't going to tell on me!"

Monica shrugged, laughing with them. "No, I said I'd think about it."

Mariah jumped from her sister's lap, moving to stand in front of Preston. "I can sing," she announced, her hands resting on her hips.

"You can? What can you sing?" Preston asked, grinning as he took a quick glance toward Monica.

"I can sing a lot of songs."

"Would you sing one for me?"

"What you want me to sing?"

Preston's eyes danced from side to side as he searched his mind for a song title. "I tell you what. Why don't you sing me Monica's favorite song?"

Mariah giggled excited. "That's easy. I know that one good," she said, all signs of shyness gone. Clasping her small hands behind her back, Mariah began to sway slowly back and forth. As the adults looked on, she belted out a powerful rendition of the spiritual "Swing Low, Sweet Chariot." By the conclusion of her song, Preston was clapping excitedly. "She's very good," he mouthed to Monica. When the child took her bow, they gave her a standing ovation.

"Very nice, Mariah," Monica said, holding out her arms as Mariah jumped into them. "That was excellent."

Mariah turned her attention back toward Preston. "That's Mon-ka's favorite 'cause Mommy made her learn it and she had to sing it in church like I done," she stated proudly, then added, "but I sing it better."

Monica rolled her eyes, giving the child a quick tickle as she kissed her cheek. Preston smiled, his gaze racing from Mariah's face to Monica's and then to Irma's. "Wow," he said. "I'm impressed."

Before Mariah could get another word in, Diondre came through the door, gesturing for Preston.

"Tell Bill I said he better not hurt himself out there," Irma said to her son. "I am going to the mountains at the end of the month, with or without him. And if he goes, I don't want to hear one word about something hurting him."

"Yes, Mom."

"You boys have fun. Preston, we'll get a chance to sit and talk when you get back."

"I look forward to it, Irma," he said before leaning to kiss Monica's cheek. "We shouldn't be too long," he said to her softly, reaching to give a light tug to Mariah's ponytail.

"You comin' back?" Mariah asked.

He nodded. "I sure am."

The child smiled, and as the two men exited the house, she turned to Monica and asked, "What's yo' boyfriend's name again?"

Thirteen

Monica's head had barely hit the bed pillows before the telephone rang, interrupting her attempt at sleep. Reaching for the telephone, she pulled it to her ear, noting her mother's telephone number on the caller ID.

"What's wrong, Mom?" she asked, her eyes still closed.

"Nothing. I just wanted to make sure you made it home safely."

Monica nodded into the receiver. "I did. Thank you for dinner. Preston said he had a great time."

"I like him, Monica. He's an upstanding young man."

Monica laughed, pulling her body up against the headboard. "That's an interesting assessment. Upstanding?"

"He was raised well. I like that. The principles he lives by are based on solid family values. He's grounded. He knows what he wants and what he's willing to do to have those things. He doesn't mind making sacrifices to do what he needs to do. Those are nice traits for a man to have, especially a man who is very fond of my daughter."

"Did he say something to you?"

Irma chuckled. "He didn't have to. It was written all over his face."

Monica grinned into the receiver. "I really like him, Mommy. There's something about being with him that makes me very comfortable."

"I could tell. What is it about him that you're so attracted to?"

Monica thought for a moment before responding. "There is something in his eyes when he looks at me that I've never seen from any man before. It's difficult to describe, but it's as if I can almost touch that single part of him that could possibly complete me. It's exciting, and I find myself almost desperate for it. He has this conservative edge on the outside, but when you start to ply the layers apart, he's like this vast island I want to explore and discover and enjoy. He makes me giddy and comfortable, and I feel safe when I'm with him. It's the strangest thing, Mom," she finally concluded, suddenly self-conscious about the tangent she'd just digressed on.

"Should I be worried about you?" her mother asked. "He almost sounds too good to be true. All that, and him being cute, too!" Irma said playfully. "He's one good-looking man, I can surely say that."

Monica laughed with her mother. "He is definitely that, and no, you do not need to worry." She could feel her mother nodding into the receiver. "I came up with this great idea to let him know how much I'm interested in him."

Irma chuckled. "Really? Like he couldn't figure it out?"

"I'm serious, Mom. I wanted to thank him for the time we had yesterday, so tomorrow I'm going back to everywhere we went to take a photo. I'm going to get a picture of the tree at the paintball field, one of the house, one of my sofa, and a few others, and I'm going to put together a mini first-date scrapbook. Then I'm going to add a note that says how much I enjoyed spending time with him and how much I look forward to our adding to the memories in the future. That wouldn't' seem too silly, would it?"

Irma chuckled. "No, I think it's sweet. He'll like that."

"I thought so, too."

"Well, you go back to bed, and I'll give you a call later in the week."

"Thanks, Mom. It really means a lot to me that you like Preston."

"I do. It's clear that he makes you happy, and that makes me feel good. I look forward to getting to know him better."

"Bye, Mom. I love you."

"I love you too, baby. Sleep well."

Preston leaned back in the large leather chair that sat behind the stainless-steel desk in his home office. The desk's surface was piled high with exam papers, books, more books, and an array of literary articles and research documents. His Dell computer was in sleep mode, the blank screen staring back at him. Barely noticing, he sat deep in thought, his mind focused on a problem.

The light on his answering machine shone, the faint glow blinking rapidly. Since his departure, a total of fifty-six telephone calls had been received. He'd listened to the first twenty, then, unable to bear the knowledge of one more, had pushed the stop button on the machine.

Fifty-six telephone calls from Donata filled his mailbox, each one more irrational that the last. He pushed the play button for the second time, and Donata's panicked voice filled the room

"Hi. It's me. Where are you? I've been calling all afternoon. Call me back. Please."

"Dr. Walker? I'm still waiting to hear from you."

"It's like that now, huh? You can't call me to say hello?"

"Pick up. If you're there, pick up the damn phone!"

"I miss you so much, Preston. What happened with us? Why don't you love me anymore?"

"I want you so badly! I need you to hold me. I need to feel you inside me. You're the only one who knows how to make me feel good. Call me, baby! Call me the minute you get in."

"Okay, okay, okay. I'm pushing too fast, right? Okay. I'll stop. Just call me. I promise I won't push so hard. I just love you so much. Call me."

"You make me sick! I hate you! You can't treat me like this and get away with it. I'm not some whore you can use and then get rid of when you get tired. I loved you!"

Preston pushed the off button, bile rising from somewhere deep in his midsection. He fought back the swell of emotion, anguish reaching for the forefront of his mind.

He couldn't comprehend how such an incredible weekend could end on such a disastrous note. Here it was, late Sunday evening, when he should have been tucked into his bed dreaming about Monica, and he was instead trying to decide what he needed to do about this student and her outrageous obsession. He closed his eyes, taking a deep breath. Oxygen filled his lungs. Stress pressed against his brow, beating an unwanted rhythm inside his skull. Confusion tainted his emotions, holding hands with anger, disappointment, and blatant disbelief. How had he gotten himself into this mess, he questioned. What in the world had he done to the girl to make her act so absurdly? He sighed, blowing out the same breath he'd sucked in just moments earlier.

Reaching for the telephone, he pulled the receiver into his hand, pressing it against his chest as he reviewed his options. With a second, third, and finally a fourth thought, he dialed 911 and waited for an operator to answer so that he could file a formal complaint and get some professional assistance with his growing problem.

Fourteen

"If you're headed home, the accident on I-85 northbound has finally been cleared away. The traffic downtown has eased up, and your ride shouldn't be too, too bad. This is Monica James, and you're tuned to the best of the best, WLUV radio, the station that loves hearing what you want to say, and loves playing what you want to hear. I'll be back after a quick word from our sponsors."

As the radio banter ended and music started playing, Preston reached to dial Monica's private line. She picked up on the first ring. "Hello?"

"Monica, it's me, Preston. I just wanted to say hello."

"Hi, yourself. What are you up to?"

"Not much. Just listening to this incredible woman on the radio."

Monica smiled. "And how did your day go?"

"Pretty busy. The school year's almost over, so there are always a million and one things that need to get done."

"Will I see you later?" Monica asked, nodding toward Bryan, who was giving her a signal to wrap up the call.

"I was counting on it. Thought I'd give that coffee thing one more try."

Monica's smile widened. "Don't hurt yourself. I always set the timer on my coffeepot before I leave for work. There'll be a cup ready and waiting when I get there."

"I'll bring the candy then," he said with a grin. "See you soon."

"Bye, Preston."

Preston moved to his office to shuffle through the mail that had piled up on his desk. Sitting to the left of his computer, a detailed police report loomed, capturing his attention. Its presence wiped the smile off his face. A patrol car had shown up to take a report within minutes of his calling 911. The local sheriff's department had informed him that until Donata was caught threatening him, or unless she physically assaulted him, he didn't have enough evidence to press charges or request a restraining order. Thus far, she'd not broken any laws or committed any crimes.

The officer, a large black man with a bodybuilder's physique, had questioned the relationship between them, insinuating that perhaps it was just an affair gone bad. His partner, a young white man with bright blue eyes, had echoed his sentiments, both men looking at him as if he had two heads and a tail. He'd even felt crazy trying to explain that she'd shown up half naked in his home and had been begging for his attention while he'd done absolutely nothing to warrant her strange behavior. After they left, he'd felt foolish for calling.

That morning he'd also reported the matter to Dr. Jessica Stern, head of the English Department. She'd given him the same strange looks and had asked the same questions, but had ended their conversation by promising that she'd speak with Donata before the week was out. He was hopeful that this would be the end of the matter and that Donata Thompson would just be a bad memory to leave in the past.

Lifting the report from its resting spot, he opened the top drawer of his desk and dropped it inside. He'd thought about telling Monica and about getting her opinion, but had changed his mind. He felt it better to leave well enough alone. He saw no reason to have Monica look at him with that questioning gaze the others had given him. He hadn't done anything wrong and saw no reason to give her reason to doubt that fact. He was confident the problem with Donata would soon go away.

The doorbell ringing pulled him from his thoughts. Rising from his seat, he eased his way slowly down the hallway toward the foyer, peering through the sidelights before he opened the door to welcome his unexpected guest.

Godfrey entered with a six pack of Corona beer in one hand and a bucket of Kentucky Fried Chicken in the other. "You got the game on?" he asked as he pushed his way inside. "Our boys are playing some ball! We're going to the Final Four this year!" he exclaimed, referring to the boys' basketball team's chances of making the NCAA playoffs.

Preston laughed, holding the door open. "Excuse you. I may have had company, thank you very much."

Godfrey glanced around the room, then cut his eyes in Preston's direction. "And you're hiding her where?"

"Don't be surprised when she gets here. Just close your mouth, say hello, and don't let the door hit you on your wide behind as you let yourself out."

"You need to stop dreaming. You should have taken Miss Thompson up on her offer when you had the chance. Another honey done slipped right out of your fingers, and she came signed, sealed, and delivered."

Preston shook his head. "That's one female you do not need to mention in my home. That child has lost her cotton-picking mind."

Godfrey laughed. "Here, I bought you some dinner."

Preston gave him a wry look. "Chicken and beer? I know full well you weren't thinking about me."

"Sure wasn't. The beer and chicken are mine. I stopped and got you a vegetable wrap at that Indian restaurant you like so much." Godfrey held out a small white bag in Preston's direction, then dropped it onto the countertop. "Figured you had your own joy juice," he concluded, taking a seat on the living-room sofa and switching on the television set.

The two men sat watching the basketball game, and then the local news. Godfrey stretched his arms over his head, yawning widely. "Guess that woman of yours changed her mind."

Preston shrugged, taking a quick glance at the watch on his wrist. "Not at all. She's just getting off work. I'm sure she'll be here in a few minutes."

Godfrey laughed. "You kill me. See, where you only dream about getting some action at night while you play with yourself in the shower, I have the real thing just waiting for me to show up to rock her to sleep."

"Let me guess. She's a graduate student, right? High school graduate, that is."

Godfrey grimaced, screwing up his face in mock disgust. "Much too young, my brother! I like my women with just a bit more experience. College sophomores do very nicely."

"You need to find you a woman your own age, although I doubt there's one who'd want you."

"Ouch! Do I detect a note of jealousy in your voice?"

Preston grinned at his friend. "Get out of my house. I'm expecting company and I need to be ready," he said, following Godfrey to the door.

The duo were still standing in conversation as

Monica made her way toward Preston's door. She stopped in the entrance and greeted the two men warmly.

"Hello. How are you two this evening?"

Preston leaned to kiss her lips, pulling her into his arms as Godfrey stood staring. "Monica, this is my good friend Godfrey Davis. Godfrey, this is Monica James."

"It's very nice to meet you, Godfrey. I hope I'm not interrupting anything?"

Preston shook his head. "Not at all. Godfrey was just leaving. Weren't you, Godfrey?"

"I . . . I was," he stammered, shock still moving across his face. "It's nice to meet you also, Ms. James."

"Please, call me Monica."

"Monica." He grinned stupidly. "I really enjoy your radio program."

"Thank you."

"Have you and Preston been seeing each other long?"

Monica smiled, looking from one to the other. She noted the interesting dynamics that filtered between the two men, a subtle wave of camaraderie, competition, and envy mixed together like vegetable soup. "What has Preston told you?" she asked curiously.

"Well, to be honest—" Godfrey started.

"To be honest, I told him it's none of his business," Preston finished quickly. "Godfrey was just leaving. Say good-bye, Dr. Davis."

His friend smiled widely. "Good-bye, Dr. Walker. Goodnight, Monica. It was a pleasure to meet you. I'm sure we'll be seeing each other again soon," he said pulling Monica's hand into his and gently kissing the back of her hand.

Monica winked as she pulled her hand back, then wrapped her arm around Preston's waist, pressing a palm to his chest. "I look forward to it. I'm anxious to get to know all of Preston's good friends."

Still grinning, Godfrey waved good-bye one last time before turning and heading down the walkway. Unable to resist, he turned back for one last look, getting more than an eyeful as Preston pulled Monica into a deep kiss, wrapping his body against hers, the glimmer of moonlight above shimmering over their heads.

Fifteen

Monica was glad to see midnight finally come and go. The calls had been tense this night, the audience wanting opinions on racism, reparations, and whether or not there really was a case against the singer R. Kelly. Monica's last nerve had snapped when one female caller had the audacity to profess that with the way young women were dressing and making public spectacles of themselves with their too tight, too low, too short clothing, they deserved whatever a man did to them.

Monica's terse response had bordered on rancorous, then had tipped into a valley of out-and-out ugly when she'd called the woman a whining, small-minded barracuda with the compassion of a dead hippo. She'd concluded by saying the woman was probably an anorexic dimwit with a face that resembled the south end of a mule. She'd also added the woman was probably just jealous because she lacked the bust, hips, and back end to pull off the too tight, too low, and too short styling of her much prettier, much younger sisters.

The woman's outraged gasp and expletives had forced Bryan to hit the disconnect button so fast that there had been a sixty-second span of dead air. Monica had figured the two of them would probably have to answer for it at their next review meeting. Bryan was not amused.

As Monica pulled out of the station's parking garage, she pushed the play button on her CD player, not wanting any part of anyone's radio program. She'd had enough radio to last her for at least the next twenty-four hours. A compilation of 1970s rhythm and blues filled the car's interior, and Monica's head bobbed in time to Evelyn "Champagne" King singing "Shame." Monica sang and hummed in time with the music as she headed toward town.

Glancing at the clock on the dashboard, she picked up speed, accelerating her automobile onto the inner belt line. Preston was waiting for her, the two of them having planned a late-night workout session at the newest health club to open in the heart of Raleigh.

Striving to keep up with the competition of more metropolitan cities like Los Angeles, New York, and Chicago, The Sports Emporium was a new, twenty-four-hour endeavor co-owned by two of Raleigh's black elite. One, a former Charlotte Panthers tight end, and the other, a University of Carolina law alum, had introduced themselves to Monica at a Duke Hospital fundraiser a few weeks back. Both had extended an open invitation to the club, and the tight end had passed on his private telephone number, encouraging her to use it if she was interested in a more personal tête-à-tête.

As she pulled onto the club's property, parking her car directly beside Preston's, she could feel a grin pulling at her lips. Over the past few weeks the more time she spent with Preston, the more time she wanted to spend with him. Thoughts of the man were never far from her mind, and with each lingering reflection, she found herself smiling foolishly.

Racing inside, Monica greeted the desk clerk, giving the very tall, very muscular man a wide smile and her guest privileges card. The two chatted briefly before he gathered enough nerve to ask her for her autograph. Monica laughed at that, joking that it was hardly worth the paper it was written on.

After changing into a pair of capri workout pants, her new sneakers with the swoosh logo, and a form-fitting sports bra, she headed to the workout room. Preston was already twenty reps into a set of chest presses. He stopped to grin in her direction as she approached, resting the dumbbells at his side as he sat up to welcome her.

"I was afraid you were going to stand me up," he grinned as she leaned to give him a quick kiss on the mouth.

"You know I'd never do that," she responded, her hands falling to her hips as she stood above him. "I had a caller give me a rough time tonight. I ended up staying a few minutes late to make amends to the bosses."

Preston chuckled. "I heard her. She was not happy with you."

Monica laughed with him. "Neither is management. They'll all get over it though." Monica pressed a palm against his shoulder. "You finish up what you were doing. I'm going to get my cardio in on that treadmill over there."

Preston nodded, then watched her walk away before reclining back against the bench to continue his workout. Monica's arrival had diffused any energy he'd had for working out, transforming his thoughts of exercise into fantasies that involved more intimate interaction between the two of them. He was amazed at how the woman's nearness always managed to cause his body to react with obvious wanting. He willed the onset of an erection away by focusing on the fifty-pound weights in his hands. He pushed the heavy weights up and out from his chest, testing the strength of his upper-body muscles.

As he resumed his workout, Monica completed a quick warm-up of her own muscles, then stepped onto the treadmill. She loaded one of the preset exercise programs and pushed the start button. As the machine kicked into gear, the walking pad moving steadily beneath her feet and rising to a slight incline, she found herself focused on Preston, watching him intently across the room.

Dressed in shorts and a tank top, his muscles shimmered under the bright lights, a glow of sweat dampening his cream-toned skin. Monica found herself uncharacteristically nervous in his being, apprehensive energy flowing through her veins. There was something intoxicating about his presence and whenever he stared, she found herself falling into the well of his gaze, lost like a mouse in a maze who was anticipating a reward at the end of the tunnel. Preston stirred an awakening throughout her body that caused her to breathe heavily, and just like so many times before, her nerve endings were tingling throughout her feminine spirit, heat rising like mist from her pores.

Thinking it best to change her view, Monica stepped off the treadmill, moving on to one of the weight machines. She adjusted the level of difficulty before attempting an abdominal exercise one of the trainers had shown her the previous week. Preston stepped behind her as she attempted the first pull.

"No," he said softly, reaching to adjust her arm level. "Like this. You only want to work your stomach. You need to keep your shoulders back so that you don't strain your neck and upper back. Remember, it's a standing crunch motion."

His hands grazed over her bare skin as he readjusted her position, then nodded as she rotated her core muscles in an up-and-down motion. Preston dropped his hands to her hips.

"Keep your hips stationary," he said, holding her in place as she pulled for a second time. "Twist straight from the abdomen."

"I get it," Monica said, her voice a loud whisper as she choked back her sudden reaction to the warmth of his touch. One of his hands was still pressed against her lower back. The sensation of his caress shot through her body, and Monica suddenly stepped away, allowing the handle of the pulley to draw back up against the machine.

Preston took a step toward her. "Is everything okay?"

Monica could only nod, her gaze locked on his. Her eyes danced across his features, noting every detail as she inhaled his scent, drawing the aroma of him deep into her nostrils. Monica stammered, struggling to form coherent words from her thoughts. "You . . . touched me . . . and I . . . it was. . ." She stopped, shaking her head as a smile filled her face, the desire for seduction punctuating her gaze.

Preston pulled her into his arms, leaning his face against hers, his lips close to her ear. "I know. I'm feeling it too," he whispered, the words blowing over her so fiercely that they made her toes curl in her new white track shoes. He held her tightly for another quick second, then let her go, stepping back out of her space.

"I need a cold shower," he said. "Why don't we call it quits? We can run down to the Chimney Post Diner and grab a snack. I think we need to talk."

Monica shook her head. "I'd rather have you take me home and make love to me," she said boldly, reaching out to take his hand into hers. The temperature between them had risen so intensely that Monica could feel the perspiration moving between her breasts, down past her belly button, then trickling over her feminine triangle and along her thighs.

She shot a quick glance over her shoulders to ensure no one else was in hearing range. With the exception of two men working on their biceps with the free weights, the room was empty, and neither one was paying them any attention.

Preston ran his free hand over his eyes and down his face, wiping at the moisture that had risen across his brow. Pulling Monica's hand to his lips, he kissed her fingers, the softness of his lips causing her to quiver with anticipation.

Preston smiled, his own emotions a melange of lust and confusion. "Making love to you is what I need to talk about," he said finally, his tone as controlled as he could manage. "I'll meet you in the lobby," he said as he turned, almost racing to the door of the men's locker room.

Walking her own frustration back to her clothes, Monica took a quick shower, changed, then joined him a few minutes later. A wave of embarrassment shimmered between them as they met at the front door, his leather sports bag tossed over his shoulders, hers resting on the floor by her feet.

"Why don't I follow you?" Preston said nonchalantly, opening the door to let her pass. "We can follow each other home from there."

Monica nodded her assent as they walked to their respective cars. Sliding into the driver's seat, she gave him a quick wave before starting the engine. "I'll see you in a few minutes," she chimed.

Twenty minutes later the duo pulled into the parking lot of the diner. From where they sat parked, they could see that the place was filled with a number of college students satiating their late-night hunger with burgers and fries. Preston remembered that the boys' baseball team had played their opening game under the lights in the University's new stadium earlier that night. Sensing that they had won, he imagined the celebratory meals would continue for quite some time. Stepping from his own car, he eased his way to Monica's passenger door, and knocked lightly on the window for permission to enter and take a seat.

"It may be a while before we're able to get a table," Monica said as he settled himself comfortably beside her.

"I'm sure the noise will make it difficult for us to talk, too," Preston said, as he studied her in the faint light that glowed from the diner's interior. Dark shadows danced across Monica's face, with swift waves of light from the diner's sign highlighting the warmth of her complexion at regular intervals.

Monica fought the desire to stare back as silence swelled around them. Turning the ignition key, she started the engine, then pulled out of the space, moving the vehicle to the rear of the parking lot, away from the bright lights and flow of people passing in and out of the diner's front door. As she cut the engine of the car, Preston reclined the seat slightly, shifting his body against the leather interior. He reached for Monica's hand and held it in his as he searched his thoughts. Behind his head, David Ruffin and the Temptations were wishing for rain, the subtle lyrics spilling out of the car's speakers.

"Preston," Monica started, turning to face him, interrupting the flow of his thoughts, "what's happening between us?" She stared down at his relaxed form, her gaze meeting his beneath the shadows of darkness that pressed in around them.

"All I know is that I have never felt about any woman the way I'm feeling about you, Monica."

She pressed her eyes closed, then opened them quickly. "Tell me if I'm wrong, but I think you want me as much as I want you."

Preston leaned up on one elbow. "No. You're not

wrong. But I'm not going to cross that line with you or anyone else until I'm married. I can't, and I need you to understand that."

Monica heaved a deep sigh. "I do, but—"

Preston shook his head, tracing a finger along her jaw line as he interrupted her. "But it's difficult. I know it is, baby. Monica, if you and I are serious about moving this relationship to the next step, then I want us both to want it to be forever. I don't see myself being intimate with you, then have us going our separate ways down the road. It is either going to be a total commitment we're going to want to make together, or it's not."

Monica let his words spin through her thoughts, not bothering to respond. Preston continued.

"My virginity is the one gift that I will have to give to the woman I commit my life to. It will be the one gift that she is going to know is all hers, totally and completely, without reservation. My wife will know that I loved her so much that I was willing to wait to share that gift with her and only her."

"Can you see yourself commiting your life to me?" Monica asked, her voice almost a whisper.

Preston smiled a faint smile. "So much so that it scares me to death. If you were to suddenly decide you didn't want me, I don't know what I'd do with myself."

The honesty in his eyes filled her, and Monica could feel her whole body smiling back, emotion sweeping through her as she trembled in response. Preston fell back against the seat, his hand still pressed to the side of her face. Heat billowed from his fingertips, flooding Monica's senses, and all she could focus on was the want of her lips pressed close to his. She moved toward him, lowering her torso over the gearshift as her mouth searched out his. Preston pulled her close, his hand moving to her hair as his fingers settled along the back of her head.

The kiss was sweet, smooth honey that rippled a stream over her taste buds. The rise of passion they shared sought to be relieved as its intensity struggled to consume them. Preston could feel the heat of her body against his, and the air was so still he imagined that if he opened his eyes he would be able to see the rise of steam emanating from between them. His mouth skated easily across hers, and when he parted her lips with his tongue, Monica moaned, the noise a barely audible rise of lust spilling up and out of her body.

Monica felt as if she was floating on a cloud of fog, lost in a sea of arousing sensation. The pleasure sweeping up and over her was almost too much to bear. Preston's hand softly massaged the small of her back and she yearned for the moment when he'd allow himself the joy of his hands exploring her whole body unabashedly. She sighed her frustration into his mouth, his tongue still dancing a two-step with her own.

As she moved to pull away from him, Preston lifted his body in time with hers, not yet willing to break the kiss. He was hungry for her, and his well-disciplined body had never felt more sensitive. He imagined that the slightest breeze blowing against his skin would feel like the heaviest of touches. The elongating lines of his erection pressed against his pants.

As they finally parted, the searing connection burned into both of their memories, Preston knew that Monica was the woman who completed him. Monica was the first woman he had ever seriously considered giving his most precious gift to. He pressed his lips to her cheek, his hand moving to the door handle of the car.

"I'll follow you home," he said softly. Before lifting himself from the car, he drew a finger along the lines of her face, pressing his fingertip to the edge of her mouth before kissing her one last time.

Monica watched as he manuevered his way through the four lines of parked cars to his vehicle. Once he was settled inside, she started her own car. As she pulled out of the parking lot, Preston following closely behind her, she whispered his name into the darkness, exploring the possiblities of it sharing space with her own.

"Mrs. Preston Walker. Mrs. Monica James Walker. Mr. Preston James." Laughing with joy, Monica reached for the volume button on the music and turned it up loud, joining in as the Pointer Sisters sang "Fire."

Sixteen

The evening temperatures had nose-dived, the last remnants of an El Niño weather pattern causing Mother Nature to send summer eighties dipping to fall forties. Preston and Monica sat side-by-side, cuddled on an oversized chair and ottoman in her living room, a raging fire shimmering in brilliant shades of burnished gold and red in the fireplace. The soothing sound of crackling firewood was all that could be heard in the room. Outside, the bright glow of a full moon cast an easy light through the windows, setting a seductive mood.

"That feels so good," Monica had moaned earlier as Preston kneaded the muscles in her back and shoulders, his fingertips slowly massaging the strained tissue into mush.

"Are you always so tense after work?" Preston had asked, kissing the nape of her neck before pulling her against him and settling them both against the cushioned seat.

"Not usually. I had a few tough calls tonight. One or two of them I probably could have handled better." She shrugged lightly, rubbing her back gently against his chest. Preston wrapped her tighter in his arms, grabbing her hands beneath his own. They sat quietly, neither speaking, the CD player spinning an ensemble of soft music in the background. Preston played with her fingers, his own hiding beneath her palm, searching along the line of her wrist, her forearm, then resting lightly against the crevice of her elbow. Monica could feel her muscles relaxing, each sinewy fiber shifting into a state of sheer bliss beneath his touch.

They'd spent many an evening together, nestled comfortably in each other's arms. Monica was awed by how easily they'd settled into a routine with one another, Preston navigating his schedule around her own nontraditional timetable. He would wait anxiously for her arrival home, the midnight moon sitting in the center of the ebony sky. They'd trade stories, sharing events from their day's activities until Preston would have to retire for a few hours of sleep to make his morning classes on time. On more than one occasion, Preston had bought dinner down to the radio station and he'd laughed with Bryan as the two had watched her in action.

They'd spent quite a few weekends in quiet discovery, learning more and more about each other as they hiked through the North Carolina mountains, swam beneath a rush of coastal waterfalls, and hot air–ballooned over vast acreages of farmland. Their friendship had blossomed, and Monica found herself craving the fruits of their labor.

Rubbing a heavy hand against his upper thigh, Monica could feel him tensing beneath her touch, his breathing labored as he struggled to control the rush of energy that spread though his groin, extending the length of his manhood. A rod of steel fought against the fabric of his pants, wanting to step forward and find freedom in the open air. Preston gripped Monica's wrist and pulled her hand to his lips, kissing the palm of her hand gently.

"This is getting harder and harder, Monica," Preston whispered into her ear, holding her hands as he wrapped his arms around her body. "You enjoy driving me crazy."

Monica giggled softly. "I think you've got that backward."

The man shook his head, a faint smile gracing his face. "I should be going home."

"What if I asked you to stay?"

"You know I wouldn't."

"You could sleep in the guest room."

"And where would you sleep?"

Monica smiled. "Close by."

"You're trying to wear me down."

"Yes, I am," Monica said, rolling against him until her body was elongated above his, his back pressed hard against the surface of the seat. Monica pressed her pelvis to his, grinding her body slowly against him. The rotation was unhurried and methodic, targeting just the right nerve endings to send them both to the edge of an orgasm. Closing his eyes, Preston felt his lips part ever so slightly as Monica taunted him, brushing against the rise of his erection. The sensation was exhilarating, the swell of emotions deliriously sweet. He made no efforts to stop her as she leaned her breasts against his chest, pressing tightly against him. Forcing his lids open, Preston met Monica's lustful gaze with one of his own, the duo exchanging promises with their eyes.

Inclining his head, he covered her mouth with a deep probing kiss that shook the breath from both of them. His tongue danced along the line of her mouth, meeting her tongue like two long-lost friends newly united. But before Monica realized what was happening, Preston slipped from beneath her, falling hard against the floor as he pulled his body away from hers. As the kiss broke, Monica was fighting to find words, but couldn't.

Rolling back against the empty seat, Monica

pulled her arms above her head, resting a forearm
over her eyes as Preston breathed heavily at her side.
The rise of her orgasm lingered along her thighs
and her nipples, flittering like a moth to a lightbulb
against her nerve endings. Across the room, the
flames in the fireplace danced beneath the glow of
moonlight above.

"Where do you want this relationship to go, Preston? What do you want from me?" Monica asked, still
gasping lightly for air.

"Farther than we can ever imagine it going," he
responded, his voice a husky flow of pent-up energy.
"And I want anything you're willing to give."

Monica's head swayed from side to side as she
tried to focus on something other than the intoxicating man leaning against the recliner beside her.
The heat between them had made her dizzy, his
presence an addiction she was in no hurry to let go
of.

Preston eased up on his knees, leaning on his
forearms above her. Resting his head against the flat
of her abdomen, he rubbed his cheek lightly against
the cotton fabric of her T-shirt. He heaved a deep
sigh as Monica cradled her palm against the back of
his head, stroking the tight curls of his hair.

"So, how far are you willing to go with me? And
what are you willing to give?" Preston asked, his tone
rising ever so slightly. He continued to cradle his head
against her body as her fingertips stroked his brow, his
ear, and the back of his neck. Time ticked slowly before he lifted himself up to stare down at her.

Monica met his gaze, studying the intensity that
lay behind his eyes. Shifting upward, she pulled her
body against the cushions, leaning back into the
chair. Preston moved to sit on the ottoman, his eyes
still focused on hers, awaiting an answer. His unful-
filled erection still pressed firm against the front of

his slacks, and he shifted himself gently, hoping that Monica wouldn't notice.

"I'll go wherever you take me, and give you every-thing I have," Monica finally whispered, her even tone caressing. "And I'll let you keep me for forever and a day."

"Forever and a day might not be long enough," he whispered, brushing his face against hers. "I can be greedy like that."

Monica smiled as Preston moved to kiss her mouth, his lips pressed closed. Monica stroked the side of his face with her hand, her fingertips moving past the curve of his earlobe and down his cheek, her palm settling against the line of his neck. Kissing him one last time, she pulled herself to her feet, reaching her arms toward him.

"Goodnight, Preston," she whispered softly, em-bracing him warmly as he rose to stand beside her.

"Goodnight, Monica, and thank you," he re-sponded, hugging her tightly.

As she guided him to her front door, Preston pulled her palm to his lips and placed one gentle kiss against the warm flesh. "You're in my heart, Monica. You are so deep in my heart, I'd be lost with-out you in my life. I hope you know that."

Monica grinned. "I love you, too, Preston Walker. I love you, too."

Seventeen

It was the third day of a five-day sentence, and Monica was ready to call in backup troops for added support. If she had to play one more game of Candy Land or hear her baby sister sing the Blue's Clues theme song for the umpteenth time, she would go berserk. She found herself watching the clock for Diondre's return home and her escape to the radio station, thinking she'd somehow drawn the short end of the sibling stick. Of course, Diondre declared that hearing the child cry for their mother until she was blue in the face or his reading more Little Bill books than he cared to count to get her to fall asleep more than made up for her antics while she was awake. Monica was grateful that Saturday and Sunday she and big brother would share their parenting duties until Irma and Bill returned Sunday night. Since the couple's first mountain holiday and little Miss Mariah's successful overnight with her big brother and sister, Irma and Bill had disappeared for four additional extended weekend getaways.

"Can we go see Preston?" Mariah asked, coming to lean against her sister's leg.

"Preston's not home. Do you want to go swimming in the pool?"

"Where is he?"

"He's working at the school."

"When's he comin' home?"

"I don't know, Mariah. Do you want to go swim or not?"

"I want to go to Chuck-E-Cheese," she responded, referring to the children's play center that Monica swore was an advertisement for birth control.

"Not today. We can go on Saturday with Diondre. He'll get mad at us if we go and don't take him."

"No, he won't," Mariah stated, dropping her hands to her hips.

"Yes, he will."

The child gave her a dirty look, letting Monica know that she was not going to be fooled, nor did she believe everything Monica had to say. The glare made Monica squint her eyes, giving the child a dirty glare of her own. Mariah threw up her hands in exasperation.

"I know what we can do," Monica finally said, rising from her seat. "Put your shoes on. We're going shopping."

"I don't like shopping," Mariah responded, her lips pushed into a full pout as she slipped her feet into a pair of white and pink sandals.

"You'll like this shopping. We're going to go buy costumes for you to perform in."

"What kind of costumes?" Mariah asked, curiosity getting the better of her.

"Pretty, shiny stuff made for the diva princess that you are."

"I'm not no diva princess. I'm Mariah."

Monica rolled her eyes, grabbing the child by the hand as they headed out the door. An hour later, arms laden with sequined tops, well-worn pumps, feathered hats, lacy skirts, and an assortment of thrift-shop dress-up gear, the two were headed back home. Monica had also purchased an old jewelry box hand painted with pink flowers and graced with

a little ballerina that danced when the top was
opened. Within minutes of arriving home, she filled
it with the contents of the bag of cosmetic jewelry
they'd found for one dollar. The final addition was
some of Monica's old makeup, two tubes of lipstick
and a container of blush.

"Can I get dressed now?" Mariah asked, excitement skating across her chubby cheeks. "Can I
please, Mon-ka?"

"Not yet. I have to get everything ready. You finish
your lunch, and by the time I'm finished you can
play," Monica responded as she spread newspaper
down against her kitchen floor.

Turning each of the clothing items inside out,
Monica laid them down on the floor. Searching beneath her kitchen counter, she found an unopened
can of Lysol and proceeded to give each garment a
gentle spraying. As she shook them quickly, giving
them an opportunity to dry in the warm air, Mariah
giggled excitedly. From her seat at the table she
watched her sister eagerly, stopping every moment
or so to take a bite of her chicken nugget Happy
Meal.

"Now, Mon-ka? Can I now?"

"Did you finish those French fries?" Monica asked,
rising to check the little girl's plate. Mariah nodded,
her small head bobbing up and down against her
thin shoulders. She opened her mouth widely, her
tongue weaving from side to side so Monica could
confirm that she'd indeed finished her entire meal.

Barely nodding her permission, Monica watched
as Mariah played dress up, clothes flying from one
end of the room to the other as the child tried every
combination of top and bottom that she could imagine. Mariah's exuberance kept them busy for most of
the afternoon as Monica joined in the fun, wrapping
a purple feather boa around her neck and doing an

imitation of Tina Turner performing "What's Love Got To Do With It." When Diondre walked through the door, Irma James's daughters were giggling over a secret.

"What's going on in here?" he asked, eyeing them curiously.

"Mind your business, boy," Mariah said, shaking a finger in his direction. "This here's girl stuff."

"Well, excuse me," he said. "I guess I can go back to work then."

"Oh, no," Monica said jumping to her feet. "I'm the one who's going to work. It's your turn to babysit. Grab a costume, toss on some lipstick, and have a go at it. We're singing show tunes right now."

Diondre flashed her a quick smile, his expression clearly stating that he didn't think so. "What's for dinner?" he asked, changing the subject.

"McDonald's!" Mariah exclaimed gleefully.

"No more McDonald's, Shorty. I need some real food. I get to choose this time."

"Okay. Can we get ice cream for dessert?"

"Whatever you want, Shorty. Whatever you want."

Mariah beamed, rising to tie the feathered boa around her brother's leg. "I love you, boy," she gushed, hugging him tightly. "I love you like soda pop!"

With her call sign echoing in her ear, Monica leaned back in her seat, watching as the lights on the switchboard lit up, silently announcing the number of calls and people anxious to tell her something good. She and Bryan sat laughing over Mariah antics, neither in any real hurry to pick up a call.

"Well, I guess we should get to work," Bryan said as he pushed the buttons for one more song to lead them into Monica's dialogue.

She shrugged. "If we have to. Surprise me

tonight. Just keep the calls coming, back to back. No screening."

"Are you serious?"

"Like a heart attack. I need to step up my game. I've been getting soft."

"I hear a good man will do that to a woman. My wife tells me that all the time."

Monica laughed. "Tell Danielle I said she needs to stop lying to you."

"You mean Preston's not a good man?"

Monica cut her eye at him, then fanned a hand for him to get out of her way. "Put me to work, Bryan Bailey, and get out of my business!

Bryan laughed as he retreated to his seat, adjusting his headphones against his ears.

"This is Monica. Tell me something good."

"Good evening, Ms. James. My name's Beverly and I want to talk about these young girls with all these young babies out here."

"Don't you like kids, Beverly?"

"I love kids, but babies don't need to be having babies."

"I agree, but what can we do about it?"

"I don't know, but someone needs to do something."

Mariah could hear a low sob rise in the woman's voice. "Is your baby pregnant, Beverly? Is that why you're upset tonight?" Monica could feel the woman nodding into the telephone. "Tell me something, Beverly. What's your baby's name?"

"Miranda. She just turned nineteen."

"That's not so bad, Beverly. She's an adult and obviously thinks she can make her own decisions."

The woman laughed, a strained echo that vibrated across the telephone line. "The girl's a fool," her mother said matter-of-factly. "She just had her second child. She had the first when she was sixteen."

"Ouch!"

"Oh, it gets better. Her first baby's father told her point-blank that he wasn't interested in having any children with her. Told her to her face that if she got pregnant it was over. So what does she do? She still gets herself pregnant. Sat around thinking she'd accomplished something. Imagine her surprise when the boy not only left her, but left her to marry some other girl he'd gotten pregnant six months later."

"She *is* a fool! And she didn't learn from that mistake?"

"No, ma'am. Left her first baby with me last year to go chase after some boy she met on the Internet."

"Oh, don't tell me that, Mama!"

"Yes, she did. Left him. Moved halfway across the country to be with this fool. And now, she has another baby to deal with. Came running back home 'cause her new man doesn't want any children either. Says he can't afford to be a father."

"Then he shouldn't have gotten her pregnant! But that's what child support is for, Beverly. The courts will make him do right if he's not man enough to do it himself."

The mother heaved a sigh, grateful to be able to unburden herself. "I don't know what to do, Monica. I didn't raise her like this."

"Maybe not, Beverly, but since this is how she is, then you need to decide what to do about it. Bottom line, she's grown. She's made decisions that impact not only her life but her children's and yours as well. Is she working?"

"No."

"So, she can't afford to feed and clothe either of these babies?"

"That's right."

"What about the father of the oldest child? Does he help out?"

"We get thirteen dollars a week. Not enough to buy a pack of diapers with."

"So it's on you to take care of them, correct?"

The woman nodded again. "I'm tired of this, Monica. I'm just too tired."

"I hear you, Beverly. Let me make a suggestion. Give her two choices. Planned Parenthood will help her with birth control. She needs to take some responsibility for her body. Secondly, she needs to go to school or she needs to work. If she's unwilling to do either, put her behind out. Put her out on the streets and let her fend for herself. Obviously, you don't want to put your grandchildren out, so take custody. If she can't be a responsible parent, then you do it for her. But don't let her dictate how you will be living your life. You decide if you want the responsibility of mothering your grandchildren, and if you don't, then you have the right not to. I'm sure you won't have any trouble finding another family to take those kids."

"I can't do that to my grandchildren."

"Then don't, but like I said, *you* make the decision. Don't let your daughter make it for you."

Beverly nodded again. "I will, Monica. Thank you for listening."

"Much love to you, Beverly," Monica said disconnecting the line. She spoke into the microphone. "Life is too short people for you young kids to be making a mess of things the way you do. Where's the respect? What happened to honoring your mother and your father? [And more importantly, what happened to loving yourself as much as you love your neighbor?] Someone call and tell me something good."

Monica took a deep breath before picking up the line.

"This is Monica. Who's on my line?"

"My name? Why do you need to know my name?" Donata asked, an attitude obvious in her voice.

"I don't, but it's easier for us to talk when I know who I'm talking to. But that's okay. Tell me something good tonight, caller."

"My man is stepping out on me, Monica."

"How'd you find out, girlfriend?"

"I saw them together. The whore lives next door to him. She's always running to his door looking for something."

"What did he have to say about it?"

The girl laughed. "Nothing yet. I haven't told him I know yet."

"What do you have planned for him, girl? I can hear it in your voice that you're up to something."

Donata giggled again. "I've already forgiven him, Monica. She's the one who has to pay. She's the one always whispering to him, getting in my way. She's the problem."

"Oh, please, girl. I know you know better than that. What is wrong with us women? We're so willing to blame the other female and forgive the man before he can get his clothes back on. How many times have we women blamed ourselves? Who hasn't thought that they had to have done something wrong for him to have turned to someone else? So what, that makes it okay for him, but not for her?

"A man disrespects us with another woman, and we automatically want to get mad at her. A woman cannot make a man do something he doesn't want to do. If your man is laying his pants on someone else's bed, you need to remember he's the one who made the decision to take them off in the first place."

"You would say that, wouldn't you, Miss Monica? You would want me to blame my man, wouldn't you?" The woman's tone was very hostile.

"That's right. I blame your man. If a man cheats,

the other woman didn't make him do it. He made that choice, and if a man doesn't respect and love you enough to resist the temptation, then the only thing you need to do is to decide whether or not you're willing to live with that fact in your face each and every day. If you can, more power to you. If not, kick his behind to the curb and move on, because you deserve better."

"What I deserve is to get rid of whores like you who think every man out there is for you. You're not that great, Monica James!"

Monica laughed. "Well, I know that there is only one man out there for me, sweetheart. I also know he isn't cheating on me. Unfortunately, you can't say the same. So, I think if you need to call someone out, it should be your man, not me. Instead of giving me a hard time, you need to save that energy for his lying behind. Get a life! Sounds like you could use one. This is Monica James, and I'm coming to you from WLUV–FM radio. Somebody call and tell me something good!"

Donata was pacing the floor like a caged animal. The woman had disconnected her. Had told her to get a life. She would have to pay, Donata thought, rage washing over her spirit with an ugly vengeance. Preston would be with her if it wasn't for that woman. She could have made things work between them if only Monica James hadn't been in her way. Monica James was the reason she was standing there in the dark, her heart hurting, the voices spinning out of control in her brain.

Donata stood shaking with anger, her muscles vibrating like warm jelly. The voices were getting louder, thinly veiled whispers rising to loud wails. They wanted to help her. They wanted to guide her and give her direction. The voices had come for her attention. She could hear them clearly now. She could hear them telling her how to make Monica James go away.

The night had ended early. Preston had been working on a project since before Monica had departed for the radio station and was still plugging away at it when she'd returned. They'd spoken only briefly before Monica had retired home, promising to have breakfast with him in the morning before she had to catch an airplane to Washington, D.C. and he had to leave for the university.

As Monica finished her third cup of coffee, she turned the last page of the book she'd been reading. The story had been dull, devoid of any excitement, and she tossed the paperback aside, annoyed that she'd purchased it instead of borrowing it from the library. After a quick check of the door locks, Monica eased her way up the stairs into her bedroom to change into her nightclothes. Across the way, Preston stood in the center of the room a pair of cotton sleeping pants his only attire. Monica smiled, then reached for the telephone and dialed his number. She stood at the edge of the window, peering across the way as he reached for his receiver.

"Are you all right?" Preston asked, pulling the telephone to his ear as he crossed over to his own window to stare out at her.

Monica nodded her head. "I am. I just wanted to hear your voice before I went to bed."

Preston stood staring, his hand pressed against the glass. Neither said a word, both wondering what might happen if the glass between them was to disappear and they could stand side by side in one of their bedrooms.

"You better ask me to marry you soon, Preston Walker. I'm really getting tired of you leaving me alone every night," Monica said, surprising both of them with the words that fell from her mouth. A quick wave of anxiety crossed her face as she waited for his response.

Preston took a deep breath, blowing the air out slowly. "Baby, I'm tired of leaving," he answered, a wide grin filling his face. "I love you, Monica. I love you very much."

Monica laughed softly, clutching the length of window curtain that framed the large, glass structure. Blowing him a kiss, she disconnected the line, still staring, longing painted over her expression.

Preston watched as she turned, stepping out of her clothes as she headed into the bathroom. With a sharp inhale of breath he stared as she slowly eased her blouse and bra off her shoulders, dropping them to the floor. Then bending at the waist, she eased her pants over her hips, a bright red thong following closely behind. He couldn't tear his eyes from her as she strolled casually away from him, feigning oblivion as her naked backside beckoned him to her.

Eighteen

Preston had dropped Monica off at the airport, giving her one last kiss before she disappeared through the security checkpoint and up the escalator toward the departure gates. As he pulled his car out of the airport parking lot, Preston tried to focus on his impending meeting with Dr. Stern. The woman had summoned him to her office, wanting to discuss his problems with Donata Thompson. He was grateful that there had been no further disruptions from the girl since he'd filed a complaint. Understandably though, his superior wanted to requestion his actions, review university protocol, and ensure that neither one of them had made any mistakes that could come back later to bite them in the behind. Although Preston could appreciate her efforts, he was in no mood to be bothered.

Before leaving the house that morning, his telephone had rung while Monica had stood in his kitchen, sipping the last of her coffee as she'd waited for him to finish dressing. Not recognizing the number on the caller ID, he'd hesitated before answering it. Monica had eyed him curiously until he'd reached for the receiver, pulling it to his ear. As he'd muttered a quick greeting the answering machine on the kitchen counter had clicked on, the call suddenly spilling out over the speaker. A quick wave of

panic had consumed him as he imagined Donata
being on the other end, but Godfrey's cheerful banter had greeted him instead, questioning his plans
for lunch during the day. His sigh of relief had gone
unnoticed, and he now struggled with whether or
not he should even bother Monica with the predicament he was facing.

As Preston pulled his car onto the highway, picking up speed to match the flow of traffic, a silver
Hyundai Accent pulled in behind him, allowing one
other car to glide between them. Traveling the
length of roadway, Preston's attention was focused on
his day and the taxing schedule ahead of him.

Less than three car lengths behind him, Donata
Thompson was focused on the chanting voices telling
her what she needed to do to get Dr. Preston Walker's
attention.

The radio broadcasters convention had not been
on Monica's list of things to do, but corporate management had dictated she attend, wanting to focus
attention on her, her show, and the program's continued rise in the ratings. Monica, on the other
hand, had hoped to avoid this conference. She had
particularly hoped to avoid King-John Vega, who was
scheduled to be the keynote speaker. Instead, here
she was, just minutes from her hotel and the only
man who had ever gotten deep enough under her
skin to break her heart.

American Airlines flight number 4570 from
Raleigh-Durham to Washington, D.C. had landed
right on schedule. Within minutes of collecting
her luggage and hailing a taxi, Monica found herself stepping into the lobby of the Willard Inter-
Continental Hotel. Management had balked at the
pricy reservations, but Monica had made it clear

that if she were forced to attend, at least she'd be attending in style.

Located in the heart of downtown Washington, D.C. the Willard was the grand dame of hotels. It was the best of tradition, luxury, and sophistication, and Monica had fallen in love with it the year she and Diondre had surprised their mother with a Mother's Day trip to the capital. Diondre had chosen the hotel, and both women couldn't help but agree that he had chosen well.

As Monica stepped into the luxurious lobby, with its magnificently carved ceilings, massive columns, crystal chandeliers, and mosaic floors, the memories flooded her senses and she felt herself smiling foolishly. Regaining her senses, she nodded as a bellman took her luggage. The concierge greeted her warmly, directing her to the check-in desk, and within minutes she was settled comfortably in her room, reveling in the lavish accommodations. Monica reached for her cell phone and dialed, waiting patiently while Preston's voice mail picked up the call. Then she left him a message. "Hey, sweetheart. Just wanted you to know I arrived safely. I'm headed over to the convention center in a few minutes to sign in. I miss you and I will speak with you later," she said. She also called her mother and left a similar message on the answering machine, giggling at the new greeting Mariah had left on the recorder.

In the bathroom, Monica laid her toiletries across the counter, then touched up her makeup, applying a thin coat of lip gloss to her mouth and a faint touch of perfume to her wrists and behind her ears. The turquoise pantsuit she wore fit her nicely, the cotton and spandex fabric flattering her figure. Monica admired the scrolled flower embroidery and silver-toned beads woven through the stitching that ran along the sleeves of the jacket and down the length of the pant legs. Pleased, she pulled her fingers through her hair and headed out the door and down to the lobby to explore.

She saw him before he saw her. It had not been her intent to deviate from the convention's schedule, but she'd figured a quick walk through Peacock Alley to admire the last of the cherry blossoms still in bloom wouldn't do anyone any harm. At the end of the long corridor, King-John Vega stood in deep conversation with three other men, two Monica recognized as former colleagues. His presence was as intense as she'd remembered, his imposing stature radiating confidence. At six feet, four inches, King-John embodied the royal presence his name dictated. He was solid muscle, a Hershey's dark chocolate mass of pure strength. His newly cropped haircut was low against his skull, his full lips accentuated by a newly acquired line of mustache. His hands were waving excitedly, and Monica knew this to be an indication of how intensely he was feeling about the subject matter. As she approached, she noted the absence of a wedding band around his ring finger.

Jason Ealy, a former associate at the Chicago station, noticed her approaching, his smile widening to a deep grin as he called out her name.

"Monica James! Look at you. How are you, woman?" he asked, reaching to give her a hug as the group turned their attention toward her.

"Better than ever, Mr. Ealy. Mr. Hazelton, hello," Monica greeted, her voice controlled as her knees shook with anticipation.

"What's with the "mister?" The last time we spoke you were hardly so formal," Jake Hazelton said, leaning to kiss Monica's cheek.

"I believe I called you an ass, but I thought I'd give you the benefit of the doubt this time," Monica responded before extending her hand toward the fourth man. "Hello, I'm Monica James, WLUV-FM, Raleigh-Durham, North Carolina."

"Darryl. Darryl Little, WKTZ, Sarasota, Florida," the short, round man answered, shaking her hand excitedly. "I've heard a lot about you."

Monica nodded, turning her gaze to King-John. "Your majesty, how are you?"

King-John grinned broadly, his thick chest seeming to push out even farther. "It's good to see you, Monica. I was hoping you'd be here."

"I just bet you were."

"We hear you and King are going head-to-head in that Southern market," Jake said, looking from Monica to King-John and back again.

Monica nodded slowly, her gaze still locked with King-John's. "Then I'm sure you heard my ratings are exceeding his," she responded, finally breaking the stare. "The king is slowly losing his crown to the queen."

King-John laughed, shaking his head. "The queen has had a good month. We'll see how long it lasts."

Monica rolled her eyes. "Well, gentlemen, I need to go get registered. I'm sure I'll catch up with you all later."

"I look forward to it," King-John said, reaching for her hand and pulling her fingers to his lips. As he brushed a kiss against the back of her hand, a flutter of heat threatened to drop her to the ground. Not wanting him to see that he had touched a nerve, Monica looked him up and down, then slowly pulled her hand away, reaching to wipe the kiss off against Jake's navy blue blazer. The group burst out laughing as Monica continued down the hallway, not bothering to look back over her shoulder at the four men staring curiously after her.

Monica spent the balance of the day avoiding eye contact with King-John. The day seemed to drag on forever, and when the last workshop ended, giving them two hours of downtime before the formal dinner, Monica was grateful to be able to escape back to her room. Stripping out of her clothes, she fell back against the bed, pulling the cell phone into her hand as she hit the speed dial.

Preston answered on the second ring. "Hello?"

"Tell me something good," Monica said, her voice low and inviting.

"I'm missing my girl."

"That's a very good thing," she answered, smiling brightly. "Your girl misses you too."

"How's the conference?"

"I'm ready to come home."

"Did you see your ex?" Preston asked. The thought had been spinning in his mind ever since Monica had told him about the man and their past relationship. Knowing that they were together in the same hotel had raised his anxiety level.

"Why do you sound like that bothers you?"

"It doesn't. I just wondered. You know . . ." Preston stammered.

"It bothers you. Admit it."

"Yes, it makes me nervous."

"Why?"

"Because you still have some unresolved feelings about the man."

"Where did that come from?"

"You don't think you do?"

"I think that whatever baggage I may still be carrying isn't because I'm unsure of my feelings, but that I'm still angry over how we handled things, and nothing more."

Preston took a deep breath, inhaling the silence that crossed the phone lines between them. Monica felt as if she could almost hear the questions racing in his head.

"We probably should have had this conversation before I left," Monica said finally.

Preston nodded into the receiver. "I would understand if you needed to . . ." He paused, searching for the words.

Monica laughed. "I'm glad you would, because I surely wouldn't. Preston, I love you. Yes, I'm seeing my former lover for the first time since we broke up. Yes, it made my stomach do somersaults, but not because I miss him or I still want him, but because it's just the first time we've seen each other since he left me and married someone else. But I'm glad he did. If he hadn't, who knows, we might still be together, and I would never have met and fallen in love with you. I love you, Preston. You either trust that or you don't. And if you don't, then we're wasting our time together."

"I do trust your love, Monica. I love you too, baby. Hurry home. I need you."

"Two more days, sweetheart. I promise. So, what have you got planned to do while I'm gone?"

"Well, I'm grading exams tonight. Tomorrow, Godfrey and I are having dinner with your brother, and I don't have anything planned for Wednesday. I'll probably just catch up on my sleep and dream about you coming home to me on Thursday."

Monica nodded. "Preston, what are you wearing?" she asked coyly.

He chuckled softly. "Track pants and a T-shirt."

"Take them off," Monica whispered.

Preston laughed out loud. "You're kidding, right?"

"Not at all. I want you to take your clothes off. Now."

"You're being fresh."

"I'm being serious. Take them off," she commanded again. She could almost see him pause before she finally heard the rustle of clothes on the other end.

"Now I have on my briefs and my socks."

"Good, because all I'm wearing is a black silk top and the tiniest thong you've ever seen. In fact, I may as well be naked," Monica said with a smile, her hand falling against her abdomen, her fingers gently stroking a slow line across her belly button. "If I were there I'd kiss that spot just beneath your chin. I love to nibble on that spot," she said softly.

Preston dropped down onto his living room sofa, pulling his legs up. He could feel the first quiver of energy shoot through his groin. He resisted the urge to fondle himself, fighting the sensation.

"Then I'd kiss a little lower, until I reached your nipples," Monica continued, her low voice a seductive breeze across the telephone line. "You'd like that, wouldn't you?"

"Mmmm," Preston groaned, his imagination gaining control over his body.

"I'd lick your right nipple first, then the left. I'd lick them both very slowly."

"Monica, you need to stop," he said softly, his eyes closed tight as he imagined her beside him, her mouth pressed to his chest.

"I wouldn't stop until I reached your belly button," she continued, her own hands now stroking the inside of her thighs. "Tell me how that feels," she whispered.

"It feels really good, warm and moist," he answered, "I can feel your breath hot against my skin."

This time Monica moaned. Her own nipples pressed rock-candy hard against her silk tank top. She brushed a hand over her breasts, shivering at the intense sensation.

"I can feel you hands, Preston. They're hot, almost burning."

"Where are my hands, baby?"

"All over my body." Monica pressed her thighs tightly together, one hand clasped tightly between her legs, the other toying with one breast and then the other. The knock against her room door pulled her from the reverie. The rapping was quiet at first, then increasing in intensity, and finally she heard a man call out her name.

"Monica, I know you're there. Open the door. It's me, King-John."

She took a deep breath, the whisper of a curse floating over her lips. "Preston, I'm sorry, but I have to call you back, baby."

"What's wrong?" Preston asked, panting ever so softly.

"There's someone at my door."

Preston nodded into the receiver. "Is it him?"

"Yes."

He nodded again, his hand falling from around his erect member. "I understand," he said, lifting himself up off the sofa, his erection deflating quickly.

"I wish I did, but this is a conversation he and I need to have. I'm sorry."

"It's okay, Monica. Do what you have to do."

"I'll call you later."

"I'll be here. Bye, Monica."

Dropping the telephone, Monica inhaled, filling her lungs with oxygen as she fought to calm her nerves. "Just a minute, King," she shouted, reaching for a pair of sweats from her suitcase and dressing quickly.

As she pulled open the door she eyed the man with disdain, annoyance clearly etched in her expression. "I thought you would have taken the hint when I didn't answer you the first time."

King-John laughed, leaning against the doorframe as he eyed her from head to toe and back again. "I prefer it when you're direct."

"Where's your wife?"

"I don't have a wife any more. We divorced a year ago."

"Sorry to hear it."

"Are you?"

Monica shrugged. "Not really."

The man chuckled again. "Like I said. You do direct so much better."

"What do you want, King?"

"I wanted to tell you how much I miss you. We were so good together," he said, his voice dropping an octave, the seductive tone meant to sway her opinion of him.

This time Monica laughed, shaking her head. "And when we were bad, we were really, really bad," she said. "And we definitely had more bad between us than we ever had good."

"We could change that."

"No, we can't."

"Why not?"

"Because I'm not interested. Good wasn't that good."

"Ouch! You always knew how to hurt my feelings."

"But not nearly as well as you hurt mine."

"You holding a grudge?"

"Not at all."

"You're holding something."

Monica smiled. "Your ego is still overinflated, King. But guess what? Not only do I not miss you, I rarely give you a second thought, and I surely don't love you anymore. In fact, at the rate things are going, it won't be long before you'll be nothing but a very faint memory in everybody's mind."

The man pursed his lips, her cold reception not at all what he'd expected. He shifted his weight from one foot to the other, searching his arsenal for an apt reply. Before he could get the words out, Monica dismissed him.

"Good-bye, King. I know you well enough to know that you thought you could sweet-talk your way back into my pants, but that's not ever going to happen again. This is one bed you will never be welcomed back into. Good try, though." Monica gave him a quick thumbs up as she reached to close the door. "And good luck with that radio career. Short and sweet is better than no career at all."

As she closed the door and locked it firmly behind her, Monica grinned. The dull ache in her stomach had subsided, and all she wanted was to get back on the telephone with Preston to finish what the two of them had started.

Preston sat with his elbows pressed into his thighs, his head propped against the palms of his hands. Monica had stirred his emotions, then stopped him cold. Thoughts of her were reeling around in his head and had she been close, near enough for him to touch, there was no telling what he might do. He wanted her and his wanting hurt, a sweet pain that promised a quick, delirious recovery. Monica James was like no other woman he'd ever known.

The connection between them was undeniable. The woman had opened her heart and allowed him in, matching his sensitivity with her own. She made him whole, filling that empty space that he'd become too comfortable with. He took a deep breath. Thoughts of Monica and the man who'd searched out her hotel room crossed his mind, a wave of jealousy flooding his senses.

Monica hadn't held anything back about her and Vega. She'd been up-front and honest, sparing him no detail about the relationship the two had shared. Some details could have been left untold, he'd thought at the time, envy seeping into his spirit. But that feeling had passed quickly, Monica erasing the emotion with a pledge meant only for him. She'd sealed it with a kiss that had left them both giddy, lust-filled promises seeping like sunshine between them.

Monica was testing his convictions, he thought, reflecting back on the moment that had just passed between them. Monica was the first woman to make him want to forget his tenets and give in to the cravings that riddled his body any time she was near. Monica tempted him like no other. He heaved a deep sigh.

Rising from his seat, he crossed the room to the window, peering out into the courtyard. Across the way, the night-light Monica had left on in the hallway shone through the window. As he scanned the dark landscape he thought he noticed a dark shadow pass behind the large sculpture that sat outside his door, but the moon disappearing behind a rush of clouds obscured his view. Not giving it another thought, he reached for the length of cord that closed the blinds. Behind him the telephone rang, and forgetting all about the outside, Preston, hopeful that it was Monica on the other end, rushed to answer the call.

They were in the reception area of the Texas Steakhouse waiting for a table. Side by side, they sat around a barrel of oven-roasted peanuts. Shells snapped, flew, and dropped to the floor as Diondre, Preston, and Bryan consumed the salted morsels as if they were starved.

"Your boy coming or not?" Diondre asked, sliding a fistful of nuts into his mouth. He chewed quickly, swallowing nearly as fast.

"Who knows," Preston responded as he took a

quick glance at his wristwatch. "It doesn't take much to distract him. Godfrey has FDD."

"FDD?" Bryan questioned. "What's that?"

"Female Deficit Disorder. Put him in a room with more than one woman over the age of sixteen, and he loses his mind. Brother can barely remember his name," the man said jokingly.

The trio laughed. The hostess, a young woman with large blue eyes, skin like Ivory soap, and hair the color of cornsilk, gestured in their direction, indicating their table was ready. As the three rose and followed behind her, Godfrey came rushing through the restaurant's front door.

"I didn't think you were going to make it," Preston said, extending his hand in greeting.

Godfrey chuckled. "When you say you're buying dinner, you can always count on me making it," he said, shaking hands with Diondre and Bryan as they took their seats.

Preston made the formal introductions. "Diondre James, Bryan Bailey, this is Godfrey Davis."

"Nice to meet you," Diondre responded, with Bryan echoing his sentiments.

"So what took you so long?" Preston asked.

Godfrey grinned. "One of your students stopped to talk. She wanted some advice," he answered, winking.

Preston cringed. "This man thinks he's the answer to every female problem that exists," he said, directing his comments toward Diondre and Bryan.

"My friend here is just jealous that I'm a better listener than he is. The women just like my sensitive manner."

Diondre grinned. "Just how sensitive are you?"

"Well, I don't want to brag but—"

Preston held up his hand. "Oh, spare us," he said interrupting. "The list of women he's taken advantage of is far too long for anyone to be bragging on."

"But I'm a happy man," Godfrey said, "not sexually frustrated like my friend here."

Diondre chuckled. "So, it's true?"

Preston raised an eyebrow. "Is what true?"

Diondre tossed Godfrey and Bryan a look, then shrugged his shoulders. "Well, you know how rumors get started. I just heard that you've never done the deed before. Is it true?"

A blush of color filled Preston's face as he shook his head. "Remind me to kill your sister when she gets back."

They all laughed.

Preston took a deep breath. "Where my experience may be lacking, Godfrey has more than made up for it. But yes, it's true, I'm saving myself for marriage. I think my virginity is the single greatest gift I can give to the woman I love and plan to spend the rest of my life with. And no, I'm not embarrassed, ashamed, or bothered that folks think I'm either gay, impotent, or dealing with some childhood issues. Bottom line, it's nobody's business but mine and my woman's."

Bryan extended his hand. "Well, I have to give you your props, brother. You're a better man than I ever was. I started dipping in the cookie jar when I was twelve and didn't stop until I married my wife. Now I can never get me a snack when I want it. Everything's on a schedule, and I never get to dictate the times."

"That's why I'm not getting married. There's not a woman around who's ever going to put me on a schedule. When my jones gets hungry, it's going to eat," Godfrey professed, shaking his head adamantly.

Diondre chuckled, the two men high-fiving each other as the waiter came to take their orders. As each rolled off their dinner wants, the young man jotted them down on a white notepad. "I'll bring your drinks and appetizers right back," he said as he turned and headed back down the aisle.

"I was wondering what you planned to eat when you picked the steak house," Godfrey said, leaning back against the wall, his arm tossed over the back of the booth.

"You don't eat meat?" Bryan asked.

Preston shook his head. "No, strictly vegetarian, but they do a great salmon steak here, and I figured you all might want beef."

"So, what do you two do?" Godfrey asked, reaching for a bottle of Corona the waiter had just set on the table.

"Lawyer," Diondre responded. "I have a private practice in Durham."

"Radio engineering," Bryan answered. "I let Monica James give me orders and boss me around."

"And she can be bossy, now," Diondre laughed.

Preston grinned. "I haven't had that problem."

"Yet," Diondre said with a wide smirk. "Give her some time. She's still on her best behavior with you. Playing by those new relationship rules. Her claws will come out soon enough, trust me."

"Now I'm scared," Preston said with a laugh.

"You should be," Bryan added.

Laughter rang around the table.

"You all leave my woman alone," Preston smiled. "She is not that bad."

"She's a woman. They're all that bad," Godfrey interjected.

"Speaking of," Preston said, changing the subject. "What student of mine were you administering aid to this evening?"

"Miss Donata Thompson came to see me."

"Donata?" Preston said, surprise registering in his voice.

Godfrey nodded his head.

"Who's Donata?" Diondre questioned, noting Preston's sudden uneasiness.

"A student with some serious problems."

"I don't think so," Godfrey responded. "She was concerned that you were still upset with her, but I assured her that you were just concerned about her getting help to get her through the semester." He directed his comments toward the two other men. "Little girl had the hots for our friend here. Got her little feelings hurt, and now she just wants someone to rub her boo-boo."

Diondre laughed. "You better watch that rubbing crap. Her boo-boo could land you some serious jail time depending on how old she is. And you being her teacher could make the key to the jail hard to find."

"She's past the age of consent, and I don't have her in any of my classes. So any after-school tutoring I may do doesn't have to be of the scholastic kind."

Preston shook his head, tossing the man a look of dismay.

"I miss those days," Bryan said wistfully. "Coochie whenever, wherever, whoever."

"You wouldn't change a thing," Diondre said. "You love that wife of yours so much it would hurt your heart if you two weren't together."

Bryan grinned. "Yeah. She's my baby!"

"Whoa!" Godfrey exclaimed, pointing to the television set positioned in the corner of the room. "You see that shot? That boy made that basket from the middle of the court!"

"Who's playing?" Bryan asked, turning to where the other man pointed.

As the men chatted amiably back and forth, the banter flowing easily between them, Preston made a mental note to question his friend later when they were alone. He was curious to know what Donata Thompson was up to.

Nineteen

Monica was peering into her mailbox when Donata pulled into the parking lot and exited her car. Monica watched as the young woman struggled with a number of grocery bags she pulled from the trunk of her vehicle. When the weight was evenly distributed in both of her arms, Donata sauntered toward Preston's door, dropping the recently purchased food to her feet. Monica strolled easily past her, catching the woman's eye as she watched her slip a key into the lock and push the entrance open.

"Hi," she said, waving her hand slowly. "How are you?"

"Fine, thank you," Donata responded as she lifted her packages, prepared to step inside.

"I don't think we've met. Are you a friend of Dr. Walker's?" Monica asked, staring at the girl curiously.

Donata giggled. "I'm his fiancée. I've been busy with school the past few weeks, haven't had much time with my baby. Our schedules are so crazy usually we only get to see each other after he gets home from work and before I have to go to work. I'm on the graveyard shift at the hospital. I thought I'd surprise him with a special dinner tonight. You must be his new neighbor. He's told me a lot about you."

"Has he now?" Monica said nodding her head slowly.

Donata was still giggling. "You're Monica James, the radio woman, aren't you?"

Monica gave her a slight smile. "I am."

"I love your show."

"Thank you. Thank you very much," Monica responded, looking from Donata to the key in the lock and back again.

"Well, I've got to get to work. It was nice meeting you. We should plan to get together. Preston and I would love to have dinner with you and your boyfriend sometime."

"My boyfriend?"

"The tall, nice-looking man I've seen you with. Preston said he was your boyfriend."

Monica raised her eyebrows, pausing briefly before responding. "Oh, yes, him," she answered.

"Well, it was nice meeting you," Donata said, her hand prepped to close the door behind her.

"I'm sorry. I didn't get your name," Monica said before Donata could retreat inside. Monica stood staring after her as the woman simply smiled, gave her a quick wave, and closed the door, not bothering to respond.

Pacing her living room floor, Monica could feel her anger rising. Not expecting her to return before the morning, Preston had told her he was spending the evening alone. When her conference had ended early, she'd been fortunate to get a quick flight change, landing at the Raleigh-Durham airport some twenty-two hours ahead of schedule. Her anger was quickly rising to a full rage.

Outside, the weather was turning, dark clouds beginning to fill the afternoon sky. Hers was not the only storm brewing as the threat of heavy rains lurked overhead. She peeked out the window toward the unit on the other side. Preston's friend had turned on the lights in the house, the sudden rise of darkness intruding upon her dinner preparations. The woman stood stark naked, chopping vegetables on a wooden chopping board placed in the center of the large kitchen island. Monica flung the pile of letters in her hand to the floor, pacing to the far end of the room. She reached for the telephone and dialed the radio station. After two rings, Bryan picked up the line.

"WLUV radio."

"Bryan, hi. It's me."

"Hey, Monica! How's the conference?"

"Over. I'm already home."

"You're kidding, right? You didn't stay to enjoy all that political aura?"

"No. I'm coming in so I'll tell you all about it."

"You have the night off. What are you coming in for?"

Monica shook her head into the receiver. "I need to work," she uttered, heaving a deep sigh. "Don't play the tapes. I'll be there on time."

"If you say so. See you soon."

"Bye, Bryan." Hanging up the telephone, Monica sighed again, crossing the room once again to peer into Preston's windows.

The woman had moved from the kitchen to the second-floor bedroom. Racing up the stairs, Monica peeked out of her own blinds, curious to see what was going on. Donata lay sprawled across Preston's bed, her hands racing up and down the length of her body. Monica watched as she rolled herself against his bed sheets, pressing her face into his pillows as she wrapped his covers around her. The sight made Monica nauseous, her jealousy-fueled rage spinning into a painful hurt. She suddenly felt betrayed and the bitter vile of that emotion sent her racing into her bathroom.

* * *

Three hours into her show, Bryan handed Monica a cup of black coffee. "You're hostile tonight, Monica. What's going on?"

She shook her head, taking a deep breath. "Nothing."

Her friend shook his head. "Then cut the brothers some slack. You've been hitting them below the belt with both barrels tonight. You need to ease up."

Spinning around in her chair, Monica shrugged off his comments, anger still fueling her emotions.

As the last song ended, she chimed into the microphone. "This is Monica James and WLUV radio. I want to talk about trust and fidelity. I want to know what you men think about being faithful to a woman and if it's not important to you, I want to know why. Pick up the phone, gentlemen, and call and tell me something good."

Monica cut an eye toward Bryan who was staring at her curiously. He shook his head slowly. As Monica's gaze locked with his, she could feel a sudden swell of tears rise to her eyes and she fought the sudden desire to cry. The phone lines ringing helped her regain her composure as she reached to answer the first call.

"This is Monica. Who's on the line?"

"It's Douglas, Monica."

"Where are you calling from, Douglas?"

"I'm right here in Raleigh."

"Talk to me, Douglas. Are you faithful?"

The man chuckled. "As long as my women don't find out about each other, I'm as faithful as the next guy."

"That sounds like it could get ugly, Douglas."

"There have been some close calls, but I'm juggling things pretty well at the moment."

"Why do you feel you have to lie, Douglas? Why not just be honest with both women?"

"Because you females like to act a fool on a brother when it's not necessary. If all of you weren't watching your biological clocks and thinking you had to pin a man down before that clock stops ticking, it would be easier on a man to be honest about not wanting to be tied down to any one female."

"Sounds like a coward's excuse, Douglas. You have your cake and you're eating it too, and you're afraid if the truth gets out, your plate will suddenly be empty."

"Let's be honest with each other, Monica. As you women get older, your supply of eligible men gets smaller. On the other hand, as we men get older, our supply only increases. Then too, you women come with these long lists of what a man should and should not have, and how he should and shouldn't act. The pressure can be a bit much on a man."

"I disagree, Douglas. I think a real man wouldn't have any problem with a woman placing some demands on him if they're both interested in pursuing a solid relationship. I think it's you little boys who have the problems. Too afraid to grow up and be men."

Monica disconnected the line. "This is Monica James, and I'll be right back after a word from our sponsors. When I return I want to tell you all a story about a cheating man, and when I'm done, I want someone to call and tell me something good. I want someone to help me understand what goes on in a lying man's mind."

Preston parked his car and made the walk to his front door. His day had been exceptionally long, his meetings running well into the evening, and he was tired. Isaac and Lydia Stern, the elderly couple that lived next door to Monica, greeted him warmly, stopping to shake his hand, as they themselves were returning from dinner. The trio chatted briefly before Preston excused himself to go inside, racing to beat the drizzle of rain that had started to seep down from the dark sky.

The lights blazing throughout the interior space was the first thing he noticed as he slid his key into the lock and unlatched the door. Pushing the door open cautiously, he called out hello, baffled by the smell of simmering food emanating from his kitchen. Glancing over his shoulder, he noted that Monica's downstairs blinds were drawn, blocking the gleam of a night-light that he'd grown accustomed to looking for.

He called out her name as he stepped inside, curious about how someone had been able to gain access to his home. "Monica? You here?"

Silence greeted him as he dropped his briefcase, keys, and the day's mail onto the tabletop. Stepping into the kitchen, he reached to turn off the flames blazing beneath a pot of pasta sauce, the thick aroma of fresh tomatoes, garlic, and onions wafting to his nose. On the other burner, a large pot of spaghetti had boiled dry, and the first whiff of burned food hit him square in his face. Lifting the pot from the stove, he dropped it into the sink, filling it to the brim with cold water.

"Hello, is anyone here? Monica?" he called out again, strolling back into the living room and looking around the familiar space. The dining room table was set, two place settings neatly arranged on the glass top. A bouquet of fresh flowers sat at the table's center, with a confetti mixture of hearts and stars dusted around the crystal vase. A wave of anxiety passed through Preston's stomach. In the background, the radio was playing, the song not one he recognized. Not seeing anything else out of place, he headed toward the stairwell and looked up the stairs. Above his head, the upstairs lights shone brightly, illuminating a trail of rose petals that started on the first step and beckoned him upward. Preston bit down against his bottom lip as he placed a hand on the banister and lifted himself toward the upper landing. The trail of red roses flowed beneath the closed door that led into his bedroom. Closing his eyes, Preston heaved a deep sigh, nervous energy gaining control over his emotions.

Monica wouldn't do this, he thought, stopping short of opening the door and looking inside. *Knowing how important it was to him to wait until they were married before they consummated their relationship, Monica wouldn't purposely put him in such a position,* he reasoned. *Monica wouldn't tempt him so willfully.* His hand pressed against the doorknob, turning it slowly as he pushed the entrance open.

Except for the flower petals that stopped a foot short of his bed, the room was empty. However, it looked as if the World War III had been waged between its four walls, with his possessions shattered, the bed in shambles, and the chair that sat in the corner lying on its side on the floor. His window blinds were closed, and as he crossed to open them, he noted that Monica's upstairs blinds, which had been opened since she left were also closed. Reaching for the telephone, he dialed her home number, hanging up when the answering machine picked up the call.

Drawing closer to the bed, he couldn't miss the spatter of blood that lay across the sheets, the crimson spilling across the length of the pillows, the headboard, and the floor. Preston cringed, taking a quick step back, his heart beating faster. Shock spun him to the other side of the room. Stepping into the master bathroom, he found a wealth of candles blazing around the bathtub, and the porcelain container filled with water and bubbles. Reaching a hand into the liquid, he noted that the water was still warm, not yet cold to the touch. Whoever had drawn themselves a bath had done so recently, not long gone from the spot where he now stood. Extinguishing the flames, he eased his way out of the room and back into the hallway.

Racing back down the stairs, Preston stood in a state of confusion. Clearly someone had made themselves comfortable in his home, but who? And what had happened in his bedroom? Monica's voice spilling out of the radio pulled at his attention.

"I trusted that this man was being honest with me. So imagine how surprised I was to return home early from a meeting to find another woman, claiming to be his fiancée, cooking in his kitchen. I watched her open the door with a key and let herself in like she'd been doing it forever. Then, she had the audacity to invite me and a date to join them for dinner some time. All the while this man had been pledging his love to me, making promises about our future, and I never had a clue. He'd sworn up and down that he and this woman had never been involved, that she was nothing to him. I'm hurt and I'm angry, and I want to hear what you folks think I should do about it. Someone call and tell me something good."

A dark realization fell against Preston's shoulders. A cold shiver ran up his spine, and he felt as if an icy breeze had blown through the room. He pulled the telephone into his hand and dialed Monica's personal line. When she didn't answer, he redialed the radio station's main number.

Bryan answered the line. "WLUV radio."

"Bryan, it's Preston. I need to talk to Monica."

"I don't think so. I don't think she has anything she wants to say to you."

"This is important, Bryan. I have to speak with her now. There has been a huge misunderstanding."

Bryan exhaled. "Hold on. I'll see if she'll take the call."

Preston tapped his foot anxiously as he waited for someone to pick up. He could hear Monica in deep conversation with another caller.

". . . the date had been set. I'd mailed the invitations, and as far as I knew, we were right on track to have the wedding of our dreams."

"How did you find out, Nina?"

"We'd gone shopping, and just like a man he had to run by his boy's house to pick up something. Of course, I had to wait in the car for him to get back, and I don't know why, but for some reason, I looked in the glove box of his car. I found another wedding invitation. He was scheduled to marry another woman the month before we were supposed to be married."

"What did you do, girl?"

"I showed up at the wedding. Sat in the back pew and watched him get married. I had actually met the girl before. He'd introduced her to me as his cousin. Later, when I asked her about it, she said that he told her I was his ex-girlfriend and I was trying to give him a hard time. He'd accused me of stalking him and told her he didn't want me to know about the two of them because he was afraid that I might try and hurt her."

"So you talked to her?"

"Sure did. Showed up at the reception and gave her a copy of my wedding invitation. Even showed her photos from the engagement party. Then told her I was two months pregnant and coming after him for some heavy-duty child support. I don't think their wedding night was all he wanted it to be." Nina laughed cheerfully.

"How did you get over the hurt, girl?"

"I found a really good man who loved me so hard, and so completely, that the bad memories just seemed to fade away to nothing before I even knew what happened."

"I love to hear that, Nina. Much luck to you and your new man."

"You too, Monica. We sisters are here for you. You hang in there. That man doesn't know what a good thing he's lost."

Bryan picked the line back up. "She's not going to pick up, Preston. Sorry, man. I tried."

Preston heaved a heavy sigh. "Thanks. I appreciate it. Tell her I called. I'll try to reason with her when she gets home."

Bryan laughed. "Just stay clear of the sharp objects, and you should be all right."

As Bryan disconnected the line, Preston sat down against the sofa, pulling his hands across his face. The fumes from the cooked food still filled the air, and he suddenly found it difficult to breathe. As he fought for air, his eyes caught sight of the answering machine and the light flickering to indicate incoming calls. Rising quickly, he crossed to the other side of the room and the machine and pushed the play button, the telephone receiver still clutched tightly in his palm.

"Surprise! I wanted you to have a special welcome home, Dr. Walker. You should know that I'm never too far away from you. I'm always there. Just waiting for the right moment. You can't make me go away that easily."

The laugh that followed was malicious, tinged with evil, and it snapped Preston back to the reality of just how serious his problem had become. Clutching the telephone even tighter, he dialed the local police, then sat waiting for someone to come take his complaint.

Monica had contemplated going to her brother's for the night but had changed her mind. She had no intentions of hiding. In fact, she had every intention of confronting Preston face-to-face. He owed her answers, and she had no intentions of allowing either of them to sleep tonight until she'd gotten them.

Pulling into the drive, she was surprised by the number of police cars parked in the yard. Maneuvering into an empty space, she looked around curiously, noting the officers who were eyeing her cautiously as she sauntered up the walkway. Uniformed men were filing in and out of Preston's front door as he stood in deep conversation with a tall Hispanic man who was jotting notes on a lined notepad. As Monica approached, he held up his hand toward the note taker and rushed to meet her, pulling her tightly into his arms.

"Monica, I was so worried. You wouldn't answer your cell phone, and Bryan said you left over an hour ago. I was scared to death that something had happened." He pressed a kiss against her cheek as she stood stiffly against him, her arms dangling at her sides, her expression chilly. Preston could feel his heart sinking to the ground beneath his feet.

The note taker interrupted them. "Excuse me, are you Ms. James?"

"Yes," she answered, wariness flowing with her words. "I'm Monica James. What's going on?" she asked, pulling away from Preston. A look of anger crossed her face as she appraised him, noting the hurt that wafted quickly across his expression.

"I'm Detective Antonio Ramirez, and Dr. Walker's

home was violated into this evening. He believes you
may have witnessed the woman who did it."

Preston's gaze flickered across her face. "I heard
you say on the radio that you saw a woman use a key
to enter my home. We need to know what you saw."

Monica's gaze raced from one to the other as she
absorbed the information she'd just heard. The detective was a tall man with a rich, caramel complexion, and Monica imagined he would fill a uniform
nicely if he were to ever wear one. His eyes were dark
pools of black ice, his gaze serious and intense. Monica could feel him studying her closely, curious about
her, her reaction, and any answers that might be
forthcoming.

"Yes, I did," she finally answered. "I saw that girl,
the student you said came on to you the night before
your car was trashed. She told me she was your fiancée and that she was surprising you with dinner.
She had a key and she let herself in like she was at
home." Monica lowered her gaze, taking a deep
breath before continuing. "I was so angry that I decided to go to work. I left shortly after that."

"Monica, I never gave that woman a key to my
house. Never. I swear that there is absolutely nothing
between us, baby. The girl's crazy." Preston inhaled
deeply, blowing the air out slowly. "You have to believe me."

Monica stared behind the two men, noting the officers who were dusting for fingerprints inside and
the locksmith, who knelt at the front door, changing
the locks. Her gaze rested back on Preston's face and
the plea that reached out to her from his eyes. She
shook her head at her own mistake, her quick jump
to judge him before she had all her facts. Reaching
for him, she wrapped her arms around his neck,
pulling him close as she pressed her cheek to his.
She whispered into his ear, her voice low. "I am so

He reached out to embrace her, returning her smile with one of his own. "I don't know if that's a good idea, Monica. I don't want either one of us to be uncomfortable."

Monica studied him momentarily, noting the thick line of his eyebrows and the heaviness that filled his pale eyes. "I won't take no for an answer," she said finally. "Grab your toothbrush while I go put clean sheets on the guest bed."

Preston sighed, then nodded his head. "I'm right behind you," he said. "Just let me get the lights and lock the door."

Conversation between them was limited, as they were exhausted. Monica had put on a pot of coffee and had barely consumed a third of a cup before she'd decided she really had no want of coffee at all. Excusing herself to go change into her nightclothes, she left Preston sitting in the oversized armchair, pondering what he needed to do to resolve the problems that had suddenly overtaken his life. As she headed up the stairwell, she stopped to turn on the CD player, filling the room with soft jazz. The sounds were soothing, and Preston soon found himself giving in to the relaxing tones. He looked up as Monica stepped back down the stairs, dimming the lights as she came toward him.

Monica had changed into a white sheer, lace tank top and a casual pair of cotton sleeping shorts. As she stood rubbing her hands together, massaging a perfumed lotion into her soft flesh, Preston was awed by her beauty. He stared brazenly, catching her gaze as she gave him a deep look of her own. With no control, his male anatomy rose to full attention, its extending length suddenly feeling as if it were molded in solid concrete. Never before had he been as hungry for any one woman as he was for Monica.

"I just wanted to say goodnight," Monica said softly, noting his sudden discomfort. "I left towels on the bathroom counter for you. Just help yourself to anything else you might need."

Preston nodded, his gaze still locked on her face, his condition hidden behind an *Essence* magazine he'd pulled onto his lap.

"Thank you," he whispered, fighting to catch his breath.

"Are you going to be okay?" Monica asked, her words floating on an air of concern. "You look pained." She smiled, raising her eyebrows teasingly, amused by his discomfort.

Preston chuckled as he nodded his head. Embarrassment crept across his face, a flood of red painting his cheeks, his forehead, his chin, and the tips of his ears.

Monica couldn't help but laugh with him. "I'd kiss you, but I'm afraid I'd hurt you."

He shook his head. "I think I can manage one kiss," he responded, lifting himself up to stand beside her. His desire to hold her was so intense that he could concentrate on little else. "I don't think one kiss can cause me any more trouble than I'm already in," he said his voice falling to a whisper again.

Monica wrapped her arms around him, leaning her body close to his. She and Preston stared at each other intensely, lost in the gaze that had connected them. Monica could see the love in his eyes, the emotion so pure it was like fire igniting her heart. She fell straight into the flames, her commitment unwavering. Preston leaned in slowly to kiss her, then pulled back, allowing his lips to barely brush against hers. When he repeated the motion, his movements deliberate and teasing, Monica's lips parted ever so slightly, a breath of anticipation escaping past her lips. When his mouth finally fell against hers, it was as if time ceased ticking. Monica could feel her temperature rising swiftly, the hairs along her arms standing on end. Preston pulled her into the kiss slowly, allowing the momentum to build between them. As Monica fell into the motion, unable to pull herself away, his tongue pushed past her lips, seeking refuge inside her mouth. Her tongue walked a path with his, lust leading the way.

So focused on the sensations he was causing, her lips swelling as his mouth danced slowly with hers, Monica was suddenly awestruck by the rise of his sex pressed hotly between them, pressing at the cusp of her southern quadrant. Just as daunting was the hand that had flitted across her chest, fingertips brushing at the protuberance of nipple that pressed like stone against him.

Preston moved to kiss the hollow of her neck, allowing his mouth to travel toward her breasts. He moved slowly, sampling the joy of her for the first time. As he pressed a kiss at the round of her cleavage, he allowed his tongue to lightly lick the warmth of her flesh. He savored the taste of her, warm chocolate melting against his tongue. The motion made Monica shudder, and she heard herself moan, a low escape of breath getting away from her.

Monica wrapped her arms around his back, and together the duo rocked one against the other in time to the music that played softly in the background. So lost in the intensity of the moment, Monica barely noticed when Preston eased behind her, his mouth still dancing against her skin, down her neck, and along the line of her shoulders. When Preston eased himself against her, pressing his crotch into the round of her buttocks, Monica gasped, wanting to spread herself wide and welcome him inside. She had no shame when she reached around and slipped her hands between them, caressing him brazenly beneath the denim jeans he wore. Incited by the heat of her touch, Preston moaned her name into her ear.

"Monica . . . shouldn't . . . too close . . ." he managed to whisper, the words catching in his throat. "Oh, Monica . . ."

Monica ignored him, pulling at the zipper of his pants, and easing her hand inside. Preston tensed as she touched flesh, wrapping her palm tightly around his manhood. His knees quivered, the solid muscles of his legs threatening to give out on him and he pressed himself, and her hand, tighter against her backside for support.

The music continued to move them in unison as Monica stroked him boldly, Preston setting the rhythm with the push and pull of his hips. His mouth still danced atop hers as she leaned her head back to taste him. One hand cupped her chin gingerly, allowing him access to her mouth, and her lips were swollen numb from the attention. His other hand danced from one breast to the other, pulling gingerly at the bead of nipple that had surged beneath his touch. His thrusts against her covered bottom increased, her grip tightening as they found themselves lost in the lust that consumed them.

Monica could feel her own pleasure rising in intensity when Preston eased a tentative hand between her thighs, his fingers tap-dancing a slow path along the edge of her cotton shorts, sliding the panel of her silk panties aside. As he eased his way slowly, Monica felt herself gasp at his touch, the sensation shimmering throughout her body. His fingers parted her easily and without thought, Monica separated her legs, giving him easier access to the moist cavity of her feminine treasure.

Preston massaged her slowly at first. When the sensations became too intense, her heavy panting begging for more, his manipulations increased in tempo.

"Monica, baby, Monica, ahhhh . . ." Preston called her name as if in prayer, his whispers rising as his body surged to a climax. Monica felt her own orgasm rush forward and explode between his fingers. His lips were still locked against hers, flesh melted one to the other. "I love you, Monica," he whispered into her mouth, blowing the words throughout her spirit. "I love you so much."

Spinning back around to face him, Monica echoed his sentiments, spelling her response with her tongue as it teased in to find his, small moans escaping her throat. As the CD player spun the music back to the first track for the third time, the two were still standing, locked body to body. They swayed with the heat that had rushed over them, lost completely in the memories of the other's touch, and the welcome relief that touch had brought them.

Twenty

By the time the police department and campus security had completed a search of her dorm room and had finished asking her question after question, Tijuana Fields was not a happy camper. Her sleep had been disrupted by the knocks on the door, and here it was two hours later, and she was still wide awake. With a science exam only hours away, her mood wasn't pleasant, and fellow students who continued to peek their heads in to ask what had happened had gotten the worst of her wrath.

When the telephone rang, she was just a hair shy from stringing someone up by their fingernails.

"Hello?"

"T, it's me, Donata."

"Where are you? The police are looking for you. What did you do?"

"I didn't do anything. It's Dr. Walker. The man has lost his mind. I told him I wanted to break it off, and he went crazy. I'm scared, Tijuana. I'm so scared," Donata sobbed into the telephone.

"You have to go to the police, Donata. They'll understand. He won't get away with it if you tell someone."

"I can't. I let it happen. They'll blame me."

"No, they won't. Where are you? I'm coming to get you."

"Just you, Tijuana. No one else, okay? Just you."

"I promise, just tell me where you are," her friend responded.

As Donata gave her directions, Tijuana jotted them down onto a scrap piece of notebook paper. Then slipping on her shoes and jacket, she raced out the door.

Forty-five minutes later, Tijuana found herself in a deserted part of Raleigh, with streetlights barely existent. At the end of the street, a low fire blazed from a metal garbage canister and two homeless men stood talking beside it, the flames dancing off their faces. Both looked up as Tijuana eased her Toyota in their direction, her headlights shining brightly. Thinking it wiser, Tijuana turned the car back around, just about to pull off, when Donata stepped out of the shadows and flagged her down. Tijuana gasped, shock creasing worry lines across her forehead.

As she pushed the passenger door open, she gestured for Donata to get inside. "Lord have mercy! Donata, what happened to you?"

As the young woman settled herself against the seat, closing the door behind her, tears raced down her cheeks, falling against the soiled trench coat wrapped around her body.

"It was horrible, T. He hurt me," she cried, her cries growing to full-blown sobs. "He hurt me bad!" The girl's face was badly bruised, swollen tissue pressing against rising black and blue marks. A thin line of blood had dried at the crease of her mouth, and one eye was swelling shut as she sat wailing.

Tijuana revved the engine, tearing up the road. "I'm taking you to the hospital."

Donata could hear them in the corridor, behind the pale blue curtains that kept them from looking at her as the doctor attended to her bruises. She could hear them whispering, asking Tijuana questions, asking the doctor questions, asking questions they would never get any truthful answers to.

Her voices were laughing, content. They had done well, and they wanted her to know it. She would never have thought to search out the barrel-chested man, his full beard, mustache, and shoulder-length hair reminding her of a distorted teddy bear. The voices had guided her to him, knowing from past experience that he could do what she needed done. The voices had told him how to pummel her, how to bruise her just enough to make it look worse than it really was. The voices had told her where to find him, and what she needed to do to ensure he performed his job without killing her. He had served her well, and the two hundred dollars had been worth the investment.

She laughed to herself, an inner roar of mirth that filled her and made her feel strong. That woman had been a gift from the vengeance gods. Monica James's unexpected arrival couldn't have been timelier if Donata had purposely planned it. Donata had given her an eyeful, and as the woman had stormed out of her home toward her car, Donata had known her plans couldn't go any better. Monica crossing paths with the teddy-bear man had been her only concern, but the woman had already pulled out of the drive when he stepped out of his truck and headed to the door. Ridding herself of Monica James would be so much easier. Donata smiled.

Dr. Walker would pay dearly now. The voices had assured her that it would all end well. Dr. Walker would pay for tossing her aside as if she were nothing. The professor would be thoroughly punished for not accepting her presents when she'd offered them. Donata closed her eyes, sleep consuming her, and the voices whispered her to dreamland.

Twenty-one

Commotion at the Raleigh police station was never ending, noise racing through the air seemingly at warp speed. As he entered the rear door, stopping to pick up the stack of pink paper that made up his messages, Detective Ramirez wasn't sure whether he was glad to be back in the office or not. With the officers, criminals, and victims shouting back and forth, and chaos ringing through the air, it crossed his mind that he'd only traded one hell for another. This was as bad as the misery on the streets, if not worse, he thought, his eyes darting back and forth as he assessed who was where and what they were doing.

Taking a seat at his desk, he leaned back in the leather chair, his mind floating to his newest case. With more questions than he had answers for, he was not happy with the most recent developments. He flipped the top open on the cup of coffee he'd purchased on his way in and took a sip, the liquid having cooled nicely during the short ride from Dunkin' Donuts to the precinct.

His thoughts were disrupted by the slap of file folders being tossed on his desk. He looked up at his partner, Detective Angela Keyes, and the stern expression that blessed her face. She was a petite woman, barely reaching the middle of his chest, and he likened her to a ball of fire and fury. Since the day she'd entered the police academy she'd been more than a handfull, continually challenging the system, but always getting the job done. As he looked at her now, he couldn't help but wonder how she might look with her dark hair flowing over her shoulders, its rich coloring an exciting contrast to her honey-brown skin. The tight bun at the nape of her neck was anything but flattering, as she purposely tried to draw attention away from the beauty of her delicate features.

"What's up?" he asked, reaching for a bite of his breakfast, microwaved eggs on a croissant with cheese and bacon.

"The blood samples taken from our victim match the blood samples taken from Dr. Walker's home."

He gestured for her to take a seat as he pushed a second sandwich in her direction.

"And how was your weekend?" he asked, not bothering to respond to her statement.

The woman returned a look that made him rethink his approach. He swallowed the last bite of his food, then opened the top folder and scanned its contents.

"Something isn't right with this one, Angela. I haven't figured it out yet, but something's not right."

"The guy claims there was nothing going on between them, but everyone we talk to says it looks like they were close. His neighbors say they were engaged, the students say she spent a lot of time with him in his office, and even the other girlfriend thought there was something going on with them. The woman said so on the radio, for crying out loud."

"But he has an alibi for his whereabouts. Four people claim he was at a meeting with them."

"Before or after he beat the girl up? You seem to ⁺ he has over an hour that's unaccounted for.

She says he was there, they were going to have dinner and a romantic evening, then things got rough, and he left."

"The man claims he went to Home Depot, then went to his meeting."

"Did we find anyone who saw him at Home Depot? And what did he do there? Did he buy anything?"

"It's a guy thing, Angie. He looked at the tools. Says he was killing time."

"I say he was trying to kill that girl. Wanted to cover up the fact he was doing one of his students."

"How do you explain the girl's crazy phone calls?"

"She explained them. She admitted she made them and she was apologetic. She said they had a relationship. The man was giving her mixed signals. When he wanted sex, he wanted her, then he didn't. The girl is young, Antonio, and she fell in love. She trusted him, and he abused that trust. She reacted because her feelings were hurt. She's not the first woman to act like a fool over a man who's hurt her heart. Still didn't give him a right to put his hands on her."

Ramirez shook his head, his jet-black hair waving from side to side. "Let's bring him in for questioning."

"You want me to send a car to pick him up?"

"No, he's not under arrest. Just give him a call and tell him we need to speak with him. Let him come in on his own."

Detective Keyes reached for the telephone and dialed.

Monica and Preston had managed to clean up most of the damage done to his bedroom. Preston had arranged for a cleaning service to come in and steam clean the carpets and the walls. The soiled linens and broken trinkets had all been tossed in the trash. As he passed Monica in the hallway with the last bag of garbage that needed to go out, he leaned to kiss her, his mouth pressing gently against hers.

"I'm done here," he said, gesturing behind him. "Do you need help in the kitchen?"

"No. All finished."

"Thank you. You really didn't have to help with this, you know."

Monica smiled. "I know. I wanted to." She yawned, pressing her hand to her mouth. "Oh. Excuse me," she said.

"Up late, were you?" Preston teased as they headed back down to the living room.

Monica pinched his backside, giving him one of her infamous eye rolls. Preston dropped down onto the sofa, pulling Monica down beside him.

"Things got pretty intense between us last night," he said, color rising to his cheeks.

"Did we overstep one of your boundaries?" Monica questioned, pulling her legs up beneath her as she turned to face him.

"No, but it went farther than we probably should have let it. We weren't too far from taking that final step."

Monica shook her head. "We were a good fifty feet from that final step, Preston. And for the record, I don't regret one moment of it. I hope you don't?"

Preston leaned to give her a quick kiss. "I haven't regretted anything with you." He paused. "Well, maybe that one moment when you were telling the whole state what a heel you thought I was."

Monica laughed. "I'll get that straight when I go on the air tonight," she said, wrapping her arms around his neck. "Can't have folks thinking my man is a total jerk," she finished.

As Preston leaned to kiss her for a second time, the telephone rang, interrupting their exchange. He reached to answer the call.

"Hello?"

Monica watched as his expression changed, the lines on his face turning serious. The party on the other end did most of the talking, and Preston responded with a quick "yes," "yes," "no," "I hadn't heard," "I understand," and "thank you." As he dropped the receiver back onto the hook, Monica could feel the anxiety flooding through his spirit. It hung in the air, a thick, acrid substance that tainted his good mood.

"What's wrong?"

"I've been suspended pending a formal investigation."

Monica's eyes widened in surprise. "Preston, no! How can that be?" she exclaimed.

"Donata was found badly beaten last night. She claims I did it. The police are investigating, and until I'm cleared of any charges, the university thinks it would be better that I not be around the students."

"That's not right."

"I need to call that detective—" he started as the telephone rang for a second time.

He answered it on the third ring. "Hello? Yes, this is Preston Walker. Yes. No. That'll be fine. Yes, I can be there in an hour. Thank you." He dropped the receiver back onto the hook. "That was the police. They want me to come in for questioning. I have to meet Detective Ramirez in an hour."

"I'm going with you."

Preston shook his head. "No. That's not necessary. Everything's going to be fine. I didn't do anything wrong."

Monica shook her head. "This doesn't feel good, Preston."

He pulled her into his arms. "No. It doesn't, but everything is going to work out. I have the truth on my side."

Ten minutes later, Preston locked the new lock on his front door, then kissed Monica good-bye. She stared after him as he slid into his car, started the engine, and pulled out onto the main road. Returning to her own unit, she reached for the telephone and dialed.

"Diondre, it's me. Big brother, Preston needs your help."

Preston had been studying every corner of the small interrogation room for over twenty minutes. The small enclosure boasted very little: a fresh coat of off-white paint, five chairs, and a table were its only decor. Preston sat uneasily, his hands clasped against the tabletop, his fingers entwined nervously. He still couldn't fathom how things had progressed as far as they had or what he had done to get himself in such a predicament. He had tried to appear unconcerned, not wanting Monica to know how worried he really was by the sudden turn of events. With his home being broken into, being suspended from his job, and now the allegations that he had physically assaulted Donata, he was scared. He could pretend to ignore it all he wanted, but this mess clearly wasn't going to go away.

Another ten minutes passed before the door finally swung open and Detective Ramirez ventured inside. "Sorry for the delay," he professed, dropping into the seat across from Preston, a file folder pressed tightly beneath his arm. He dropped the folder to the tabletop and heaved a deep sigh. Meeting Preston's stark gaze with his own, his eyes flickered over the man's face as he studied him.

"We have a serious situation here, Dr. Walker. As you're aware, Ms. Thompson alleges you assaulted her. The physical evidence points to her being attacked in your home, yet you claim not to have been there."

"I wasn't," Preston stated. "I have no idea how she gained access or who was with her."

"Let's talk about that hour you say you were at the store. What store was that, again?"

Preston heaved a deep sigh, his eyes still locked on the detective's face. "Home Depot. After my last class I had some time to kill before I had to be at my meeting. There was no point in my driving back home to have to come back across town, so I ran down to Home Depot. I wanted to price their gas grills."

"Don't you have a grill?"

"I need a new one."

The man shook his head up and down, the motion slow and deliberate. "Did you talk to anyone in Home Depot?"

"I had no reason to. I may have said hello to one or two of the clerks as they passed by, but I really don't remember."

"What time did you get home, sir?"

"It was close to ten o'clock, maybe ten-thirty."

"And that's when you found your home had been entered into. Is that correct?"

"Yes."

"Were you and Ms. Thompson lovers?"

"No."

Ramirez paused as if waiting for Preston to flinch. The man would not be moved and so the officer nodded, then proceeded with his questioning. "How would you define your relationship with Ms. Thompson?"

"She was my student, and I was her teacher. That's all."

"How did Ms. Thompson get a key to your home, Dr. Walker?"

"I don't have a clue."

"She says you gave it to her."

Preston's jaw tightened and he swallowed hard. "She's a liar."

A knock on the door drew the officer's gaze from Preston's. Detective Keyes gestured for her partner's attention, and the two whispered softly in the entranceway. Preston inhaled, taking a deep breath to fill his lungs and ease the tension pressing on his midsection.

"Well, Dr. Walker, it seems your attorney is here," Detective Ramirez stated, opening the door wider to allow Diondre to enter.

The man extended his hand toward Preston. "Sorry I'm late. I was in court when Monica called. Got here as quickly as I could."

Preston smiled a weak smile, nodding his head. "Thank you," he said, appreciation dripping from his tone.

Diondre nodded, then turned back to the two officers watching them. "Is my client being charged with anything, Detective?"

"No. He came voluntarily to answer some questions to assist us with our investigation," Ramirez replied.

"Then we're finished here," Diondre stated matter-of-factly.

Diondre and Ramirez eyed each other briefly, both pulling themselves up tall, establishing territory. "Your client shouldn't make any plans to leave the state. We will probably have some additional questions for him," Ramirez concluded.

Diondre smiled. "Either charge him or leave him alone, Detective. I will not have my client harassed by you or any of your staff," he said, his gaze falling briefly on Detective Keyes.

The woman glared. "We'll be in touch, Counselor."

Ramirez watched as Preston and Diondre exited the office and proceeded out the building. He continued to stare as they climbed down the short length of brick stairs to their respective cars, stopping to speak briefly, before driving off, one behind the other.

"He's guilty as sin," Detective Keyes stated, walking up behind him to stare where he did.

The man met her gaze, then shook his head. "No. I don't think he did it. I think he's telling us the truth." He turned back toward his desk, barking orders as she followed behind him. "Get me everything you can on our victim. Go back as far as you have to go back, but I want to know every little secret Ms. Thompson thinks she has."

Preston sat comfortably in Monica's home office, with Diondre giving him a list of things to do and not do. He listened intently, grateful to have an ally on his side. Monica had retreated to her bedroom to lie down, giving the two men an opportunity to speak in private.

"You understand that anything you tell me is held in the strictest confidence?" Diondre said as they were concluding their meeting.

"I do."

"And you've been completely honest with me? There's nothing you might have forgotten, or you think wouldn't be relevant so you're not sharing it?"

"Diondre, I've told you everything."

"Why do you think she's doing this?"

Preston shook his head. "I don't know. As God is my witness, I don't know."

Diondre nodded. "Well, let me get to work. I need

to find out everything the police know and anything they don't. I would think that if they thought this case was as strong as it appears on the surface, they would have pressed charges against you by now. Either way, we'll need to be prepared. You have my pager number, so use it if you have to. I'll call you after I meet with the university. Until you're formally charged, there is no reason you can't work. I'll get you reinstated as quickly as I can."

"Thanks, man. I appreciate it. I really do."

The man smiled. "Since you're on the record, what's the deal with you and my sister? How serious are you two?"

Preston grinned, meeting the man's eyes. "I'm in love with your sister. I'm hoping she'll make an honest man of me some day soon."

Diondre chuckled, extending his arm as the two men shook hands and bumped shoulders. "At least you play golf. I would hate to have a brother-in-law who didn't play golf."

The two men laughed as Diondre led the way out of the room. He stopped to pull a can of soda out of the refrigerator, popping the top as he continued toward the door. "Tell Monica to call me later," he said as he made his exit.

"I will. Thanks again," Preston said as he waved good-bye, closing the door behind the man.

For a quick minute Preston thought about retreating across the courtyard to his own home, but decided that was not where he wanted to be. Climbing the steps to Monica's bedroom, he peered in cautiously, fearful of disturbing her rest.

Monica lay sleeping, her body relaxed against the wealth of pillows, the coverings pulled back and folded against the foot of the bed. She had slipped out of her slacks and blouse, and lay only in a lace babydoll top and matching bottom, the pale lavender color shimmering against her warm complexion. The sight of her caused his temperature to rise, and Preston suddenly found it warm in the air-conditioned room. He stood watching her for some time, marveling at the magnitude of his emotions for her.

Slipping quietly into the room, Preston released his necktie and undid the buttons of his white dress shirt. Folding the articles of clothing neatly, he dropped them against the seat of the wing chair that sat in the corner of her bedroom. He slipped out of his black dress shoes, reaching to set them beneath the corner of the queen-size bed. He inhaled deeply, then blew the wealth of breath out of his mouth, blowing it slowly over his lips into the air. With his pants still on, he eased his body against the side of the bed. Stretching the length of his frame down against the mattress, he shifted to curl himself up against Monica. The movement caused her to open her eyes, and when she saw him, she smiled.

"Are you okay?" she asked softly, nestling herself against the arm he'd wrapped around her.

He nodded, leaning to press his lips against her forehead and her eyelids, and resting finally against her mouth. The kiss was soft, an easy breeze that passed between them.

Monica closed her eyes and allowed sleep to repossess her. As Preston lay staring, he could feel his own lids becoming heavy, and with his fingers entwined with hers, he succumbed to the rest that beckoned him, falling soundly asleep beside Monica.

Twenty-two

"Ever been in love, people? Ever been so head over heels for that special someone that it had you hiding in the bushes outside their home? Have your emotions for another person ever had you making a fool out of yourself? This is Monica James, and I want to hear your story. Call and tell me something good."

Monica clicked the off button on her microphone as Bryan hit the play knob for the requisite advertisements. He turned as Monica joined him in the sound room, coming to stand at his side, stealing a quick bite of the sliced apple pie his wife had sent with him.

"I can't believe this mess with Preston!" he exclaimed. "How's he handling it?" he asked as he pulled his fork back from her hand.

Monica shrugged, a slight push of her shoulders. She swallowed before speaking. "I don't think he wants me to know just how bothered by it he really is. But I can see the stress is beginning to get to him." She took a second bite of Bryan's pie, wiping at her mouth with a yellow paper napkin.

"You're really into this guy, aren't you?" Bryan asked, his tone serious.

Monica gave him a quick smile. "He's a pretty special man, Bryan. He makes me happy."

Her friend nodded. "Well, not that you asked for my two cents, but for what it's worth, I like him. I think he's been good for you." He reached to squeeze her hand. "But that's just my two cents."

Monica leaned to give him a kiss on the cheek. "It's worth a lot to me," she said as she sauntered out of the room. Settling back against her seat, she pulled the microphone into her hands and waited for his cue, both of them monitoring the flickering lights on the switchboard.

"This is Monica. Who's on the line tonight?"

"Do I have to give my name?" a male voice asked. His deep baritone filled the airwaves.

"No, not if you don't want to," Monica responded. "So, what's your story, friend?"

"I loved a woman once, loved her good, too. Ya know? Then things started going bad, and I didn't handle it too well."

"What did you do?"

"We started growing apart, and I couldn't figure out why, so I started following her. It won't no big deal at first, ya know? But then it got out of control."

Monica could hear the hurt painted in the man's voice. She took a quick breath, then pushed him for more. "What did you do to her?"

The man paused, silence filling the space.

Monica pushed again. "Come on, friend. Tell me something."

The man continued. "Well, we had plans to go out this one night and she cancelled on me last minute. She said she was sick, but I just knew it was to see some other guy."

"Had she been dating other men that you had seen?"

"No, but I just had this feeling. I sat outside her apartment for a few hours and then, when I saw the lights go out, I climbed the fire escape and broke in through a window."

Monica shook her head at Bryan, who was spinning an index finger in the air beside his head. "Then what happened?" she asked.

"Nothing really. I sneaked in and found her sound asleep in bed. Alone."

"I can hear it in your voice that something else was going on also. Talk to me. Tell me why this was such a big deal for you."

The man heaved a deep sigh. "When I broke in, I had a gun. It was loaded and cocked, and if she had been with anyone, I would probably have used it."

"That's serious, friend. Are you and this lady still together?"

"Naw. I had to let that go. I realized that night that it was driving me crazy."

"Good for you. Any advice for a man who might be thinking the same thing right now?"

"Tell him it's not worth it, Monica. Tell him there's always a better way. Tell him a friend said so."

Monica smiled. "Thanks, friend. You stay strong, brother."

"Thanks, Monica."

"This is Monica James and WLUV–FM radio, bringing you the best talk and the best sounds. Sometimes, people, we need to recognize when a relationship is toxic so we can get out of it before it steals our soul. If you're in a relationship now that you know isn't healthy for you, find your strength in someone else's story and run. Run, don't walk. Run, and run as far as you can before it's too late. I want to hear your story. Call and tell me something good. Who's on the line?"

"Hi, Monica. My name's Patricia."

"Tell me something good, Patricia."

"A year ago I was being stalked by my husband's girlfriend."

"Whoa, girl! Your husband's girlfriend? That sounds serious!"

"It got pretty bad there for a while. You know the story, Monica. You think you've got the perfect man, everything seems like it's sugar at home, and then out of the blue you find out your man is doing you dirty out in the streets." The woman took a deep breath, then continued.

"The first time I saw her, this heifer had the nerve to show up at my child's day care. Was sitting on the hood of my car when I came back from dropping my baby off. She wanted to know if my man and I are still together. I asked her what she wanted to know for. Of course, I didn't get an answer, but I told her no. I told her if she wanted his stank behind she could have him. When I left her, I went right to his job and went off. I was like a madwoman."

Monica laughed. "Did you hurt him, Patricia?"

"I should have. Anyway, he swore up and down that he didn't know anything. Swore there was nothing between them. Then the phone calls started. Witch called up asking for him, and when I asked who was calling, she wanted to know why I needed to know. Then when he got on the telephone, she hung up. I had to change my telephone number two times. Then she really got crazy."

"What did she do?"

"The fool started following *me* around. Everywhere I went, there she was. Parked in the lot at my job, and behind me at the supermarket, church, even the mall. Finally, I had to ask what her problem was and she told me that if I wasn't around she and my man could be together. That I was in her way. I told her I wasn't her problem because he was free to do whatever the hell he wanted. I didn't have any holds on him. But I have to tell you, Monica, it scared me. It scared me good. I still remember when that girl in Long Island shot her lover's wife. I wasn't looking to be a statistic."

"I can understand that. How did you manage to finally get rid of her?"

"The last straw came when she showed up one morning, ringing my doorbell, wanting to know if he lived there. Then this fool is going to walk outside with her to set her straight. Well, I walked right out after them. She was crying and carrying on about how she might be pregnant and he was causing her all this stress, so I flat-out asked her what was going on. She told me she loved him and he loved her and they wanted to be together and I wouldn't let them.

"I told that crazy twit that if she was stupid enough to get pregnant for a man not even knowing where he lived, then she deserved whatever she got. He stood there the whole time, swearing that she wasn't pregnant by him and he didn't know what her problem was. I called the police and filed for a restraining order. Two weeks later she was walking in circles around my neighborhood. I knew that she wasn't going away, and since he didn't seem to be able to do anything about her, I would."

"What did you finally do?"

"When school got out, I packed my kids and my house and I moved across the country. Didn't even leave a forwarding address. Told him that with or without him I was out of there."

"Did your man stay?"

"No. He still insists that he did absolutely nothing to make her act that way. He swears up and down she was just crazy."

"Do you believe him?"

"I want to. He has my heart, so I want to trust that he wouldn't hurt me like that."

"Whatever happened to the other woman?"

"For the first few months we heard she was trying

real hard to find us. She showed up at my mother's house pretending to be an old friend of mine from school. Claimed she lost my address and telephone number. When my folks told her they'd pass her information on to me, then she wanted to know where he was. She got ugly, and my father booted her behind out. Then she went to my old job looking for a forwarding number. Her mistake was using my maiden name and pretending we were related. Everyone knew she wasn't any kin to me."

"Wow, that's some story! You hang in there, girlfriend."

"Monica, I have to say one more thing."

"What's that, Patricia?"

The woman's voice trembled ever so slightly. "I may want to believe him, but I'm no fool either. I wrote a letter detailing every episode with her. In it, I said that if anything should ever happen to me then they needed to look at her first and my husband second. Then I sent a copy to my sister, my lawyer, my best friend, and the local police departments here and at my old home."

Monica chuckled. "Love surely doesn't have to mean stupid! I'm proud of you, Patricia. You stay strong. This is Monica James. Call and tell me something good!"

Donata drove down the tree-lined street, cursing the unrelenting heat and the broken air-conditioning in her car. She and her entourage of personalities were doing battle, the voices winning dominion over her body. Nothing was going as she wanted it to, and it was all Monica James's fault. Her hands gripped the steering wheel tighter as she drove past the entrance to Preston's home, willing herself from pulling into the parking lot and going to Preston's door.

The woman had been angry the first night, but something had happened to change her mind. She'd apologized over the radio, sending word to "the love of my life" that she believed him, she trusted him, and she would stick by him no matter what. She'd professed her love to an audience of thousands, and the calls that had followed had encouraged her, given her public approval, and called Donata crazy.

No one had mentioned Donata's name outright, but she knew what the other woman was insinuating with her request for stories about scorned lovers and crazed stalkers. The memory enraged her, and Donata hit the gas pedal, sending the car racing down the roadway. Taking a quick glance in her mirrors, she fought to control the angry voices, the ones berating her for not moving against Monica James sooner.

Monica James. The name left a bitter taste in Donata's mouth, and she bit down against her tongue, drawing blood between her teeth. Monica James would pay for what she'd done. Preston had been hers. It had all been planned, and then that woman had come, interfering, willing him away.

One voice shouted over the others, the tone soothing, calming her spirit. It spoke slowly, pulling at her attention, and Donata tilted her head slightly to hear what it had to say. Turning the car around, she drove back in the other direction, making one last pass by Preston Walker's home. The voice encouraged her, and she could feel herself smiling, her lips lifting upward. It would be easy. The voice was crystal clear now, and she understood exactly what she needed to do.

Twenty-three

Service ended later than either of them had anticipated, it being the first Sunday of the month and a communion Sunday. The church mothers had greeted Preston warmly, whispering that they could now take Monica off their prayer list, her having finally found herself a man. "We'll pray for a quick wedding and pretty babies," Sister Bernadette Perry had whispered in Monica's ear. "Lots of pretty brown babies."

Tossing Preston a quick glance, Monica had nodded, amused by the interest in her love life, the prayer line more like an impromptu game of telephone among the senior citizens of St. Luke AME Church. The altar call had given them more reason to wag their tongues when Preston had led her by the hand to the front of the church, the two of them falling to their knees in the act of devotion. His hand had held hers as both had offered praise for the blessings bestowed upon them, and had given witness to the love that had brought them together. After a moving sermon from the pastor, and three passes of the collection plate, they'd made their exit. As they had moved through the doors out of the vestibule, Sister Perry had winked toward Diondre, shaking a wrinkled finger and a gray head in his direction. "We'll pray harder for you, Brother James.

Your turn's comin'. I can feel it. I just know one of these girls will make you a mighty fine wife," she'd cooed with glee.

An hour later, the trio pulled into the driveway of the family home, Diondre blowing his horn at the little girl who played in the yard. Mariah came racing to greet them, her patent leather shoes kicking up the freshly cut grass beneath her feet.

"Mon-ka," she cheered, rushing into her sister's arms. Monica hugged the child warmly, then watched as she wrapped her arms around Diondre's neck and then Preston's, kissing both their cheeks before kicking to be put back down.

"I got a new dress," she sang, spinning around for them all to see the pink and white lace frock falling against her short legs.

"So did I," Monica laughed, walking a circle around the little girl, showing off her new Nordstrom's purchase. Mariah giggled. "Where's your mommy?" Monica asked, grabbing the child by the hand.

"In the kitchen, kissing Bill."

"Excuse me?" the older daughter said, raising an eyebrow at the two men behind her.

"Mommy's in the kitchen kissing Bill. It's yuck!" the child chimed, her face grimacing in disgust.

"Since when do you call your father by his first name?" Diondre asked, tapping her on her bottom with the palm of his large hand.

Mariah glared in his direction, pressing a hand against her ruffled panties as she rubbed where her brother had patted her. "His name's Bill."

Irma greeted them all at the door. "Mariah, I've told you that you are to call him Daddy. You aren't grown. Keep it up, and I'm going to give you licks."

The child rolled her eyes. "I like Bill."

Monica shook the little girl's hand. "I like Daddy better."

"He's not your daddy. He's my daddy."

"Baby girl, you are acting right up today," Bill said, rising from his seat in the kitchen to shake hands with Preston and Diondre. He leaned to kiss Monica's cheek. "Keep it up and I'm not going to save you from that spanking you keep asking for," he said, staring down at Mariah.

The child shot them all a dirty look, then crossed her arms as she stomped out of the room. Diondre chuckled softly and Monica couldn't help smiling as Preston shook his head at them to not encourage her.

"Excuse me," Irma said, wiping her hands against a dishrag and following her youngest child out of the room. "I have to adjust my daughter's attitude."

Diondre pretended to cringe. "I remember those days. Monica used to get a lot of attitude adjustments."

The family laughed as Monica nodded her head over the memories.

"So, how are things going?" Bill asked, looking from one to the other.

"It's been a long week," Diondre answered, glancing at Monica and Preston.

"I'm glad for it to be over," Preston added.

"Have the police given you any more information since that woman broke into your home?"

"No, sir." Preston shook his head. "They've got me in limbo right now. I'm grateful that Diondre was able to get me reinstated at work, though."

Bill shook his head, shifting against the kitchen chair. Irma returned, annoyance still painted across her face.

"Your daughter is about to wear out my last nerve," she said as she peered into the oven to check on the roasted chicken.

"When she's bad, she's my daughter. When she's

good, she's your child. Ain't this some stuff," Bill said
with a chuckle, his head moving from side to side.
Irma gave him a look that said she was not amused.

"Where is she?" Bill asked, peering around toward
the living room.

"In her bed. She needed a nap. That's half her
problem. Thinking she's grown is her other problem. That and those two letting her get away with so
much stuff the other week, she still thinks she's on
vacation."

Diondre held up his hands. "I didn't do it." He
pointed toward Monica. "It's all her fault. It's that
girl thing they have between them." The others in
the room laughed as Monica cut her eye in his direction.

Irma pointed to the stack of plates atop the table.
"Well, you and your sister should set the table so we
can eat. Bill is hungry. Preston, give me a hand with
these dishes, please."

"Yes ma'am," Preston grinned, rushing to help
the matriarch with the platters of food she'd finished
filling. "Everything looks wonderful, Irma."

The woman smiled, handing him a large tray of
dinner rolls and a bowl filled brim-high with but-
tered broccoli. Reaching atop the stove, she grabbed
the macaroni and cheese, and candied yams, carefully setting the containers in the middle of the
table. Within minutes, they were all gathered around
the circle, the table blessed and their mouths chewing contentedly. There was minimal conversation,
with the wealth of energy spent enjoying the delica-
cies that Irma had spent the morning preparing.

Smacking his lips, Diondre pressed his palms to
his stomach. "That was good, Mom. That was real
good."

"Thank you, son. Preston, did you have enough?
I can get you some more if you're still hungry."

"Irma, thank you, but I'm full. Everything was delicious. I have to get your recipe for the glazed carrots. They were incredible."

Irma smiled. "Just boil you some carrots until they're fork tender, add a stick of butter and some brown sugar to taste, then cook them on low until the sauce caramelizes. It's really very easy."

"Well, I will have to try them when I get home. I really enjoyed them and the macaroni. I won't ask for that recipe. I'm sure I'd ruin that one."

The woman chuckled. "Monica can make the macaroni and cheese. That's an old family recipe. We just use the ziti instead of that tiny elbow macaroni, and four different types of cheese."

"Plus enough heavy cream and butter to send you into cardiac arrest," Monica added, pulling her last forkful into her mouth.

"I could use me a nap now," Bill said, shifting his chair back.

"Isn't there a game on?" Diondre asked.

Bill nodded. "Baseball on ESPN," he said. "A doubleheader."

Irma shook her head, rising from her seat. "I don't care what you do, Diondre, but you'll do it after you help Monica with the dishes."

"I can help her," Preston volunteered.

"No," Irma stated firmly. "Diondre and Monica can do the dishes. I'd like you to give me a hand with something else."

Monica cut her eye in her mother's direction but said nothing.

"Bill, Preston and I will be out in the backyard for a few minutes. Keep your ears open for Mariah. She won't nap too long." She leaned to kiss her husband's cheek.

As she turned to walk away, Bill gave her a quick swat on the rear end. "Don't you scare that boy away," he said jokingly. "We won't be able to live with this girl if you scare her boyfriend off."

Irma giggled as Monica gave them both an incredulous look. Diondre burst into laughter.

"I won't hurt him too bad," Irma said as she led the way out the rear door. "Took her long enough to find this one. If he gets away, I don't know what we'll do," she said, her words fading as she made her exit, Preston close on her heels.

The modest three-bedroom home had been Irma's pride and joy since the day she'd found herself able to put up a sizable down payment to secure a mortgage. Diondre and Monica had grown up with grass to run upon, in a family neighborhood that was not only safe, but afforded them the best educational opportunities. Its rear yard was a narrow half acre lot of land with a white picket fence, a well-worn children's play set, a sandbox, and a multitude of vibrant flowers that bordered the perimeter of the property. Irma spent many an afternoon weeding her floral beds and tending to the growth of vegetation. The garden area had always been her personal sanctuary no matter how many children ripped and roared though the yard.

As she and Preston sauntered toward the edge of the property, which bordered an expanse of state-owned preservation land, she appraised her handiwork, making note that she needed to thin out the wealth of hostas threatening to run rampant. Preston's gaze followed Irma's as she pointed out her prize rosebushes and the hydrangea, which she called her favorite informal flower. As they neared the teak bench that sat beneath a trellis of climbing ivy, Irma's tone turned serious.

She cleared her throat before speaking, then met Preston's stare with an intense gaze. "My daughter is a very special woman, Preston."

"Yes, ma'am. She is definitely that."

Irma smiled. "A special woman deserves a pretty special man," she stated, raising an eyebrow in his direction, her intense gaze still locked on his face.

Preston could only nod.

"Monica never knew her father, and although Bill has been an incredible parent to all of my children, I think there is a part of my daughter that has always yearned for a man to be the source of strength she imagined a father would be. But I was adamant about teaching Monica that she didn't need a man to accomplish what she wanted.

"And I think that because I was so ambivalent about relationships myself, she knows any man she chooses to share her life with should be around only if she wants him to be."

Preston nodded again, sensing that something else was brewing in Irma's mind. The woman reached into a basket resting on the lawn and removed a pair of pruning shears. She moved to cut three peony stems, pulling the flowers to her nose.

"My daughter loves you, Preston, and I believe that you're good for her. You seem to understand that not only does she need your support, but also that she needs you to let her be the woman she's destined to be."

"Thank you," Preston said softly. "And I do understand. I love Monica very much. She means the world to me."

Irma held up her index finger. "Don't thank me yet, Preston." She dropped back to the seat beside Preston, its position ideal for viewing the manicured lawn in its entirety. "I know you love her, but I'm not at all happy about this mess you've got her caught up in."

The man pressed his eyes closed and took a deep breath. Opening his eyes again widely, tears threatened to fall past his lashes as his emotions washed over his face. "Irma, I would give anything to not have had this happen to Monica. It was never my intent to do anything that would ever hurt her. But you can trust that no matter what, I will do whatever it takes to ensure she stays safe."

Irma nodded slowly. "What you might want may not be enough, Preston." The woman blew a heavy sigh. "My ex-husband was a very jealous man. He could also be very brutal. What neither of my children know, and I am going to trust that you keep this between us, is that their father and I are no longer together because he tried to kill me. At the time, I didn't even know I was pregnant with Monica, and Diondre was just a baby. Too young to remember. But the man allowed his emotions to get the best of him, and he actually tried to do me harm. I was able to get away, but I also had to go into hiding for a very long time until I was certain we were safe."

Preston reached to stroke her hand as Irma wiped a tear from her eye.

"I don't ever want Monica to know that kind of fear, Preston. No woman should ever have to live in fear that someone is going to hurt them in the name of love. This woman clearly has the capacity to harm somebody because of her infatuation with you, and I don't want my child to be caught in the cross fire. Is that clear?"

Preston nodded. "I promise you, Irma. Nothing will ever happen to Monica. I swear I will keep her safe."

"You had better. I will not be a woman you'll want to deal with if my child gets hurt because of something you've done, or whatever this woman seems to think you've done."

Preston nodded his understanding as Irma got to her feet.

Irma headed back to the house, her slow gait

showing she was in no particular hurry. "Monica says you two have been talking about getting married?"

"Yes, ma'am."

Irma smiled. "When you do, elope. Get it over with, and call everyone after the fact. That's the best way to do it."

Preston chuckled. "Monica says she wants a small wedding."

The woman's mother laughed. "My daughter would. Well then, think about having it here in the yard. It's always so beautiful out here, and this is one of Monica's favorite spots."

The James–Turner family stood waving good-bye as Diondre pulled his car out of the driveway, chauffeuring Monica and Preston back home to Raleigh. Irma stood staring long after the car had pulled out of sight and Mariah and her father had retreated inside, hand in hand, to watch the Cartoon Network.

She hadn't known what she would say to Preston until after the words had fallen, but once they'd eased over her tongue, she was glad for them. She had always been proud of Monica and her accomplishments, the young woman's fierce independence a badge of honor her mother had bestowed upon her. Her daughter had matured into a woman any mother would be proud of, but the single greatest thing Irma had worked diligently to shield her child from now threatened to nip too close to the young woman's heels.

Irma had never wanted Monica to feel true fear. Irma herself had experienced far too many years of the harsh emotion, and she knew all too well how thoroughly debilitating it could be on a woman's spirit. When Monica had called to tell her about Preston's problem, letting it slip that the woman had threatened her harm as well, Irma had heard something in her child's voice that had alarmed her. To anyone else it would have seemed like nothing, but Irma was all too familiar with the initial denial fear could incite. Denial, turning to despair, then dropping a body headfirst into a pit of paralyzing fright. A pit deep enough to keep a soul trapped beneath it forever.

She would never allow that to touch either of her girls. Never. And she had thought it important that Preston know so. A cool breeze wafted against her skin and she felt a chill shiver up her spine. Turning, Irma headed back inside, her baby girl and a Bugs Bunny rerun calling her name.

Twenty-four

The last interview had been revealing, the informant offering information and details the duo had wished for. As Detectives Rodriguez and Keyes returned to their vehicle, Angela Keyes shook her head in disbelief.

"She had me fooled completely. I thought that girl was telling the truth."

Detective Ramirez nodded, giving his partner a quick glance before refocusing on the road. "Ms. Thompson is very good. That's why she was so convincing."

"Yeah, but I interviewed her twice. I never suspected a thing, and I'm usually better than that."

"Yes, you are," Ramirez responded, "but Ms. Thompson is a rare breed. Her criminal intent is motivated by illness. That adds a whole other dimension to what she's capable of."

Dejection washed over the woman's expression. "But I should have seen it," she said softly.

The man pressed his hand over hers. "She didn't want us to. She hid it well."

The woman shook her head again, incredulity flowing like floodwater over her. Particulars about Donata Thompson's history had begun to fill in a number of blanks for Keyes and Ramirez. With each new detail, the picture that had once been an incomplete puzzle for them was growing clearer and clearer.

The discovery of an expunged high school charge had been the first significant tip. Donata had been charged with assaulting a fellow student, whom she alleged was involved with the boys' basketball coach. Donata had also alleged that she was dating the man. The coach had filed suit against Donata for harassment. Since Donata had been a juvenile, the issue had been settled out of court. With promises to keep her nose clean for a period of four years, she had the blemish wiped from her files. It had been fortunate for both officers that the coach remembered all too well his problems with Donata Thompson.

The young woman's college career at Meredith College was cut short when she was accused of threatening a female science teacher. Donata had claimed the woman was experimenting with chemicals that would steal Donata's mind. Donata's crush on the woman's basketball-star husband had facilitated the girl's delusions. A one-year recovery period in a private health facility was thought to have cured the girl's problems. That was, until she met Dr. Preston Walker, and he became her new object of obsession.

The last conversation between the two officers and a homeless man known only as Brick had exposed a good deal of information about Miss Thompson and her late-night activities the evening she claimed Dr. Walker had assaulted her. One name in particular had gotten their attention, and the duo were headed to the east end of town to track its owner down.

"Why is that name so familiar?" Keyes asked, turning in her seat to face him.

"Tank, aka Warren York, has been arrested at least four times this year that I know of. We collared him the last time for assaulting his wife. You remember, the woman with the broken jaw and fractured collarbone he forced out of the car on the highway because she'd purchased the wrong pack of cigarettes."

Recall washed over her as a flashback of the poor woman's face and battered body flickered through her mind. "I do remember. He was a real winner," she said sarcastically. "Said he got his kicks hitting on women."

Ramirez nodded. "That's him, and I'm really curious to know what business he and Ms. Thompson had together."

Although it was still early afternoon, a number of seats were taken along the long, wooden bar that lined the wall of Casey's Bar and Grill. Ramirez scanned the deadpan faces that barely acknowledged the detectives' arrival, the quick looks falling back to half-filled glasses. Detective Keyes tapped him against the upper arm and pointed to the pool table and the large, barrel-chested man who leaned like a heavy side of beef against it. The two approached him cautiously, and his gaze caught Ramirez as the man stepped in front of him.

"Mr. Tank. Long time no see."

The man shrugged. "Not long enough, obviously."

"We need to ask you some questions."

"About what?"

"Let's take it down to the station."

The big man glared, his thick eyebrows becoming one full line above his eyes. "And what if I don't want to?"

Ramirez smiled. "I don't recall asking," he said smoothly. "I was telling."

Tank heaved a deep sigh, filling his massive chest with hot air that he spat out in Keyes' direction.

The woman stood sternly, staring him down from

head to toe. "What happened to your hand?" she
asked, gesturing toward the row of black and blue
marks that covered his knuckles.

He snarled. "I hit something."

"It must have been something hard."

"No, I just hit it hard," the man said, the foul odor
of his breath hitting her squarely in the face as he
grinned obscenely.

Ramirez gestured toward the door. "Now, you
have a choice. You can make this very easy, or you
can make it difficult. Either way, you're going to the
station. Now let me know how you want it to do it."

Tank slammed his pool cue against the table, then
reached for a ten-dollar bill that sat at the table's
center. The man who'd been prepared to play with
him turned an about-face, knowing that the exchange between his associate and the officers was
over, and there would be no game with Tank that
afternoon. The cops had won; Tank was going to be
playing by their rules instead of his own.

A warrant had been issued for her arrest. Donata
could only shake her head at the absurdity. The two
officers who'd heard her story wanted her to think
they knew something, but she knew better. They
didn't know anything. Least of all, they didn't know
where she was or what she had planned. She smiled,
pulling herself up against the double bed in the
tastefully decorated bedroom.

Her friend Tijuana had begged her to turn herself in, but Donata couldn't. Not yet. Not until she
was done and her mission was completed. She had
unfinished business with Preston and that woman.
The two of them had been laughing at her, overjoyed when the detective knocked on Preston's front
door to deliver the news about the warrant. They

hadn't known that she could see them clearly, that even now, as they strolled from one unit to the other, having a cookout with their family and friends, she was right there, one eye keeping a check on things. As close as she was, Donata knew she'd have no problems knowing when the time would be right for her to carry out her last act against them.

There was a whisper in her ear, and Donata listened intently, a wicked grin flooding her face. It would be too easy. The voices were jubilant, overjoyed at the prospect of settling the score. And only when her mission was finished, when there was nothing else left for her to do, would she be able to leave. The prospect of packing her things and disappearing was beginning to grow on her. She knew that there was someplace where someone was waiting for her, excited about her coming. Donata nodded as the voices promised that her presence would be accepted the next time.

Rising from the bed, Donata peered out the window, watching as the couple played host and hostess to the crowd gathering in the rear courtyard. Preston stood over the grill, a large white apron over his casual shorts and cotton T-shirt. Monica sat at the patio table, a small child sitting comfortably in her lap. They were all laughing and Donata winced, their joviality inciting a sudden well of ire within her.

Moving into the other room, she raged. A sudden glimpse of the old woman's eyes and the rise of tears that filled them made Donata stop short, inhaling deeply as she fought to still her anger. A quick in-and-out exchange of air made her feel better, and she welcomed the onset of calm. She smiled down at the couple who lay anxiously against the queen-size mattress.

Isaac Stern struggled with the wealth of duct tape that held him hostage against the delicate quilt that covered the bed. Donata shook a finger at him, shaking her head.

"You really don't want to do that, Mr. Stern," she said, dropping down against the bedside beside his wife's body. She rubbed a hand against the old woman's knee. "We wouldn't want anything bad to happen to Mrs. Stern, now, would we?"

The man ceased struggling, his eyes pleading with the girl to leave them both alone. A tear rolled down his wife's face, and he watched as Donata reached a finger to brush the offending flow away.

"I know you can understand, Lydia. May I call you Lydia?" Donata asked, pressing a finger to the duct tape that covered the woman's mouth. "I know you can understand. Sometimes we women have to take command of a bad situation and make it right. I'm only trying to make things right. I promise, it won't take long, and then you two can go back to doing whatever it is you do here all day." Donata gave the woman a wide smile.

"My fiancée thinks he can get away with hurting me, but I can't let that happen. He cheated on me, Lydia. He cheated with that cheap tramp that lives next door. You really should get better neighbors." The girl blew out a heavy sigh. "What kind of woman would I be if I let him get away with it?"

Donata stood back up, reaching for a JC Penney's bag on the floor of the large bedroom. She pulled a brand new trench coat and a lace lingerie set from its interior. Holding the garments up to her body as she stood staring at her reflection in the mahogany-framed mirror, she was pleased. All she needed now was the perfect hairstyle to complete her new ensemble. She turned to face the couple, ignoring the fear across their faces.

"What do you think?" she asked. "Isn't this perfect? My new boyfriend is going to love me in this. I just know it." Donata spun around the room, humming softly, imaginary music swirling around the conversation dancing through her mind. She grinned, cocking her head as if hearing someone call her name. "See! I told you!" she exclaimed excitedly. "Everyone agrees. Everything is going to be just fine!"

The heat from the gas grill had finally eased down, but not before Diondre and Godfrey had waged a battle for the last T-bone steak. Inside, Diondre, Godfrey, and Preston lounged in front of the television set, knee deep in the New York Knicks-New Jersey Nets first round playoff game. With Bryan Junior pretending to keep score, Bill and Bryan Senior played horseshoes in the far corner of the backyard. Bryan's daughter, Tanya, was being dragged from one point to another by Mariah, while the older females sat watching everything from the glass-topped table that sat under the large umbrella on Monica's patio.

"Do they have any idea where she might be?" Danielle Bailey asked. "I would think you and Preston would still be on edge until she's in custody."

Monica shrugged. "The detective said her family believes she's headed to Wilmington, to her grandmother's home. Apparently, any time she knows she's in trouble, that's where she retreats to. They say she's called there a few times already."

"You still need to be careful," Irma said, bristling ever so slightly as she caught her daughter's eye. "You don't know what that woman might do."

"We're being cautious," Monica replied, before changing the subject. "Danielle, how's your business? Bryan said you were thinking about moving the store," she said, referring to the women's specialty clothing shop her friend owned.

"It couldn't be better. I'm thinking I need to ex-
pand into a larger space. I've been seriously consid-
ering adding a line of clothing for girls."

"Very nice," Irma said. "I'm always looking for
clothes that don't make Mariah look like she's three
going onto thirty."

Danielle nodded, her shoulder-length bob waving
against her honey-brown complexion. Her large
black eyes widened in agreement. "Exactly. Every
time I have to shop for Tanya, I get annoyed. She's
only eleven, and some of the styles make her look
like a hooker-in-training. I hate it. It's also hard because so many of her friends are wearing all these
midriff tops and tight bottoms, and she wants to
wear what she sees them wearing."

The three women turned their attention to the
two girls, who were dancing side by side in the center of the small yard. Mariah was giving out orders,
wanting to lead the activities.

Irma laughed. "My child is a mess!" she exclaimed
as she shook her head. "Tanya is so good with her."

"Tanya loves little kids. She says she wants to be a
teacher when she grows up."

Monica smiled. "I don't know how you both do it.
Kids wear me out."

The two mothers grinned in her direction.

"It grows on you," Danielle said with a wry smile.

"You just do what you have to do," Irma added.
"Besides, you and Preston have plenty of time to decide whether or not you want to have children. And
when you do, it will be the best decision for the both
of you."

Monica shook her head as she rolled her eyes.

Irma laughed. "It's okay to be unsure, Monica, but
I know that if you do decide to have children, you will
be just fine. You're wonderful with Mariah. Preston is
even better. The two of you will be great parents."

"Well, thank you, but personally, I'd rather not be bothered," Monica said. "Being a big sister and surrogate auntie is enough for me."

"Have you and Preston talked about kids?" Danielle asked.

Irma laughed. "Kids! They need to get past the issue of sex first!"

"Mom!" Monica exclaimed, embarrassment flushing her face.

Danielle laughed with her. "Well, that would certainly help," she said fighting to stifle her giggles.

"You both need to stop," Monica said, in a hushed whisper, glancing through the patio door to ensure Preston had not heard them.

Irma flipped her hand at her daughter, still laughing. She and Danielle both leaned in conspiratorially.

"I have to tell you, Monica, when Bryan first told me about Preston, I didn't believe it."

"I still don't believe it," Irma said smirking.

Monica rolled her eyes. "Well, trust me, it's very true!"

"That's too funny," Irma whispered back, "especially since Monica's fast behind couldn't wait to lose her virginity."

"Was she fast, Irma?"

The woman laughed, nodding her head.

"I was not!" Monica said with a deep chuckle.

"Yes, you were," her mother responded, "and mark my words, one day you'll have a daughter just like you. Then you'll see what fast is."

"I've told you. Children are not on the top of my to-do list. Preston and I are not concerned about having a baby."

"You say that now," her mother said, "but we'll see."

Danielle laughed. "Forget it, Monica. You're cursed now. Irma's hit you with that mother voodoo." The woman pointed to her youngest child, the young girl teaching Mariah a new music-video strut. "My mother cursed me with that one. Bryan and I weren't thinking about a second baby, but then she said she wished I had a girl just like me. It was all over after that. I spit out my reflection nine months later."

Monica's eyes spun in their sockets. The trio was interrupted as Mariah came racing toward them. "Mon-ka? You want to see my new dance?"

"I saw it," Monica answered, leaning down to the little girl's eye level. "I saw you and Tanya shaking your bottoms over there."

"I was singing, too!"

"You sing beautifully, Mariah. Where did you learn that song?" Danielle asked.

"From da radio." Mariah leaned on her mother's knee. "Mommy, can I stay with Mon-ka? Can I? I want to sleep in Mon-ka's room with the special sheets she got me for my bed. Can I, Mommy? Please?"

"Mariah, Monica has to get ready for work on Monday. She has things to do. Maybe you can sleep over next week."

The child pouted, her bottom lip pushing out past her chin. Tears pressed at her eyes.

"Don't you do it," Irma admonished, her pointed finger inches from the child's face. "Don't make me give you something to cry for."

Monica laughed. "It's okay with me. If Diondre says he'll take her back home tomorrow, then she can stay."

"Are you sure?"

Monica nodded. "We'll be fine. We can watch movies with Preston tonight," she said aloud, then added, muttering under her breath, "because we sure won't be doing anything else."

Danielle and Irma laughed, the two children eyeing them curiously.

Irma smiled, pulling at her youngest daughter's

pigtail. "Monica says you can stay, but you need to ask your brother if he will bring you home tomorrow, because I'm not coming back to Raleigh to get you."

"Hey, boy!" Mariah shouted loudly, racing into the house. "Mommy says you have to bring me home tomorrow. You have to! Okay, boy?"

An old Cosby rerun played on the television. Mariah sat against Preston's lap, her head pressed into his chest as she slept soundly. Beside them, Monica sat leaning against Preston's arm, not far from falling off to sleep herself. She rubbed a hand down her sister's back, then lifted herself up off the sofa.

"I should put her to bed," she said softly, moving to lift the child from Preston's arms. He shook his head as the child stirred, her eyes opening for one quick second before she closed them again, dropping right back to sleep. "I'll do it. You don't want to wake her up," he said quietly.

Monica smiled as she followed him up the flight of stairs, Mariah snuggled comfortably in his arms. In the bedroom closest to her own, Monica pulled back the covers, exposing Mariah's freshly washed pink and purple striped sheets. Preston laid the child gently against the mattress, stepping out of the way as Monica pulled off the little girl's sneakers and socks. When Mariah was down to her flower-printed underpants and matching T-shirt, Monica tucked the covers around her and kissed her goodnight.

Seconds later the two adults stood in the living room, wrapped in a warm embrace. Monica leaned her body against Preston's, pressing her lips to his. His gaze was tender, a loving touch as he broke the connection of their mouths, pressing his palm to her cheek. The two swayed quietly together, lost in the splendor that filled the space around them. Monica marveled at how safe she felt locked tightly in his arms, his hands pressing against her back, the length of his fingers kneading her flesh affectionately.

Preston sensed her comfort and held her tighter, wanting to cushion her from any anxiety that may have threatened her spirit. "Maybe I should sleep on your sofa tonight?" he said, concern rising in his voice.

"Don't you start," Monica answered. "My mother is worrying enough for the both of us."

"Your mother is right to worry. We need to be smart. That crazy girl paid someone to beat her up. We don't know what else she's capable of."

Monica sighed, her cheek pressed close to his as she whispered in his ear. "I'm really not worried. The detective promised to make sure a patrol car kept watch in the complex, so someone will see her if she shows up. Besides, I don't think she's interested in getting caught. I seriously doubt if we'll be seeing her any time soon."

Preston nodded, inhaling the scent of her deep into his nostrils. As he blew the air out past his lips he gave her a quick squeeze, the dropped his lips back against hers.

The quiet in Preston's townhome was broken by the ringing telephone. When no one answered, the answering machine clicked on. "I'm unable to take your call at the moment. If you'll please leave your name, number, and a brief message, I will return your call. Thank you."

The machine beeped.

"Hey, Preston. It's me. Godfrey. I just wanted to thank you and Monica for the invitation this afternoon. I had a great time. Hey, by the way, does Monica have any single friends you can introduce me to? Call me. Bye."

With one last beep and a serious of clicks, quiet returned. Preston had just pushed his key into the lock when the phone rang for the second time. He let it roll over to the answering machine, too exhausted to go rushing for the call. As the tape shifted into play, a brief silence spun out of the machine, and then Donata's voice floated into the room. Preston stood frozen, his hand having barely left the doorknob behind him.

"I'm never going away, Dr. Walker. Even now, I'm so close I can see the fear on your stupid face. I'm going to make you pay for what you've done to me." The woman laughed, her glee swiftly changing to a low sob. "I just wanted to love you. That's all. I could have been good for you, but you had to let her mess things up between us. I'm going to make you pay for that. And I'm going to make her pay, too."

As the call disconnected, Preston felt a chill pass through him. Opening the front door, he stared out across the courtyard. Monica's lights had faded into darkness. Only a sliver of moonlight shimmered against the grass-covered ground. Stepping outside, he glanced from one end of the yard to the other. Nothing but darkness filled the space around him. Going back inside, he locked the front door and closed all the blinds. Dialing Monica's telephone number one last time to check on her, he couldn't shake the uneasy feeling that Donata Thompson was indeed somewhere close, watching them.

Twenty-five

The sun had risen with such vibrant intensity that it infused energy in each ray of warmth that spilled down over the earth. Monica inhaled the urgency of it, wallowing in the luxury of its touch against her skin. The clear blue sky had beckoned her outside, and as she had stepped out the front door to inhale the view she couldn't imagine anything coming that could spoil so perfect a Sunday morning.

After taking a quick sip of her morning coffee, the aroma of the first cup wafting to her nostrils, she walked barefoot across the bright green carpet of freshly cut grass. As she rang Preston's doorbell, she turned to face her own unit, keeping her eyes focused for Mariah, who had still been sleeping soundly.

"Good morning, beautiful," Preston said, stealing a quick kiss as he opened his own door and stepped outside to greet her. "What are you doing up so early?"

"It's too pretty out to sleep. Have you had breakfast yet?"

"No. I thought I'd offer to take you and Mariah to IHOP for pancakes."

"I like that idea."

"Do you want to go to church?"

Monica nodded her head. "I do actually, but I think

I'd like to go to that new church Danielle was telling us about. I think it's Horizons Christian Ministry. It's off of highway 54. She said the service is only an hour, and the dress code is extremely casual. I hear they have a great program for children, also. And since Mariah doesn't have Sunday clothes, she can wear her shorts and sneakers and not be out of place."

"If you want, we can also drive to Asheboro Zoo this afternoon. She'd like that."

Monica grinned. "That sounds like a lot of fun."

Preston took a quick glance down at his watch. "I can be showered and dressed in about thirty minutes. What time is service?"

"Eleven o'clock. We actually have time to eat first, do church, and be on the road by noon."

Preston nodded, then gave her another quick kiss. "Why don't you call and see if Diondre wants to join us?"

Monica smiled. "I will. Let me go get my girl up so we can get ready."

Preston watched as she made her way back across the courtyard and entered her home. The smile that had graced his face faded slowly. He knew he would have to tell her about Donata's call. Last night when he'd called the detective, the police still had no clue to the woman's whereabouts. That fact concerned him, but he didn't want his worries to affect Monica. Spinning around on his heels, he closed and locked the door, then headed up the stairs to dress.

"Mon-ka? Can we go see the monkeys at the zoo? I like the monkeys!"

Monica grinned at her sister. "Stop shouting. I'm sitting right here. Yes, we can go see the monkeys."

The little girl returned her sister's smile, watching as Monica applied a faint line of eyeliner to her lids and brushed a coat of pale color across her lips. "I want lipstick."

"You're too little for lipstick."

"Just a little. Please?"

Monica cut her eyes in the little girl's direction, then searched her makeup tray until she found a half-used tube of strawberry Chapstick. "Here. This is your lipstick. Just use a tiny bit, then put it away in your drawer in the bedroom."

Mariah's smile almost filled her face as she pushed herself against Monica's elbow to stare at her reflection in the makeup mirror. She lined her lips with the flavorful lip coating, grinning widely as she did. "I want to go show Preston," she exclaimed, jumping up and down excitedly.

"You can show Preston in a few minutes."

The telephone on the nightstand rung, and Monica rose from her seat to grab the receiver. "Hello?"

"Good morning. How are my girls this morning?"

"Hi, Mom. We're doing fine. Headed out the door, actually."

"Oh? Where are you two off to?"

"Diondre's on his way over, and we're going with him and Preston to church, and then we're driving to Asheboro to the zoo."

Irma laughed. "Well, I guess I won't worry about Mariah. I just hope you and your brother can survive."

"You aren't worried about Preston?"

"Preston's tough. He can hold his own. He doesn't let Mariah run all over him the way you two do."

"Thanks."

"I'm just being honest."

Mariah pulled at her sister's elbow. "I wanna go show Preston my lipstick," she whined, dragging her words like fingernails against a chalkboard.

Monica gave her a hard look. "Here, say hello to your mommy."

Pulling the receiver to her ear the little girl stuck her tongue out at Monica. "Mommy, can I go show Preston my lipstick?" she asked, greeting her mother.

"What lipstick?"

"Monica gave me lipstick."

"I gave her a Chapstick!" Monica shouted over the child's head. She gave Mariah a light pinch. "Tattletale!"

Irma chuckled. "Mariah, you better behave for Monica. Do you understand me?"

"Uh-huh. Can I, Mommy? Can I go show Preston?"

"If it's okay with Monica. You listen to what your sister tells you."

Mariah dropped the phone, racing for the door.

"You stop, Mariah," Monica shouted as she pulled the phone up from the floor. "I swear. Hold on, Mom."

Mariah ignored her as the child rushed down the stairs and pulled at the front door. "Mariah, don't you step out of this house," Monica chastised, calling down from the second floor.

"But I want to go see Preston," the child whined for the second time. "I wanna see him now!"

Monica could hear the screen door opening. "You wait at that door until Preston says you can come over," she shouted back down the stairs. She could hear the child muttering under her breath as Monica switched to her second line and hit a speed dial number. Preston answered on the second ring.

"Hi. Everything okay?"

Monica nodded into the receiver. "Mariah wants to come see you. I'll try to slow her down, but I just wanted you to know she's headed to your door as we speak. I'm not dressed yet, and she's having a fit."

Preston laughed. "I just finished putting on my pants. I'll go right down and meet her."

"Thank you." Monica clicked back to her mother. "Is everything okay?" Irma asked.

"Yes, ma'am. I just wanted Preston to know Mariah was on her way over. She tore out of here."

"Mariah has a crush on Preston. I heard her telling her father that he was her new boyfriend."

"Bill must have loved that. Mariah's been saying he was her boyfriend since she learned how to talk."

"He'll get over it. Daddies have to share their little girls sooner or later."

Monica smiled, walking to the window to peer across the way. In the parking lot, she saw Diondre as he pulled into an open space and exited his vehicle. Preston's front door was wide open, but there was no sign of him or Mariah.

"Let me go, Mom. Diondre's here, and I need to go rescue Mariah's new boyfriend before she drives him crazy."

Irma laughed. "You all have fun, and stay safe."

After throwing on her own clothes, she headed down the stairs. Monica checked to make sure the coffeepot was turned off and the sliding doors were locked. Grabbing her keys and purse, she stepped out the front, waving to her brother and Preston, who stood talking at the man's front door.

Preston smiled as she approached. "What happened? Mariah change her mind?"

Monica's face fell, a wave of panic flooding through her as her eyes skated back and forth in seach of her sister. "Didn't you see her? Didn't she come to your door?"

Both Preston and Diondre instantly reacted to Monica's look of surprise, dread suddenly filling the morning air. Turning back to her front door, Monica unlocked it and pushed it open, shouting Mariah's name as she rushed through the house. Behind her, Diondre raced to the pool and children's play area, doing the same. Preston scanned the parking area, searching for anything unusual, then began knocking on the line of front doors, waking his neighbors from their sleep. As the three of them regrouped in the center of the courtyard, neither of them needed to say the unthinkable out loud. Mariah was gone.

It had been too easy. The little girl had danced alone into the courtyard, and before anyone could see her, Donata had coaxed her to the Sterns' front door and pulled her inside. The young woman laughed hysterically as she watched the child struggle with the duct table that held her captive beside the old people on the large bed. It had been much too easy.

Retreating down to the kitchen, Donata looked around the brightly decorated room. Lydia Stern had painted the space a bright yellow, the color almost blinding with the bright sun that flooded through the windows. The curtains were a white and yellow checkered print that coordinated with a collection of chickens and roosters that were throughout the room. Ceramic chickens on the counter, a chicken painting on the wall, chickens on the potholders, even a teakettle in the shape of a chicken. Donata chuckled, wondering what she might collect when she got old and senile. *It won't be chickens*, she thought, still laughing to herself.

After searching inside the refrigerator, she pulled out a dozen eggs, four slices of bacon, two slices of Amercian cheese, and a large tomato. Her grandmother had always kept the tomatoes in a basket in the center of the table. She shrugged. What did the Sterns know about tomatoes? They'd never worked a farm. Donata would bet that neither one of them would even know what to do if they had to pluck a tomato from the vine.

As she cracked her eggs into a glass bowl, she heard the doorbell ringing and the rise of voices that rang through the air on the other side of the door. She could hear them calling for the little girl, the panic and fear rising like thick mist to coat the inflection of their words. Without flinching, Donata pulled a fork from the kitchen drawer and pulled it through her eggs until they were beaten into a froth. On the stove, a saucepan had started to warm nicely, the cold pat of butter dropped against the Teflon beginning to melt and sizzle. As Donata poured the egg batter into the pan, filling the center with the tomatoes and cheese, she could hear the blare of sirens pulling into the parking lot outside. The voices were singing in her head, and she smiled, humming along softly.

Twenty-six

Bill held Irma's hand, squeezing her fingers with his right hand as he steered the car with his left. Traffic along Interstate 40 was moving rapidly, but neither of them noticed as he exceeded the speed limit to move them toward Raleigh as fast as possible.

Irma fought to hold her tears. They billowed at the edges of her eyes, threatening to betray emotion she wasn't yet willing to share. Her children would need her strength, and she was determined not to fail them.

"Everything is going to be fine," Bill said softly, as if reading her mind. "Hopefully, they will have found her by the time we get there."

Irma's gaze caught his, and in his brief glance between her and the roadway she wanted to believe him. She desperately wanted to trust that their baby girl would be waiting, safe and sound, when they arrived.

Irma leaned to press her cheek against her husband's shoulder. She inhaled the scent of him, the mixture of Dial soap and Brut cologne consoling.

Bill repeated himself, reiterating how it would all end well. "Have faith," he said. "God will keep her safe."

As they pulled into Monica's housing complex, a uniformed police officer waved them to stop, requesting proof of identification.

"My name's Bill Turner," the man said as he

passed over his driver's license. "That's our daughter who's missing."

The officer waved them in, radioing news of their arrival to someone else. As they stepped from the car, hurrying up the walkway toward the flow of activity, Monica rushed forward, pulling herself from the officers gathered around her, Diondre, and Preston. Tears stained her cheeks as she ran into her mother's arms.

"I'm so sorry, Mommy. I should never have let her out of my sight. It's all my fault."

Irma held her oldest daughter tightly, her own tears finally dripping past her lashes. "Shhh," she whispered softly. "You stop that nonsense. You have no reason to blame yourself. Now stop that crying," she said, her tone firm.

Bill wrapped his arms around them both, echoing his wife's sentiments. "Monica, you and your brother have always been very responsible with Mariah. We trust both of you. Your mother and I know you didn't do anything to put our baby girl in harm's way." He turned to Diondre, Preston, and the officer who had joined them. "Do we know anything yet?" Bill asked, directing his question to the three men.

Detective Ramirez extended a hand and introduced himself. "Mr. Turner, we've already initiated the Amber Alert."

"I'm sorry," Bill said shaking head. "What's that?"

"The Amber Alert is an emergency-response system. As soon as a child is reported missing and we've ascertained that he or she might possibly be endangered, we launch the system to alert the public of any critical details that would enable us to locate the child sooner. We've already passed on pertinent information about your daughter, including her photo, to all the radio and television stations in the state and the Internet. We've also issued an all-points bulletin for Donata Thompson. We believe she may have had something to do with this."

Irma bristled. "You mean that crazy woman may have my baby?"

Monica hugged her mother as the man responded. "We're not sure, but it's highly possible. We've set up a command station in your daughter's home here, and I have every one of my officers working on this case."

Preston reached out to hug Irma, his gaze meeting Bill's. "I take full responsibility. None of this would have happened if I had been able to do something about that woman."

Irma shook her head, pressing her palm to his cheek. "I need you to take care of Monica right now. All of us need to stop trying to take the blame for what has happened. We need to focus on finding Mariah." She turned to Detective Ramirez. "Now, will someone please tell me what else you people are doing to find my child?"

"We're searching the entire complex. There's no way she could have gotten far," the man said with a nod, directing his comments to Mariah's parents. "We were just establishing a time line for your daughter's disappearance. Ms. James says she was on the telephone with you when Mariah disappeared, Mrs. Turner?"

Irma nodded. "Yes, it wasn't quite nine o'clock. I remember the exact time because Reverend Price was just finishing his television sermon. Bill, my husband, watches Frederick K.C. Price every Sunday morning from eight to nine, like clockwork."

"And you spoke to the child?"

"Yes. She wanted permission to go see Preston. I told her she could only do what Monica said was okay for her to do."

"Can you think of anything else?" the man asked

as he added comments to his notes, scribbling quickly as she spoke.

Irma took a deep breath. "Monica switched to her other line to call Preston. She wanted him to know that Mariah was on her way over. I could hear Mariah in the background having a fit to get out the door."

Detective Ramirez focused his gaze on Monica. "What happened after you called Dr. Walker?"

"He said he would go right down to meet her. He had just finished dressing, and I didn't have my clothes on. I heard Mariah at the door, then I didn't hear her. I assumed she'd gone straight to Preston's. When I looked out the window, I saw my brother arriving, and Preston's door was open. I thought Mariah was already inside the house."

"How much time passed between you being on the phone and looking out the window?"

"Maybe a minute or two. It wasn't long at all."

Preston picked up their account. "After Monica called me, I came right downstairs and opened the door. Monica's door was open, but Mariah never came out. I waited a few minutes and I was about to walk over to see what was keeping her when her brother showed up."

Diondre nodded his head. "That's right. We said hello, and before we could say anything else, Monica stepped out. We immediately realized Mariah was missing and after we searched around and couldn't find her, we called you guys."

The detective nodded. "You didn't see anyone leaving as you drove in, Mr. James?"

"No. Not a soul."

"Ms. James, is it possible your sister walked outside before you called Dr. Walker?"

Monica shrugged. "It's possible, but I told her not to go out the door until she saw him. She's usually very good about listening."

Irma chuckled, an unconscious giggle to ease a sudden wave of anxiety. "Detective, my baby can be very hard headed. She wanted to go to Preston's, and she didn't want to wait. You could blink an eye, and she'd be out of your sight before you knew it." The woman struggled not to cry, leaning her weight against her husband. The man grabbed for her hands. "Find my child," she whispered. "Please, Lord, let them find my child."

Detective Keyes joined her partner as he stood alone in the center of the courtyard. The man's mind was racing as he fought to process this new turn of events.

"What's going on?" she asked, leaning against the marble statue as she appraised him.

"It's just too neat a job. From what I figure there was, maybe, a four- or five-minute window of opportunity for someone to see the child, grab her, and then disappear without being seen. There's no indication that she was driven away, and nothing to say she was taken away on foot. We have enough witnesses in the perimeter of the complex that can attest to the fact that they didn't see or hear anything, and if that child had walked off, someone would have seen her. What did the door-to-door turn up?"

Keyes glanced down at her notes. "Not much. All of the neighbors were home and have been questioned, with the exception of unit seven and unit three." She pointed to the corner unit at the end of the complex. "The Glaston family resides in unit three, and their neighbors to the immediate left say they've been on vacation and aren't due back for another week. That couple had a key, and we went in to check but it was clear."

Ramirez nodded. "And what's the story with unit

seven?" he asked, pointing to Monica's immediate neighbors.

"Mr. and Mrs. Stern. The older couple we interviewed about Dr. Walker, remember? From what we've determined they were scheduled to leave for a family reunion in New York today. They have a daughter in Mebane who confirmed she spoke with them yesterday, and they're supposed to contact her when they arrive. Dr. Walker also said their car was in the parking lot last night, but it was gone this morning. He says they usually leave it in long-term parking at the airport when they leave town."

The man's head continued to bob up and down against his shoulders. "We have to find this child, Angela. I don't care what it takes, I want her found alive."

"King-John is in the house, and you're listening to WTIC, 98.3 FM radio. The state police have issued an Amber Alert for a missing child believed to have been abducted from a Raleigh home earlier this morning. The little girl, four-year-old Mariah James-Turner, was last seen wearing a yellow top with white flowers, denim shorts, white socks, and pink tennis shoes.

"The police believe she may be in the company of a woman identified as Donata Thompson, a student at State University. Ms. Thompson may be driving a silver Hyundai Accent with North Carolina license plate number LINBRAV. If anyone believes they've seen this child or have any information about her whereabouts, you are asked to contact your local police department.

"On a personal note, little Mariah is the baby sister of one of Raleigh's premier radio personalities, Monica James. From our family to hers, we want her to know that our prayers for Mariah's safe return are with her and her family. This is King-John Vega, the crown prince of talk radio, bringing you the news first, fast, and accurate."

They had broadcast her picture on television, showing the photo she'd taken after the spring dance the year Coach Dixon hadn't let her love him. It was a good photo, she thought as she stared at the television screen, the sound muted. On the bed, the child had finally stopped crying, drifting off to sleep, her body pressed close to Mrs. Stern's. The old woman and her husband had cradled themselves protectively around the little girl and lay staring at Donata cautiously, a shadow of rage burning in both their eyes.

Donata ignored the looks. She had explained to Lydia why she needed to do what she'd done. She'd told her repeatedly that Dr. Walker had to pay for how he'd treated her. That he had to suffer for choosing that woman over her. More importantly, though, Monica James had to pay for taking her man away. He had been hers until she'd come sneaking along.

Donata moved to the window to peer outside. Nightfall had finally come and settled in. The afternoon heat had lifted, and the warm air outside was comfortable. From where she stood, she could barely see into his windows, the angle distorting her view. She knew he was there, though. She knew he sat waiting inside with that James woman, and the rest of them, waiting for some hint of news. In the courtyard, the police had been joined by local news crews and everyone was still scurrying back and forth like annoying bugs. The voices were ready, and Donata smiled. The time had come.

* * *

Preston had followed when Monica pulled herself away from her family and retreated upstairs to the bedroom he'd converted into a small exercise room, a weight machine, some dumbbells, and a treadmill its only furnishings. She stood staring into space, her spirit bruised, and as he stepped in the room beside her, it tore at his heart to see her so pained.

Stepping up behind her, he wrapped his arms around her torso, pulling her gently against him. Monica leaned back into his chest, allowing him to catch the brunt of her weight, her whole body suddenly feeling too heavy for her to carry alone.

"She's never been away from any of us before," Monica whispered. "She's probably so scared."

Preston tightened his grip, hugging her closer. "Mariah is tough. She's going to be fine. They're going to find her."

Monica nodded. "I should never have let her out of my sight," she said, repeating the thought that continued to race through her head. "I should have known it wasn't safe."

Preston spun her around, his hands pressing heavily against the round of her shoulders. "I don't want to ever hear you say that again. This was not your fault. No one could have predicted this happening. Right now, you have to stay strong. For your mother, and for Mariah. We don't have time for you to feel sorry for yourself right now. We have to get your sister back safely. That's all we need to focus on. Is that clear?"

Monica's gaze met his, their eyes connecting in understanding. She nodded her head. "You sound like my mother."

"Your mother is an amazing woman. And you're just like her, don't forget that."

Monica moved to wrap her arms around him, pressing her face into his chest. "I'm glad you're here," she said, wallowing in the warmth of his body.

Preston brushed his lips against her forehead. "I wouldn't be anywhere else," he said. "Nowhere."

As they stood, holding each other tightly, Irma watched quietly from the door. Her oldest child would be all right, she thought, watching her offspring and the man whose love poured like rain around her. Monica would be fine, and as soon as they found Mariah, so would she.

The moment was interrupted as Detective Ramirez called from the stairwell below. Irma turned to stare down at him as Monica and Preston caught sight of her standing in the entrance.

Ramirez called out again. "Ms. James, we have a call for you. It's a Mr. Bailey, and he says it's urgent! He says it's about your sister."

The trio rushed down the stairs, Monica grabbing at her telephone in the policeman's hand. "Bryan, what's up?"

"Monica, you need to get to the station, now."

"What's going on?"

"She called. Donata called looking for you."

"Bryan, hold on." She pushed the speaker button and hung the receiver up. "I've put you on speaker. I want everyone to hear this. What did she say?"

Bryan's voice echoed out into the room. "She said that if you want to see Mariah again, then you need to get on the radio and start talking to your callers. She said you and she need to have a long talk."

Monica's eyes raced from one face to the other as her family and the police stood staring at her. The seriousness of the situation was planted deep in the lines of her expression. Monica nodded toward the instrument. "Did she say anything else?"

"She said to bring Preston with you. No one else. She said if any of the police leave with you she'll see, and she'll hurt Mariah. She said she wants to hear you in thirty minutes, and the clock is ticking. Those were her exact words."

A chill shot through Monica's body, and she pressed her eyes closed. As she opened them, resolve flowed through her bloodstream. "We're on our way," she said before she disconnected the line. "Get me a playlist, mark out my air time, and be ready to roll the minute I get in the door."

"I'll go with you," Detective Keyes said, having arrived midconversation.

"No. She said alone. Just me and Preston. We're going alone," Monica responded.

"It's not safe . . . ," Detective Keyes started.

Ramirez held up a hand. "Call for a unit out of station South to meet them there. Plainclothes, two officers only. They should arrive first. Tell them to camp out at the main door and keep an eye on who's coming and going."

"No," Monica interrupted. "The main door is locked after six o'clock. Employees come through the garage. Security mans the gate. Guests enter through a side door that leads right into the security office, and then into the main stairwell."

The man smiled. "Very good. They should park themselves outside the side door and get someone in the office with the guard to keep an eye on the garage. Also, call Bell South and tell them to start a tap on every line that goes into Ms. James's switchboard. We need to be ready to trace that call. Can you keep her talking, Ms. James?"

Monica returned the smile. "Talk is what I do best, Detective."

Twenty-seven

Preston paced the floor in the sound booth behind Bryan as Monica adjusted her headphones and waited for her cue. Her call sign rang in her ears, and then Bryan pointed his finger, indicating she was live and on the air.

Monica's voice flowed into the microphone, strong and determined, any edge of anxiety lost deep in her enunciation. "This is Monica James and WLUV radio. It's Sunday night, and I'm here by special request tonight. We have a lot to talk about, people, so start ringing my lines. Someone call and tell me something good."

The trio watched as the switchboard lit up, calls flashing emphatically. Monica reached to answer the first line. "This is Monica. Who's on my line?"

"Monica, this is Mrs. Lewis. Did you find yo' baby yet?"

"Not yet, Mrs. Lewis."

"What you doin' at work then? You didn't do nothin' to that baby, did you?"

"No, ma'am. But I'm here right now hoping to get my little sister home safe."

"'Cause, you know, folks might think you done something, you there on the radio like you ain't worried."

"Trust me, Mrs. Lewis. I'm very worried, but I have to be here for Mariah."

"Well, good luck, dear. We'll keep that po' baby in our prayers."

"Thank you, Mrs. Lewis. This is Monica James. Someone call and tell me something good."

"Yo, Monica! This is Dozier from downtown Raleigh!"

"What's up, Dozier? What do you want to tell me tonight?"

"My woman ain't acting right, Monica. She acting like she don't want me no more. What should I do?"

"Get yourself a new woman. If yours doesn't want you, why waste your time and hers? Get over it, brother. Move on. Let her find what she does want elsewhere, and you do the same."

"I don't think so. She owes me. I've put too much into this."

Monica heaved a deep sigh. "Get over yourself, Dozier. You deserve a woman who wants the same things you do. A woman who wants to make you feel special. That's what we all deserve, someone who makes us feel special." Monica's gaze met Preston's and he answered with just a faint bend of his lips, a smile pulling at his heart. "Don't you deserve to be treated like a king, Dozier?"

"Sure I do."

"Then why are you willing to settle?"

"Who says I'm settling?"

"You have to be settling if you're willing to hang on to a woman who doesn't want you. Let's be for real. She doesn't want you. She doesn't want you to be her king. If that's not what she wants, then what makes you think she's going to treat you well?"

"She will. She can change."

"That's why you're calling me, complaining that she won't act right, because she's going to change, right? I don't think so. Be a man, Dozier, not half of one. There's a woman out there who will be more than you could have ever imagined if you're willing to treat her as well and let her love you. You deserve that, and if you don't know it, then you need to sit down and make out a long list of why you should be treated like a king. If the list is too short, then maybe you need to think about changing how you are, and not how some woman is."

"Yeah, okay. Yeah," the man muttered. "Thanks. I'm gone call you again sometime. Thanks, Monica."

"I feel like some Heather Headley tonight, people. Here's my girl singing *Fulltime*, and when I come back, I want to talk about my man. I want to tell you why my man is so special and why he's all mine. Because he is. He's all mine, and there's not one woman out there that can say otherwise. And if there's any woman who thinks she can, then let her bring it. Let's get this settled once and for all."

Monica pulled the headphones from her ears, standing to stretch her legs as Preston and Bryan rushed into the room.

"What are you doing?" Bryan asked.

"Do you remember a few weeks ago, a woman called and got hot with me because her man was stepping out on her? She gave me hell because I wouldn't encourage her being angry with the other woman?'

Bryan nodded. "Yeah, so what?"

"It was her. It just clicked. Remember, the woman was his neighbor? She said she was going to make the woman pay. And she was angry with me for no apparent reason at all. It was Donata. I'd bet my last dollar on it."

Preston raised his eyebrows, studying her closely. "So what have you got planned?"

"We've been here for over an hour now, and nothing. She hasn't called. They haven't found her lurking outside. Nothing. But I bet I can get her angry enough to want to call. If I can provoke her, the police will be able to trace the call, and with any luck it'll lead us to Mariah."

"Are you sure you want to do that?" Bryan asked. "What if it sets her off and she does something crazy?

"She has my baby sister. I have to do something."

"Let me call Detective Ramirez and see what he thinks," Preston said, as he dialed the number on his cell phone.

"Well, do it quick," Monica responded, dropping back down into her seat. "I'm back on the air in three minutes."

Detective Ramirez was sorting through details in his mind, some so small that no one could have imagined them having any bearing on the case, and least of all be of any value to his solving it. The brevity of time was what puzzled him most, how a grown woman could steal a child in a span of three minutes and disappear as if she'd not been there. The complex was too enclosed for someone not to have seen something. He strolled to stare out of Dr. Walker's window, staring into the unit across the street and his team of officers staffing telephones and trying to get a lead. As he stared through the glass, Angela stood in his line of sight, barking out orders with such authority that it made him smile.

Irma came to stand at his elbow, staring where he stared. They stood watching the flurry of activity across the way, neither bothering to speak, both lost in their own thoughts. Irma finally broke the silence.

"Preston watched my daughter through this window. I think they fell in love just standing here watching each other."

Ramirez turned to stare at the woman. He smiled

a faint smile. "Dr. Walker's a lucky man. Your daughter seems like a remarkable woman."

"Yes, he is. Both of my girls are one of a kind."

The man nodded, refocusing his attention across the way.

"Is she married?" Irma asked, gesturing toward Angela, who had turned to stare back at them.

"No."

"What about you?"

"It's difficult to maintain a relationship in this job, Mrs. Turner. I stopped trying many years ago."

Irma chuckled. "Maybe it's time for you rethink that. If you stand here long enough, you may decide to change your mind."

Ramirez laughed at her bluntness, his gaze meeting Angela's. Pulling himself away, he moved back to the center of the room and the radio program the rest of the family was listening to. Monica was putting a caller in his place, and he had to admire her directness. The man had sputtered, lost his train of thought, and then changed the subject, but Monica refused to let him go until she'd given him more than an earful. It made for good radio, and he was surprised, having never bothered to listen to the program before. As Monica promised to return, hinting at the conversation that was to follow, everyone in the room cut their eyes from one to the other. Irma nodded her head slowly.

"What's she going to do?" Diondre asked, looking from his mother to Bill and back again.

"She's going to make that girl talk," Irma said. "She's going to help them find Mariah."

As they all sat, suddenly anxious, the telephone rang, and Ramirez reached over to answer it.

* * *

She was pacing the floor, anger rising like bitter bile. The old people and the child were watching her, anxiety sweeping over their expressions. The radio was low, but they could hear Monica and the conversation she was having with her callers. Donata's enraged strides were wearing a path against the pine flooring, her high heels digging into the wood. Monica had challenged her. She had told everyone that Preston Walker was hers and hers alone. Then Preston had gotten on the radio with her and the two of them had laughed. They had laughed at her and he had professed that not once, since the day he had met Monica James, had any other woman even crossed his mind.

When Donata slammed her fist into the bedroom wall, the trio lying across the bed top jumped, and the tears that had just stopped falling from Mariah's eyes began again. Donata pointed a finger in the little girl's direction. "This is all your sister's fault. She did this. She thinks she's special, but she's not. She's going to be really sorry for what she's done."

Donata pulled the radio from the wall, slamming it against the floor. Mariah jumped, her small body twitching in fear at the crazy woman who was calling her sister and Preston names. They stared at each other for a brief moment, and then Donata turned the television back on, turning it to the twenty-four-hour cartoon channel. As she stormed out of the room, racing down the stairs to reach the cell phone in her purse, Lydia Stern pressed her forehead to the child's. As Mariah rolled close against her, she heaved a deep sigh, and her husband lay quiet, lost deep in prayer for them all.

Bryan had been clearing the telephone lines as quickly as the calls were coming in. Across the airwaves, Monica and Preston were holding court, sharing intimacies with an audience of thousands who'd tuned in to listen to the drama being played out in their own backyards. As Brian picked up the line, Donata's fury rang heavy, spilling out into the room.

"Tell Monica James if she wants to see this brat again she needs to get on the line right now."

"Hold one moment, please. I'll put you right through," Bryan answered. He lifted himself from his seat ever so slightly and tapped the glass window. When Monica looked in his direction, he nodded his head and signaled her to pick up the second line. Reaching for his private line, Bryan pushed the button for the security office, setting the wheels in motion for the police to trace the call.

"This is Monica James. Are you calling to tell me something good?"

Donata laughed. "You'd like that, wouldn't you?"

"Sure, I like good news. So what's yours?"

"I want to tell you a story, Ms. James," Donata said, spitting Monica's name past her lips.

"Let me hear it. Tell me something."

At the Walker home, Monica's family and detectives Keyes and Ramirez were listening intently.

"That man you want to claim isn't so special. I know. He treated me bad. I tried to be nice to him. I went out of my way to show him how good he and I could have been together, and he threw me out. He threw me out like I was garbage. What kind of man does that?"

"Sometimes we make the mistake of choosing the wrong man to give our hearts to, Donata. It doesn't make the man a bad man for someone else." Monica's tone was low and soothing as she listened for the clues in Donata's voice that would give her an indication of the woman's mood. "I've done it a time or two myself."

"He wouldn't love me. He should have loved me.

I tried to do what I thought he wanted. He should have loved me."

"He cared about you, but he couldn't care about you the way you wanted him to. That happens sometimes."

'What made you so special? Huh? You go around acting like you know everything, and you don't know anything.'

"No, I don't know everything. So why don't you tell me? Tell me why you're so angry, Donata. Who was the first person to make you sad? Who was it that didn't love you?"

Donata froze, the question surprising her. Her gaze ran around the living room of the Sterns' home, stopping at the framed photographs that sat on the coffee table, the bookshelves, and the walls. One in particular caught her eye, and she rose from where she sat to run her finger against the glass.

"He should have loved me," Donata said, her voice dropping to a loud whisper.

Monica prodded her for more. "Who? Who should have loved you?"

"My daddy. He didn't love me. I tried to be a good girl, and he still wouldn't love me."

Monica's gazed rested on Preston, who was watching her closely as he followed the exchange.

"Did your father leave you, Donata? Is that what happened?"

Donata snapped back to reality, flinging the image of Mr. Stern and his daughter against the floor, shattering the glass. "You don't know anything about me!" she shouted into the receiver.

Monica cringed as the sound of breaking shards echoed in the background. "No. I don't. But I know what it feels like to have your father leave. My father left me, too. I've never even met him. So you see, I do know what it is to have someone you love not love you back. My father didn't love me, either."

Silence filled the space, each woman waiting anxiously for the other. Donata resumed her pacing.

"Mariah has a father who loves her very much," Monica said softly. "His name's Bill, and he misses his little girl, Donata."

"Shut up, shut up, shut up," Donata chanted, speaking to the voices.

"I can't do that, Donata," Monica answered. "This is talk radio. I have to talk, and I want to talk about my baby sister. Her name's Mariah, and Mariah is only four years old. Mariah's a very special little girl. She loves to sing and she loves to make new friends. She's never been away from her family before, and I imagine she's pretty scared right now. You've been scared before, haven't you, Donata? It's not a nice feeling. I don't want Mariah to be scared. I need you to help me, help her, Donata. Please."

Donata continued chanting. "No, no, no, no. . . ." She fell to the floor, pressing her head into her lap, trying to still the rush of noise that seemed to flow through her.

Preston reached out to grab Monica's hand, infusing her with the strength to press on.

Donata finally spoke. "I wanted to be Dr. Walker's present. He should have special presents. But he didn't want mine."

"He wanted you to give your presents to someone else. Someone who deserved them and would treasure them always. He wanted that for you because he cares about you, Donata. Dr. Walker really wants things to be good for you."

"Everyone else understood," Donata continued, ignoring Monica's comments. "My friend Lydia said she wanted us to be very happy together. She said we made a nice couple. But then you messed that up." The bitterness returned to Donata's voice.

"No, I didn't," Monica said firmly. "And you know this, Donata."

Donata tilted her head, searching for sounds in the air that were not there. "My friend Lydia said I was a nice girl, and you wanted her to think I wasn't."

"That's not true, Donata."

Donata laughed, a strange chuckle that seemed to rise from some dark spot in her. Dropping the telephone to the floor, Donata sat rocking her body back and forth, losing herself in the volume of the voices. Anxiety pulled at the pit of Monica's stomach. In the control booth, Bryan was gesturing with his hand, slicing his fingers back and forth across his throat.

"This is Monica James and WLUV radio. We'll be back after a word from our sponsors."

The telephone line was still open as Bryan gestured for the two of them to join him.

"What?" Monica asked, pushing anxiously into the room. "Were they able to trace it?"

Bryan's expression was blank as he looked from Monica to Preston. "She's calling from her cell phone. They can't pinpoint her whereabouts."

Monica shook her head, her body beginning to quiver with panic. "I've got to get her talking again. I've got to get her to tell us where Mariah is."

Preston reached out to hug her. "Monica, be careful. This girl is fragile. There's no telling what she might do."

"I have to try, Preston," she whispered, clutching at the front of his shirt. "I have to keep trying."

Detective Ramirez had returned to the window, listening to Monica and Donata. His gaze raced from one door to the other as he reacquainted himself with his surroundings. Donata had called the old woman a friend, he thought, replaying the conversation over and over in his head. When he'd spoken to the couple during the investigation of the girl's alleged assault, they'd thought the woman was Dr. Walker's fiancée. "Such a sweet little thing," Mrs. Stern had said, noting that the two of them had shared a cup of tea with Donata Thompson in their home. He turned to his partner and gestured for her to join him out in the courtyard.

Angela followed obediently, listening as he barked out orders. "Call the old couple's daughter. Ask her if she's heard from her parents. Either way, we need permission to enter the premises. Get it."

"What are you thinking?" Keyes asked, her gazed locked on his intense expression.

Ramirez gestured toward the unit beside Monica's. "I'm thinking that if I grabbed a little girl and needed to get away quickly, hiding close by might be the best route for me to take. And I'm also wondering why a couple who has gone on holiday would leave their television on," he said, pointing to the faint glow of blue light that shimmered out the darkened upstairs window.

She didn't hear the door as it was slowly pushed open or the footsteps that followed. She couldn't hear the taped music that had replaced Monica James on the radio, or Monica still calling out her name from the telephone. She couldn't hear anything, her entire being lost in the embodiment of noise that filled her head, indistinct voices saying too much and then saying nothing.

The little girl had a father, she thought to herself. She'd had a father once, too. Monica James's father had left her. Monica's father hadn't loved Monica, but Donata's father had loved Donata. A smile filled the expanse of her face as the tall man lifted her from the floor, speaking words she couldn't understand. She smiled at the man warmly. "My father loves me," she said. "I'm his favorite girl."

The woman who guided her outside to the police car said something to her, but Donata paid it no attention. She could hear her father talking to her, whispering in her ear how much he loved her. She wasn't interested in hearing anything else.

Back inside the Stern family's home, Detective Ramirez pulled the cell phone from the floor, lifting it to his ear.

"Hello, Ms. James?"

"Detective Ramirez? Is that you? Did you find Mariah?"

"I have someone who wants to speak to you." He handed the phone to Mariah who stood waiting anxiously at his side.

"Mon-ka? Can we go to the zoo now? Please, Mon-ka?"

Twenty-eight

Irma and her two daughters sat side by side in her rear yard, the trio eating chocolate ice cream cones. Ice cream dripped down Mariah's chin onto her pale yellow T-shirt and floral printed skirt. She had been running nonstop for most of the day, challenging her brother, father, and Preston first, then her mother and sister. When the men had escaped to the golf course, the James women were put on the hot seat, chasing after the little princess, who was ruling the day. Ice cream had come as a welcome reprieve from hopscotch, hide-and-go-seek, and tag.

For the umpteenth time since her child's safe return, Irma wrapped her arms around the little girl and hugged her tightly.

"You squeezing too hard," Mariah grunted.

Monica and her mother laughed out loud, the noise ringing through the floral-scented yard. Jumping from her seat, Mariah raced toward her swing set as the two women stared after her.

"I want to ask you something," Irma said, her gaze still focused on Mariah.

"Yes, ma'am?"

"Do you really think your father didn't love you?"

Monica cut her eyes toward her mother. Memories of her conversation with Donata spun through her mind. "There was a time that was all I thought.

Then after a while, it didn't matter much because you loved us so much. Since I was never without love, I didn't have reason to miss it. Donata wasn't that lucky."

Irma nodded. "It's sad about that poor child. She's had a hard life."

Monica nodded her agreement.

Irma cleared her throat before speaking again. Her eyes remained locked on her youngest child. "Your father loved you and your brother very much. But the man had some problems, Monica. He didn't know how to just let love be what it was going to be, instead of trying to force it to be something it wasn't. I've never said this to you or your brother, but you need to understand that your father leaving wasn't about either of you. It was about him and me. Your dad loved you, in his own way. Don't ever think otherwise."

Monica smiled, reaching her hand out to stroke her mother's palm. She nodded her head up and down, the motion slow and endearing. "I know, Mom. I've always known."

The duo sat in silence, caught up in their own reflections as ice cream melted sweet and creamy against their tongues. Mariah heard the men returning before Monica and Irma did, and raced to the front as the car pulled into the driveway.

Irma shook her head. "I want to go chase behind her every time she takes off, but I know I can't. I don't want her to grow up being afraid to be independent."

Monica nodded. "I know. I'll go this time." She smiled widely, and Irma smiled back. Minutes later the sisters returned with the males of the family close beside them. Irma grinned as Monica and Preston entered hand in hand, their fingers clasped tightly together. Mariah was sitting atop her father's shoul-

ders, her arms waving wildly over her head as she
sang the chorus to "I Believe."

"There's my other baby," Bill chimed, leaning to
kiss his wife's cheek. "What have my girls been up to?"

"Just enjoying this beautiful weather," Irma answered, pressing herself against the man's body as
she wrapped her arms around his waist.

Diondre looked down at his watch. "We need to
get on the road," he said, turning to Preston and
Monica. "I'm meeting Godfrey and Antonio Ramirez
for drinks, then we're going to the club."

Irma rolled her eyes. "You're getting too old to be
hanging out in clubs, Diondre. Need to find you a
woman to settle down with."

He reached out to tickle his mother. "Never. I'm
enjoying this bachelor life."

Preston laughed, shaking his head. "I'm glad
someone is because personally I've about had my fill
of it."

Monica grinned, leaning to kiss her man's cheek.

"Mommy, can I go stay at Mon-ka's house? Please,
Mommy? I wanna go with Mon-ka!" Mariah said
pleadingly.

Monica laughed. "Nope! Not this time, Shorty
Cake. Monica isn't going to be home. I have to go
away for a few days."

"Oh, where are you off to?" Bill asked.

"Las Vegas. Preston and I are going to Vegas for
the week."

With eyebrows raised, Irma turned to stare at
them both. She smiled, an all-knowing expression
gracing her face. Nodding her head slowly, she
reached out to kiss their cheeks, wrapping her arms
tightly around them.

"I think we should have a nice party in the backyard here when you two get back. Something special
to celebrate. What do you think, Monica?"

She grinned at her mother and nodded. "I think that would be very nice."

"What are we celebrating?" Diondre asked, looking from one to the other, then to Preston and his stepfather. "What's going on?"

Mariah giggled. "Mind yo' business, boy! This is secret girl stuff!"

Preston felt buoyed by the wave of emotion that flooded his spirit. He didn't know if the excitement he was feeling was a result of what he knew lay ahead for the two of them or if it was simply the vibrant energy of the city. Both he and Monica had felt it even before the plane had landed at McCarran International Airport in Las Vegas, both of them consumed by the city's incomparable energy.

With Monica's hand clasped tightly in his, the two of them had decided to explore the famous Las Vegas strip, shedding their traveling clothes for casual shorts and T-shirts. Preston had insisted on adjoining hotel rooms until after the impending ceremony, and Monica was still shaking her head at the absurdity.

"It's a total waste of money, Preston. It really is."

"Maybe, but if we had one room, you and I both know we'd be celebrating the honeymoon before the wedding."

Monica sighed, then giggled, squeezing his palm against hers. "I love you, but you're driving me crazy."

Preston wrapped his arm around her waist, pulling her close to his side. "That's a good thing."

The evening weather was comfortable, the day's high temperatures finally falling into the low seventies. A cool breeze was blowing, and dusk was settling in quickly. Both were intent on accomplishing two things: obtaining the appropriate marriage license and deciding where they would finally end their separate life journeys and begin a new one bound together by their love. Fifty dollars cash and two signatures had accomplished the first goal at the Clark County Marriage Bureau. They were hopeful that their evening exploration would accomplish the second.

"Where did Bill and your mom get married?" Preston asked, looking up and down the busy street before they attempted to walk across to the other side.

"Graceland Wedding Chapel."

"You're kidding, right?"

Monica shook her head. "No. An Elvis impersonator walked her down the aisle. That's where Aaron Neville of the Neville Brothers was married. He's one of Bill's idols."

Preston laughed, the warmth of the sound flooding over Monica. "Then I think we just have to get married there."

"I think not," Monica responded, still giggling herself.

Preston wrapped his arms around her and hugged her tightly. "It doesn't matter where I marry you, Monica James. I just know that when I do, I will be the happiest man in the world. But I have an idea and I want you to trust me. Will you let me plan this for us?"

Monica smiled up at him, curiosity wafting over her face. She nodded slowly, joy spilling out of her eyes. "As long as there won't be a rendition of *Blue Suede Shoes* in the background, you can have complete and total control."

Twenty-nine

The whirlpool tub was filled to the brim with warm, floral-scented water the color of a clear summer sky. White and yellow rose petals floated over the liquid surface as Monica lounged beneath the water. Lifting her left hand, she marveled at the exquisite ring that adorned her finger, its large stone announcing to the world that she was the wife of Dr. Preston Walker.

The smile that graced her face had been there since she awoke that morning and prepared herself for the day that had now changed her world. The morning had been blissful, starting with breakfast in bed in the bridal suite of the famous Bellagio hotel. The morning had included Preston's first surprise of the day, a bound collection of handwritten love poems written by him especially for her. His words of love had brought the first wave of tears to her eyes, and she had spent the better part of the day fighting back the other waves that had threatened to consume her.

As lunchtime approached, her own private assistant had arrived to help her dress, bringing Preston's second gift, a white satin gown that fell ankle high, the bodice embroidered with tiny pearls. A simple crown of white roses and orchids had adorned her hair. With her mother's antique pearls around her neck, and the diamond and pearl drop earrings given to her from her brother, she'd been a vision of beauty.

The third surprise had been one of the single greatest moments in her life. She had opened the hotel room door expecting Preston to be standing on the other side. Instead, Bill had stood regally in a black tuxedo, a bouquet of one dozen white roses tied with a satin ribbon in his hands. Bill had kissed her cheek and with tears in his eyes had reminded her of a father's duty on his daughter's wedding day, noting how proud he was to be able to give his eldest daughter's hand in marriage to a man as fine as Preston. Her mother, brother, and sister had stood waiting at the end of the hallway. Both women had fought not to cry, willing away the tears that escaped past their thick lashes and spilled over their cheeks.

Before the ceremony began, Preston had given her one last surprise, leading her to a reception area of the Bellagio to introduce her to his mother and his two aunts. The three women had appraised her, then had reached out to hug her warmly, welcoming them into their family. Mrs. Adele Walker was a small woman, barely reaching five feet two in low heels. As she'd smiled warmly at Monica, it was Preston's eyes that looked up at her, his smile that washed over her, the ivory tones of his skin that glistened beneath the bright lights. He was his mother's child, her image stamped upon his person.

"My baby boy is lucky to have found someone who's made him this happy," she'd whispered into Monica's ear as they'd sat together, getting acquainted. "I'm so happy for the two of you."

The two sisters, who had never married and had no children of their own, had chimed in gleefully. "It's about time Preston settles down," Glenda, the eldest sister, had chuckled. "Now, maybe we can get

some grandbabies!" Bernadette, her younger twin by
six minutes, exclaimed. The three women had made
her laugh, had made her feel comfortable, and as
they had waited for the final preparations to be completed, the two famiies had melded into one.

With their families watching, Preston and Monica
had celebrated their vows on a terrace overlooking
Bellagio's Lago di Como beneath an expansive back-
drop of a Tuscan landscape. The setting had been
magnificent, and as Monica had spun slowly in
place, taking in the sight, she knew that Preston
could not have chosen a better place for their ceremony.

The walls around them had been tinted a warm
golden patina. The flooring was a toasted marble,
and in combination with the azure blue of the waters
below, the atmosphere was seeped in romance.
Their moment of jubilation came after their exchange of "I do's" when Preston leaned to take his
first kiss and the waters of the Bellagio Fountains
soared skyward, as if sending prayers for their happy
union straight up to the heavens. Mariah had giggled excitedly, throwing her arms out widely as Diondre scooped her up, lifting her to his shoulders. The
three siblings had grinned from ear to ear. Bill had
wrapped his arms around his wife, kissing Irma as
passionately as he'd kissed her the very first time.
The moment had been surreal.

Now as Monica wiped the moisture from her skin
with an oversized towel, its plush threading baby soft
against her body, she shivered with anticipation. She
couldn't begin to imagine ending so perfect a day
and reveled in a myriad of fantasies about the impending wedding night.

A silk gown and matching robe lay across the chair
in front of the ornate dressing table. It was an elegant
design, just shy of being translucent, and as she

slipped it on over her head, the pale, cream-colored lace panels lay like a second skin against her perfumed body. As Monica stood in the mirror admiring her reflection, nervous energy filled her. The gown left little to the imagination, highlighting every curve of her voluptuous body. Her breasts stood at full attention, her cleavage swelling full against the softness of the fabric. The silk was cut low in the back and draped subtly over the rise of her buttocks, fabric falling in a smooth line to the floor. As she brushed her fingers through her hair, she felt beautiful, and she wanted to be beautiful for Preston.

He was standing nervously by the bedside when she entered the magnificent bedroom. Standing only in a pair of black silk sleeping pants, the garment contrasted nicely with the pale, bare skin of his broad chest. Monica couldn't help but gasp at the sight of him, her desire seeping out of her eyes.

Candles flickered light around the dim room, catching the hint of sheen that glistened from the scented moisturizer that was on Monica's skin. Preston took a step in her direction, his eyes widening at the sheer majesty of her presence. "You are a goddess, and I am here to serve your every need," he whispered softly.

Monica could feel herself blushing with anticipation as he appraised her, his eyes flowing from the top of her head down to the floor and back again. As his gaze swept over her, Preston could feel his breath slipping away, shaking the essence of his foundation. She was exquisite, and she was his. Preston felt as if he could stand there and stare at her forever, and as she lifted a hand toward him, reaching out to him with her eyes, he had to will his shaking legs to keep him standing.

He held her at arm's length, and as he whispered that he loved her, Monica parted her lips in surren-

der. His first kiss was slow, the beauty of it like the
first brush of sunrise against a morning sky. The intensity built in fervor, heat rising between them, and
as his tongue searched out hers, he eased her down
against the bed. Monica could feel him pulling her
soul from between her lips as his body skated lightly
against hers, his hands pressed against the bed at her
sides. Never before had she known pleasure to be so
intoxicatingly sensual.

The first wave of his touch teased her, wafting like
a feather over her shoulders and down the length of
her arms. Preston lifted himself to stare into the
depths of her eyes, and as his gaze locked with hers,
he began to undress her, slowly easing away the fabric of her gown to savor the feel of her flesh. As he
slipped the thin straps off her shoulders, his large
hands glided over her, his fingers dancing with joy.
Preston left no surface untouched, acquainting
himself with every inch of her. He pulled gently
against her nipples, causing them to flower like precious jewels against his palm. His soft tongue followed his fingers, and he felt as if he'd found
heaven on earth and had been given permission to
linger there forever.

Monica felt herself melting as she wrapped her
arms around him, and held on, her nails digging
into his flesh, her mind lost in her rising desire. She
knew that she was his and that he belonged to her,
and that knowledge fed her passion like wood on a
burning fire.

Everything within him was screaming at Preston to
take her, to push himself deep inside her. Wanting to
feel her hot and flush with need beneath him, his
longing pulled at the length of his manhood, extending the flesh into a solid stone of pure lust between them. "Oh, Monica," he cried out, her name
rushing over his tongue. He took her face into his

hands and kissed her again, his need for her raging against the fullness of her lips.

Lifting her torso, Monica pushed against him, rolling him back against the bed. Straddling her body over his, she pushed her pelvis into him, savoring the rush of heat as he burned hot against her skin. Fabric was bunched wildly around her waist, as Preston pushed and pulled to expose her nakedness. Lifting the gown up and over her head, she threw it to the floor behind then. A wide grin pulled at Preston's mouth as he eyed the fullness of her breasts swaying like ripe fruit above him. He savored her nudity, etching the memory of it into his brain. As he lay beneath her, his hands paying tribute to every inch of her brown flesh, Monica inhaled the beauty of him, wanting to sample the sweetness of him against her tongue.

Preston gasped when she licked the lobe of his ear, gliding her tongue along the lines of his face until she reached one nipple and then the other. Her tongue ran a slow race up and down his torso. It left him breathless. He opened his eyes and met her gaze as Monica smiled down at him. Seduction filled the darkness of her eyes. She pulled at the ties that held up his pants and pushed them down over his hips. Preston lifted his buttocks as Monica freed him from the confines of the silk bottoms. He raged solid, his pulse throbbing in his maleness, and when Monica clasped his organ tightly between her thighs, the room spun in sheer ecstasy.

"Is this really your first time?" Monica said coyly, teasing him against the warmth of her secret treasure, her slow gyrations making it difficult for him to breathe.

He nodded, his mouth falling open as Monica toyed with him, pleasure shooting through his nerve endings as he gasped for air.

"Then, I promise to be gentle," she whispered, lifting herself up and hovering shamelessly above him. Preston grinned with anticipation as she reached between them to grab his manhood, sliding her palm over his fullness. He quivered at the heat of her touch. It was pleasure beyond his imagination as Monica impaled herself slowly, taking the length of his manhood deep inside the dark chamber of her womanhood. She rode him slowly, the thrust of her hips resonating through his body.

Preston moaned, calling out her name in ecstasy. "Oh, baby. Monica, baby," he chimed, unadulterated lust coating his words.

Lifting his torso to hers, Preston pressed his chest to her chest, her breasts kissing the muscular lines of his torso. With his palm resting against the back of her head, he pulled her mouth to his, kissing her with greedy abandonment. Thirty-plus years of sexual prudence spilled like water from a faucet out of his pores. As Monica rocked against him, a rush of heat started deep in his midsection, spreading down into his pelvis and along his thighs, curling his toes, his fingers, and the tiny hairs along the nape of his neck.

As Monica plunged her body against his, stroking his body boldly with hers, flashes of light filled the room and blinded him. Sweat beaded against his brow as he felt her mouth drawing a path against his neck, then along the cleft of his chin, her lips finally settling back against his. As Monica blew breath into him, Preston felt himself losing complete control.

"Monica, I'm coming," he muttered hoarsely against her lips. "Oh, sweet baby . . ."

As Monica dropped herself down against him, his hand clutching her buttocks tightly, she felt him explode deep within her, the tremors of his orgasm bringing down her own. The sensation was overwhelming. With complete surrender, Monica shouted his name, her body quivering its carnal release.

They lay one atop the other, their bodies still connected. Preston kissed her face, pressing his lips to her eyelids, and the tip of her nose, then nibbling at her bottom lip.

"How'd I do?" Preston asked timidly, his breathing returning to a semblance of normalcy. "I didn't want to disappoint you."

Monica smiled, hugging him hard against her. "You done good, Dr. Walker. You done very good."

He smiled back. "I'll get better with practice," he said. "I promise."

Monica kissed him quickly. "Trust me, you'll be getting plenty of practice."

Preston laughed as he held her close.

They lay in the quiet, reveling in their first moment of intimate connection. Monica was suddenly aware of the faint sound of music that trickled from the sound system in the room. She smiled again, pressing her lips to his cheek. "Thank you," Monica whispered.

Preston looked at her anxiously.

"Thank you for waiting for me," Monica smiled.

The man hugged her tightly. "I can't imagine having waited for anyone else. I love you, Mrs. Walker," he said, his smile caressing.

Monica smiled back as Preston rolled her onto her back, his pelvis still locked with hers. Monica spread herself open as he rotated slowly against her, inciting the quiver of a second erection to full attention. Kissing her boldly, he loved her slowly, and sweetly, over and over again, until they both fell back against the bed consumed by exhaustion.

As sleep was pulling them beneath the warmth of her blanket, the moon outside was exchanging places with the sun, the first rays of her greeting beginning to peek through the open windows. Monica rolled her body close to Preston's, snuggling deep beneath his protective embrace. She smiled, tilting her head to whisper in his ear. "The first thing we're going to do is buy a house, a big one."

Preston chuckled. "On ten acres with no neighbors."

"Why no neighbors?"

"I want us to be the only ones looking in our windows."

Monica laughed, her eyes fluttering open and then closed, as promises of visions in windows danced in her dreams.

Conclusion

Preston stood over the soundboard with Bryan as Monica's call sign opened the evening's show. He thought she looked incredible, her face flushed with excitement. Her skin glowed and her eyes were bright, exuberance wafting through her spirit. She'd let her hair grow longer, the extended length barely touching her shoulders, and he thought her even more beautiful than the day he'd first laid eyes on her.

Their love for one another had grown deeper and deeper with each passing day. Even then, as he stood watching her, he wanted to pull her into his arms and drop the rest of his body into the chasm of her soul that his heart had fallen into. He took a seat against a wooden stool as Bryan passed him a set of headphones to listen in.

"We're having a party down here at WLUV-radio, people! Before I start taking your calls, there are a few things I need to do tonight. I have some business that needs to be completed before I can say good-bye.

"The last three years have been an incredible journey for us. You have been a remarkable audience. There is no radio personality out here who can say they have loved every minute with you as much as I have. My thanks and gratitude go out to Raleigh-Durham and every one of you who helped me make this show the number one show in the southern region!

"I'm excited to be taking this next journey, and I'm blessed to have good friends and an incredible family by my side. The Monica James Show will premiere next week on WRAL-TV, and I promise that I'll be bringing it to you with the same energy and the same vibe that has kept you coming back here every night since I arrived. I have a lot to talk about and I want to hear what you all have to tell me.

"Now, before I open the phone lines tonight, I have to make a call myself this evening. There's someone I need to send a special message to."

Monica pushed the speed-dial button on the switchboard at her elbow. The telephone in the control booth rang, and with a wide grin, Bryan pointed a finger at Preston and nodded for him to answer it. Eyes bulging, Preston lifted himself from his seat to stare out at Monica. A devilish grin danced across her face.

"Hello?" he answered timidly, dropping the headphones to the table and pulling the receiver to his ear.

"Good evening. This is Monica from WLUV-FM. Is this Mr. Romantic?"

Preston chuckled softly. "Yes, it is. What can I do for you, Monica."

"My listeners and I just wanted to know how you're doing on that romantic home front. Are you and that woman of yours still enjoying the romance?

"Yes, we are. She's made me an incredibly happy man."

"And are you making her an incredibly happy woman?"

Preston laughed aloud. "I think so. But if I wasn't, I'm sure she would let me know."

Monica laughed with him. "I'm sure she would. Well, before we say good-bye, that woman of yours has something she wants to tell you. Are you sitting down, Mr. Romantic?"

A flush of color tinted Preston's face as a wave of nervousness filtered through him. He dropped back onto the stool, cutting an eye toward Bryan, who was still grinning at the two of them.

"Mr. Romantic, just wanted to wish you a very happy first Father's Day!"

Confusion painted Preston's face as he looked from Monica to Bryan and the Christmas tree that was lit in the corner of the studio. Father's Day was six months away, and surely he wasn't anyone's father. His eyes widened as understanding suddenly seeped through him. Monica grinned, her smile filling the room with joy, and she nodded at him slowly, the palm of her hand falling to her abdomen.

"Congratulations, Mr. Romantic! And I love you very much."

Dropping the telephone, Preston rushed into the other room, wrapping his arms around Monica, their excitement still filtering across the airwaves.

"I love you," Preston whispered, pressing his mouth to hers, the kiss as breathtaking at the last one and the one before that. "I love you so much."

Monica smiled, then reached for her microphone. "This is Monica and WLUV-FM. We'll be right back after a word from our sponsors."

With the advertisements rolling, Monica returned her husband's hug, pressing her hand to his cheek as he leaned to kiss her belly button, wishing his unborn child a warm welcome.

"So," Monica said teasingly. "How long do you think you're going to want to keep me and this kid of ours?"

Preston laughed. "I think forever and a day will do nicely."

Monica smiled. "Doesn't sound long enough to me."

As Bryan counted down her ten-second signal,

Monica kissed her husband one more time, then pulled the microphone to her lips, settling herself back against her seat.

"This is Monica Walker. Someone call and tell me something good!"

Dear Friends,

Love can be an avalanche of emotions, sending us sky-high one minute before dropping us head-first into the ground the next. This story, *Forever and a Day*, was an exciting story to write as I worked to capture the intensity, the frustration, the incomparable magnitude of love and its ability to possess, motivate, and take the human spirit hostage.

I pray that this story makes you laugh, smile, and reflect on the love and passion in your own lives. To all of you who've written to express your support, who've shared your personal stories with me, I thank you. You are each so incredible and I'm always overwhelmed by your outpouring of love. Each time I do this, I hope that I'm able to leave you satisfied and nourished, knowing that you are truly loved.

Again, thank you so much for your support, and please visit me at my Web site and continue to send me your comments.

With much love,

Deborah Fletcher Mello
www.deborahmello.com

ABOUT THE AUTHOR

Deborah Fletcher Mello has written four books to date and says that weaving a story that leaves her audience feeling full and complete, as if they've enjoyed an incredible meal, is the ultimate thrill for her. Born and raised in Stamford, Connecticut, she now calls Hillsborough, North Carolina, home, where she resides with her husband, sixteen-year-old son, and three dogs.